LIKE
MOTHER
LIKE
DAUGHTER

ALSO BY DAWN GOODWIN

The Accident
The Pupil
Best Friends Forever
The Pact
What I Never Told You
When We Were Young

LIKE MOTHER LIKE DAUGHTER

DAWN GOODWIN

HEAD
of ZEUS

An Aries Book

9 7 5 3 1 2 4 6 8

A catalogue record for this book is available from the British Library.

ISBN (PB): 9781803283715
ISBN (E): 9781800242203

Cover design: Meg Shepherd | Head of Zeus

Typeset by Siliconchips Services Ltd UK

Printed and bound in Great Britain by
CPI Group (UK) Ltd, Croydon CR0 4YY

Head of Zeus Ltd
First Floor East
5–8 Hardwick Street
London EC1R 4RG

WWW.HEADOFZEUS.COM

For Dad.

I watch them through the window, a witness to everything and nothing all at once, disbelieving, terrified.

She lies in the bed, still, too still. A chill passes through me. I take a step forward, press up to the glass. Then I hear the whir of the machine, see the hospital-issue blanket rise and fall. I exhale again too.

The girl in the chair next to the bed looks younger than her seventeen years, her auburn hair pulled untidily into the nape of her neck, long strands loose around her unsettlingly pretty face. She is wearing a grey sweatshirt that swamps her small frame as she crouches in the uncomfortable chair. Her forehead is pulled tight and her fingers pick at each other as she watches. Her phone is balanced on her knee, but she is ignoring it. Her eyes see only the girl in the hospital bed. Occasionally, her eyes flick to the lines and numbers on the screen next to the bed, the blips and dips, the ticks and whirs, as it does the hard work of breathing for the patient.

The two girls are as still and as quiet as each other. Yet, nothing about this place is restful. Squeaking soles on disinfected linoleum, beeping machines, hushed voices, all amplified against a low-level hum of anxiety and pain. I jump with every door that opens, each trolley that trundles past. I marvel at how still they are behind the glass, those two girls who not so long ago were full of life and teenage energy, all sass and attitude.

The black coffee in my cardboard cup is cold, but I sip at it anyway, grimacing at the bitterness.

Where do we go from here? How will this end?

And how the hell did we get to this point?

1

Lisa

Six Weeks Ago

Lisa Marco stopped abruptly as the double doors to the school hall slapped back into place behind her. Familiar smells bombarded her: sweat, stale air and canteen grease hanging suspended in the air, bringing back unwelcome olfactory memories of her own school days. Teenage angst dripped down the woodchip wallpaper. The wall panelling bore the scuffs and stains of every kick, stumble and fall.

No matter how many times she walked into this school, it was still like stepping back in time, triggering memories of disappointing report cards and comments about not living up to her potential.

She told herself she was being pathetic. This wasn't her school and she wasn't a teenager any longer. She was a married mother of two and this was just the annual school quiz night, where the fish and chips were delivered with a sizable portion of parental guilt.

Still, she couldn't deny that some things never changed.

There were bullies everywhere, even when you were a grown-up.

Lisa took tentative steps towards the main hall. For a while, events like these had been fun, years ago when the kids were in primary school and the parents needed an evening to let their hair down, drink too much and pretend to still be young and outrageous, only to be home by midnight for the babysitter. The kids were teenagers now though and it felt like the grown-ups were trying too hard to hang onto their rapidly fading youth when they were actually bone tired, intolerant of too much noise, and wanted to be at home watching *The Great Pottery Throwdown* in their slippers.

So why am I here?

Because she didn't want to give them something else to gossip about. The whispers had finally died down over time, but it wouldn't take much for them to start up again. She wasn't going to give them a reason to say she was that parent who never did their bit, didn't put their hand in their pocket for a fundraiser or throw their support behind school initiatives. So she convinced her husband, Ben, to turn up with her every year. They drank the cheap wine and laughed at the headmaster's stale jokes while she bit her tongue against the barbs and jibes.

Lisa looked at her watch. Ben was late. He had said when he'd left for work that morning that he would meet her at the school, that he had a light day for a change, only one short appointment in the afternoon, and then he would be home after a detour to the gym. Since then, he hadn't answered her calls or replied to her texts. Lisa had stood outside the school gate for a bit, the end of her nose turning cold, then when her last text to him remained unread, she'd reluctantly made her way inside on her own.

She was annoyed. He knew what it was like for her, how she hated arriving on her own, especially here. She stood in the doorway to the hall as other parents filed around her, jostling with handbags and sharp elbows. Lisa fixed her top, reached down to adjust the bottom of her skinny jeans where they had started to bunch up around her knees, and wondered if the wedge heels were a bad idea. Everyone else seemed to be wearing immaculate, white trainers. She had thought the wedges made her look taller; now she realised they looked like she was trying too hard. The dark red nail polish on her toes was chipped in places and completely missing on the third toe of her right foot. She could've done with socks just to hide that.

Someone was waving at her from across the hall. It was Sally, who had a wide smile on her face and a full glass of white wine in her hand. Relieved, Lisa waved back and weaved through the chairs towards her.

'Lisa, you're here! Where's Ben?' Sally said, peering over Lisa's shoulder. Sally made little effort to disguise her obvious crush on Lisa's husband – on anyone's husband, for that matter.

She was a soft ball of a woman with a button nose, a bubbling laugh and a crown of tight, strawberry blonde curls. Her round glasses magnified her eyes, giving her face a bug-like quality, and she had permanently reddened cheeks, as though she was in the midst of an eternal hot flush.

'Ben's running late, but he'll be here,' Lisa replied, giving Sally a brief hug.

'Oh, good. He's always such an expert in the sports round.'

Lisa smiled and took one of the empty seats next to Sally's husband, Trevor, a balding, mild-mannered man who said very little and wore a pullover on even the hottest day. Today's pullover was a purple, paisley affair, complete with a dribble of something down the front. Despite his fashion sense and lack of conversational skills, he had an uncanny knowledge of trivia and had been known to get quite animated during previous quiz nights.

'Hi, Trevor, how are you?'

'He's fine, aren't you, Trev? Been brushing up on his general knowledge,' Sally answered for him. Trevor grunted and took a healthy swig from his bottle of beer.

'I've bought a bottle of wine already. Have a glass, Lisa,' Sally continued, indicating the sweating bottle in the middle of the table, half of which was already gone.

'Thanks,' Lisa said and poured herself a moderate glass. 'I'll get the next one.'

Sally squealed at something over Lisa's shoulder, making Lisa spill some of her wine over the lip of the glass. Her heart sunk as she turned and saw Christina Valdecchi weaving through the tables towards them, trailed by a chunky man with a bald head and a greying wizard beard. The Hawaiian print of his shirt was as aggressive as the leopard print stretched tight across Christina's jiggling chest as she teetered on a pair of very high platform stiletto heels. Vindication for Lisa's wedges at least.

Sally bounced in her flat ballet pumps, a wide smile on her face. 'Oh yay! Christina is here!'

'Oh, yay,' Lisa muttered and took a big gulp of her wine,

now wishing she had filled her glass to the brim like Sally had. The wine was bitter and made her wince.

'Chris! You're here!' Sally shrieked. Trevor flinched and lifted his beer to his lips again. 'And who's this dishy fella?'

'This is Colin,' Christina replied with a proud grin. Colin looked bemused at being in a school hall on a Friday night.

'Hello, Colin,' Sally flirted. 'What's your specialist subject then?'

'Ornithology,' he said in the gravelly voice of a heavy smoker. Up close, his Hawaiian shirt strained across a middle-aged paunch, his eyes were bloodshot and Lisa noticed crumbs in his beard.

'Ooh, what's that then?' Sally said.

'The study of birds,' he replied with a wink and was rewarded with a giggle and eyelash flutter from Sally.

Lisa fought against the urge to roll her eyes and lost.

'Lisa,' Christina said tightly.

'Christina.'

'Meet my new boyfriend, Colin. You flying solo tonight?'

'Ben is coming, he's just running late. An important meeting at work.' She didn't know why she felt the need to justify anything, especially not to Christina.

'On a Friday evening? I have a feeling that meeting may have been in the pub,' Christina goaded.

'Oh, I'm sure not. All work and no play at the moment. We hardly see him.' Lisa turned to Colin with a wide smile. 'Colin, so nice to meet you. Welcome to the team. Considering our table, don't expect anything too intellectual tonight.' She flicked her eyes at Christina for emphasis.

Christina glared at her, then dismissed her with a sniff

and turned away. 'Wine!', she proclaimed before emptying the rest of the bottle into a glass.

Lisa 1; Christina 0.

The woody scent of male aftershave reached her before she heard a deep, smooth voice over her shoulder. 'Lisa, you're looking good.' She turned to see Owen Teegan leaning on the back of the spare chair next to her. 'No Ben tonight?' he said softly.

'He is coming,' she replied. 'No Lena?'

'She's getting the drinks.'

Lisa looked towards the bar area and saw Lena Teegan, her statuesque legs in tight, white jeans and her long hair like pale-yellow silk rippling down her back.

'Owen! You're here!' Sally proclaimed yet again. 'Where is your beautiful wife?'

Owen pushed away from the chair and turned to Sally. 'Sally, a vision as ever. You'll be pleased to hear that Lena is at the bar ordering some more wine.'

'Excellent, we need more wine. Where are you sitting? Over here next to me, I hope?'

'Sally, I wouldn't be able to control myself, so I think I'll keep Lisa company. Hi Trevor, alright, mate?' Trevor grunted once more as Owen sat in the empty seat next to Lisa.

Lisa felt heat rise in her cheeks.

Most of the tables were full, the volume of excited chatter rising and falling in waves. Amid a buzz of activity around the stage, the school headmaster, Mr Rawlinson, appeared from the wings, approached an outdated sound system and began to fiddle with a microphone. There was the obligatory squeal of static from the microphone. Rawlinson was a very tall and wide man who walked with a shoulder stoop that spoke of someone looking to hide their vastness. On the very few occasions that Lisa had had reason to talk to him directly, he had towered over her and yet had managed to look everywhere but at her face.

Owen leaned over and said, 'Are you ok?' Lisa turned towards him, but her reply was interrupted by Lena, who slid with excessive grace into the chair on the other side of Owen, deposited two full bottles of wine on the table and kissed her husband on the cheek. The scent of lilies and vanilla wafted over Lisa.

'Oh, you two are too cute!' Sally proclaimed, then added unnecessarily, 'Lena, you're here! And you brought wine!' She was insufferable. No wonder Trevor chose to ignore her.

'Sally, how are you?' Lena's voice was as silky as her hair and carried a trace of a Swedish accent. She smiled and placed her hand on Owen's thigh. Lisa turned away.

Sally gulped at her wine, her eyes dancing. 'Good, thank you, Lena. All good. You look as amazing as ever.'

'Thank you,' Lena replied, without offering a return compliment. 'Hi, Lisa. Lovely to see you again. It's been too long. No Ben tonight?'

'Oh, he's coming, just delayed at work, I think.' Lisa looked at her watch. He was over half an hour late and still had not replied to any of her texts.

Christina cackled loudly on the other side of the table as Colin whispered in her ear. The microphone squealed again.

Trevor slurped at his beer. Lisa could feel a headache settle in behind her eyes.

Rawlinson coughed loudly, which the microphone managed to pick up very clearly. 'Good evening, parents, teachers, friends. Welcome to our annual quiz night and I'm delighted to see so many of you here.' Most people ignored him and carried on chatting. 'As always, all proceeds go straight to the PTA, so please make sure you keep your glasses filled throughout the evening. Every little sip helps.' He chuckled. 'Sharon is going around with the answer sheets and some pens, and we will be ready to start in a minute or two.'

A large lady in a floral skirt and sensible shoes shuffled between the tables, handing out sheets of paper and biros.

'Ooh, here we go! I'll do the writing though, yeah? Let's not forget last time,' Sally said. The whole table swivelled to look at Lisa, who blushed. She had been granted the responsibility of the pen last year and had scribbled two answers in the wrong box in haste, which had cost them third place by only one mark. Despite the fact that they were playing for nothing more exciting than a box of Celebrations chocolates, it had clearly not been forgotten.

Owen caught Lisa's eye and winked. She smiled back, but sank a little lower in her chair when Lena caught her eye too.

Where the hell was Ben?

The first round was general knowledge, which passed in a blur of whispered answers layered over each other, but with the team ultimately then going with whatever Trevor said. There were a few that Lisa felt confident she knew, but she sat back and contributed little. A brief argument broke out when Trevor was adamant that US President Joe Biden's middle name was Robinette, which Colin proclaimed loudly to be 'absolute bollocks'.

The table next to them seemed to be finding most of their answers on Google and an older man across the hall was stalling for time by asking Rawlinson to repeat questions while his teammates conferred frantically. When the round ended, the school band, consisting of five spotty boys with identical floppy hair and a petite girl wearing the tiniest crop top and excessively baggy, low-waisted jeans, popped up onto the stage and murdered 'Don't Stop Me Now'.

Another bottle of wine was emptied as the second round began. Lisa chewed at the skin around her fingernail and wondered if it was time for her to exit stage left. She was still contributing nothing and the evening had turned into a painful experience some time ago. She glanced at Owen and Lena. They were chatting in low voices. Lena seemed to be annoyed at something.

'We're going to need some more of this,' Christina said loudly and cracked open another bottle as Rawlinson proclaimed that the next round would be flags of the world.

Lisa started to get to her feet, but Colin beat her to it, declaring that flags all looked the same to him and he didn't know his Uganda from his Ghana, so he was better off going to the bar. Trevor mumbled something about presidents not being Colin's thing either, then paled as he realised that he had said it out loud. He followed after Colin, muttering apologies for his uncharacteristic outburst.

Lisa looked at her phone again. No messages. She fired off another text to Ben.

Where are you? At least let me know if you are not coming at all. I'm giving it five more minutes, then I'm going home.

'You ok?' Owen repeated in her ear.

'Yes, yes, just wondering where Ben has got to, that's all. It's not like him to not get in touch.'

'I'm sure he'll be here in a minute. The trains are probably a nightmare. He hasn't missed much, has he?' Owen was about to say more, but Lena tapped his arm and spoke to him, thin words that Lisa couldn't hear over Christina's loud cackling as she gossiped with Sally behind her hand.

As it turned out, Sally was a bit of a flag boffin and answered most of the round single-handedly, leaving Christina outsmarted. She declared loudly that Sally was 'smarter than she looked', causing Sally to purse her lips in annoyance. Lisa's headache was palpable now, with a nasty bitterness on her tongue from the cheap, school-issue wine.

As the round ended, Christina said, 'Lisa, I think it's your shout for drinks, isn't it? Just because Ben isn't here doesn't mean you don't get to put your hand in your pocket.'

'Oh, yes, of course.' Lisa blushed in embarrassment, annoyed at herself for giving Christina ammunition. 'I was going to get the last one, but Colin got there first.'

Christina raised a cynical eyebrow and muttered something about a likely story.

'Leave her alone, Chris. You know Ben and Lisa are usually the first to get a round in,' Owen replied. 'And the way you and Sally are drinking, we'll all be bankrupt before the night is out.' He pushed his chair back and stood up. Lisa felt the lightest of fingertips brush against the back of her neck, so light that she wondered if she had imagined it. Goosebumps rippled across her skin and heat flared at the point of contact.

'What a bunch of fucking losers you lot are!' a voice boomed over them then and Lisa turned to see Ben standing in front of her.

2

Lisa

Now

A phone was ringing somewhere. Lisa heard it through her sleep. She sat up, groggy, confused, unsure where she was. She looked around. She was on the couch, still in her clothes, the television on. The phone stopped, then started ringing again straightaway. She fumbled with the blanket that was covering her legs, then felt the vibrations coming from the side of the couch. Her phone had fallen between the cushions.

It was close to midnight. Nothing good ever came from a phone call at this time of night.

She looked at the screen of her mobile and saw that it was a call from Christina. Why the hell was she calling her? Should she even answer? She hesitated, but curiosity won out.

'Hello?'

'Lisa?'

Christina's vice sounded strangled, tight.

'Christina, why are you calling me?'

'Lisa, is Ben with you?'

'He's in bed. Why?' Lisa had been annoyed that he had come home from work, eaten his dinner alone again and then taken himself off to bed. After she had cleared away his dishes, Lisa had made herself comfortable on the couch with glass of wine, a bowl of crisps and a crap film on Netflix. The film was still playing away to itself, not finished yet. The bowl had been knocked over and Lisa suspected that her dog Jester had eaten the crisps. She must've been asleep for a good hour. She wiped at the dried dribble on her chin.

Christina said nothing more. A trickle of panic ran down Lisa's spine. She got to her feet. 'Christina, you're frightening me. What's going on?'

'Lisa, there's been an... accident.'

Lisa swayed. 'What kind of accident? Is Emma ok? Let me speak to her!'

'I don't know much, but the girls – there's been an accident, that's all I know. Someone called an ambulance and they've been taken to hospital.'

'What? What do you mean? They're having a sleepover – at your house. What on earth has happened? What have you done?'

Now it was Christina's turn to sound confused. 'Yes, the sleepover is later, but they went to the gig first. You did know about it? The gig?' She was breathing heavily down the phone into Lisa's ear. 'Look, we can talk about this later. We need to get to the hospital. They've gone to St George's. I'm on my way there now. I can come and get you on the way if you like?'

'I don't need any favours from you. I will get there on my own.'

Lisa hung up the phone, her brain swelling and throbbing. She thought for a moment, then picked up her phone again and called Emma's mobile.

This was a mistake. It had to be. Emma would answer and it would all be fine. It would be a misunderstanding – or Christina playing some horrid trick on her.

The call went to voicemail.

Ok, that in itself didn't mean much, did it? She may have run out of battery. She was supposed to be at a sleepover with Sophia.

Her finger hovered over the photo of her daughter on the phone's home screen.

But what if something had happened?

Oh God, what if Christina was telling the truth?

3

Christina

Six Weeks Ago

Christina realised with delight that Ben Marco was drunk.

Not just drunk. Inebriated.

She had clocked him as soon as he sidled into the school hall, the doors swinging loudly behind him. She noticed how he rebounded off the chairs instead of walking around them, the tell-tale sway in his stance as he stood at the makeshift bar at the back of the hall and ordered a beer.

She smiled to herself. This was going to be priceless.

Christina kicked Sally under the table. Sally frowned and looked sharply at Christina, who merely nodded in Ben's direction. Sally looked over to the bar and shrugged at Christina in confusion.

'Ben,' she mouthed.

Christina couldn't wait to see Lisa's face when she saw Ben weaving his way towards them.

'What a bunch of fucking losers you lot are!' Ben said loudly when he finally ricocheted over to the table. Several heads at neighbouring tables swivelled towards them. Lisa paled.

Ben's shirt was untucked, his top button undone, his tie loose and askew. Christina had never seen him so dishevelled.

This was just delicious to watch.

'Ben! You're here!', Sally said, but even her usual enthusiasm was dampened. She bounced over to hug him, then recoiled as a wave of alcoholic fumes hit her.

Ben sloped around to where Lisa was sitting. 'Am I late?' he said.

Circles of red had appeared high on Lisa's cheeks. She replied mildly, 'Only a little bit. So glad you're here now, though,' and accompanied it with a tight smile as he barely pecked her on the cheek.

Ben fell into the chair next to Lisa and slammed his beer bottle onto the table. Beer frothed up the neck.

'Looks like you may have started even earlier than us,' Christina said to him. 'Long day at the office, was it?'

He grinned at her. 'Something like that, but I also need to be pissed to get myself through this fresh hell tonight.' His voice was drunk-loud. A bespectacled woman at the table next to them scowled in their direction.

Lisa looked mortified.

'I was about to send Lisa for more wine as it's her round. She hasn't bought one yet,' Christina said.

Ben turned on Lisa. 'Bloody hell, Lisa. That's not cool.'

'It's not... I...' Lisa stammered.

Owen intercepted. 'We all keep getting there first – figured you could do the buying – when you eventually turned up, anyway.'

Tension flickered like a faulty lightbulb as the two men

sized each other up. Then Ben said, 'Fair enough. It's a man's job to look after his wife, after all.'

The quizmaster announced that the next round would be sport and a few scattered men cheered.

'It's fine. I'll go,' Lisa said. 'Sport is more your thing than mine, anyway.'

She scurried out of her chair.

Christina watched her go, feeling short-changed that there hadn't been more drama, then Owen said, 'I'll help her carry,' and followed after Lisa. Lena raised an immaculately plucked eyebrow, not lost on Christina.

She leaned over and rested her hand on Ben's arm. 'Ben, this is Colin, my new boyfriend,' she said over a rugby question being belted into the microphone.

'Alright, mate,' Colin said warily.

'Shh, I missed that question!' Sally hissed.

Ben said, 'Another fella, Christina? How many is that this year? Sal, the answer is seven.'

There was no one in the queue for drinks and yet Lisa and Owen took quite some time returning with the wine. They seemed to be having quite a discussion about it, considering there were only two types of white wine to choose from. Lena watched them the whole time, her lips pulled so tight they had all but disappeared.

Ben had changed position to angle his chair so that he was in the aisle between the tables, manspreading his legs so that no one could get past. Lisa had to step over him when she returned to her seat. In return, he slapped her on the bum and Christina snorted at the look of disgust on Lisa's face before she sat down primly.

The evening had certainly taken an interesting turn.

*

The questions rumbled on; the rounds stacked up. Greasy fish and chips were served during an interval when the famous faces picture round was put in front of them to consider while they ate. Christina was starving, wanted to shovel every last salty, vinegar-drenched chip into her mouth, but Lisa was nibbling at just the fish, pushing the batter to the side, and Lena hadn't touched any of hers, so Christina ate half and scooped the rest onto Colin's plate to remove temptation. Only Sally ate every last scrap.

Lisa was adamant she recognised one of the photos as Irish author Sally Rooney but Christina shouted her down, telling her it was definitely a politician. Christina had no idea if it was or not, but she was annoyed at not being able to finish her chips and the flicker of doubt that passed over Lisa's face when she was put on the spot made Christina feel a little better. It turned out it was Sally Rooney. Christina merely said with a smirk, 'Oh dear, we should've believed you,' to Lisa after the answers were announced. No one else seemed to care, but Lisa's skin was practically bubbling with repressed fury.

Lisa kept looking over at Lena, who was without doubt the most beautiful woman in the place. Her very presence seemed to be making Lisa feel awkward. Every time she looked at Lena, she would tug at her shirt or smooth down her hair, sink a little lower in her chair, and it was blatantly obvious that Lisa felt small and beige next to the statuesque Lena.

While they waited for the scores to be added up, the table finally had some actual conversations. Inevitably, Sally brought up the recent school reports that had been issued and, in her typical passive-aggressive way, Lisa managed to tell all of them that her daughter Emma had been given A*s for her predicted grades without actually saying it. Sally kept quiet – her twin boys were not known for their intelligence.

Christina didn't care either way. She had taught her daughter, Sophia, that there was more to life than studying in order to sit in an office all day. There were pushy parents who wanted their little darlings to be the next generation of surgeons and lawyers and architects, but she just wanted her daughter to be happy.

It was Lisa's smug delight that annoyed Christina. She was the worst of those parents because she hid her ambitions behind a gossamer fabric of judgement of everyone else around her. But Christina knew what Lisa was really like beneath that layer of superiority. They had known each other long enough for Christina to know what kind of parent Lisa really was.

Christina could feel the wine buzzing in her head like a hive of bees and her mouth was dry. She wished she'd eaten all the chips, but the trays had been cleared away. By the time the results of the quiz were announced, Christina felt almost as drunk as Ben looked. Sally was also reaching the loudly inebriated stage and Trevor was falling asleep in his chair, a drip of curry sauce drying on his chin.

Then came a moment of absolute horror when their team was declared to have come in last place. As a smatter of applause rippled through the hall, Ben got to his feet and started whooping and hollering loudly in celebration. The rest of their table were stunned into humiliated silence, but Christina leapt to her feet and joined in with Ben's hollers. The headmaster looked on in disdain until Ben and Christina collapsed back into their seats.

'Such party poopers, you lot!' Christina said, a little out of breath.

There was far more applause as the team at the table next to them was crowned the winner, despite clearly cheating, then everyone was scraping their chairs across the floor as they got to their feet and began to fold away the tables.

'We should help them clear up,' Lisa said quietly. Christina noticed Lisa hadn't had anything else to drink after Ben had turned up. He, on the other hand, had sunk a fair few more beers.

'Yes, we should,' Owen agreed and started to fold up his and Lena's chairs. Lisa collected some glasses in her fingers. Colin and Sally ignored Lisa and Owen. Sally was as drunk as Christina and now openly flirting with Colin. Christina didn't mind. Sally was harmless and frankly Colin could have her if he found her, with her round, moon face and chunky thighs, more attractive than Christina. Meanwhile, Lena was inexplicably trying to engage Trevor in conversation, despite the curry sauce on his chin and his obvious disinterest.

'Christina, are you going to fold up your chair?' Lisa said.

'Oh, shut up, Lisa. There are plenty of people helping and I'm not finished with my glass of wine just yet,' Christina snapped, just as Lisa reached for the glass that still had a bit of wine in it. 'In fact, there's still some in the bottle.' She upended the bottle into the glass, then sloshed the remainder into Lena's glass. 'Here you go, Lena, you'll join me, won't you?'

'Oh no, thank you. I've had way too much already and I'm hoping to do a 12 kilometre run tomorrow as part of my marathon training.' She passed the half-full glass back to Christina. 'You are more than welcome to have it, though.'

Christina rolled her eyes, then handed the glass to Sally. 'What about you, Sally? Can you stop flirting for one minute to down this? I can't imagine you're running anywhere tomorrow.'

Sally flushed, chose to ignore the veiled insult with a giggle. 'You are such a bad influence, Chris.' She never seemed to notice the loaded comments Christina made at her expense and it had become a bit of light entertainment for Christina to see how many unnoticed gibes she could get away with. Sally just wanted to be liked, which made it too easy. Christina swallowed down a knot of guilt that swelled in her throat. It was just banter, after all. Sally didn't mind.

As if to prove her right, Sally did as she was told and necked her wine, inhaled sharply, then slumped into her chair, which then toppled backwards onto the floor. Sally was left flat on her back with her legs in the air, ballet pumps flapping, ample thighs wide open. Christina burst out laughing while Trevor tried to upend her.

Lisa rushed away with a folded chair in her hands, mortified as faces round them tutted and scowled.

'Bloody hell, you alright, Sally?' Owen said.

Sally started to laugh, but her cheeks were puce with humiliation.

'Fuck me,' said Ben, then started to laugh too.

The headmaster stomped over to them and engaged his best authoritative voice to say, 'Right, I think you've all had enough, don't you? Time to go home. The way out is over there.' He raised his arm and pointed to the saloon doors to the hall.

Christina, Ben and Sally looked at him, then burst out laughing again. He flushed, lowered his arm and walked away.

'Come on, you're all coming to our house,' Ben said.

'Ooh, fabulous idea,' Christina replied. 'You up for that, darling?'

'Damn right I am,' Colin replied with a grin.

'Yay!' Sally said. Trevor didn't look like he knew what was going on, but the curry splash was now gone at least.

'What about you, Owen? Or are you off to beddy-byes?' Ben said.

This was a side of Ben that Christina hadn't seen before. Barbed comments that poked at Owen, provoking him, like he was playing the same game that she was with Sally. Pissed Ben was much more fun than Sober Ben.

'I have a run tomorrow, like I say, so we won't join you,' Lena said.

'Yes, but that doesn't mean Pretty Boy here can't carry on with us, does it?' His words swam into each other, softened with alcohol but sharp with a sting, nonetheless.

Lena shrugged. 'He is welcome to join you if he wants to. I am not his keeper.' She looked annoyed.

'There you go then. What's it going to be, Pretty Boy? A cup of cocoa at home or a beer with those of us who know how to have a good time?'

Lisa scuttled back to the table and reached between them to grab her handbag from the floor.

'Everyone is coming back to your house, Lisa. Should be

a right laugh,' Christina announced with glee, made that much sweeter when Lisa gaped at her.

'Really? Tonight?'

'Yes, we're all in. Just waiting to see if Owen is coming too,' Christina added.

'But the girls are home,' Lisa said lamely.

Christina didn't attempt to hide her judgement as she rolled her eyes. 'Shouldn't they be out having fun?'

'Emma is studying for her mocks,' Lisa said tightly.

'Her mocks are two weeks away. Lighten up, Lisa! She's seventeen – loosen those apron strings!'

'So what's it going to be then, Owen?' Ben interrupted.

Christina looked between Owen and Ben, who were now glaring at each other, two alpha males trying to decide who could piss the furthest.

'You're on,' Owen said.

4

Christina

Now

Despite what had happened between her and Lisa, she would never wish this on either of them. She sat in the car park of the hospital, not wanting to go in, but knowing she couldn't avoid it. The sky was pitch black and the air smelled like rain that hadn't fallen yet. She gripped the steering wheel with shaking hands as she thought about all the time that had passed until they had reached this point.

They used to be such good friends in the early days, her and Lisa, when the girls were starting school together. Christina remembered turning up to the reception year mixer in the park a few weeks before school started, not knowing anyone as she had only just moved into the area after Sophia's dad had left her high and dry.

The move had cost her a small fortune after her marriage collapsed. She had sold up in order to move to a nicer area where the schools were good enough for Sophia to be anything she wanted to be. Their little terraced house was way more expensive than she could afford, but it meant she was within walking distance of a primary and secondary school with excellent reputations and a good art programme – because of course Sophia would be an artist like her mother.

Christina had even given up her passion for sculpture and taken a full-time job at the local doctor's surgery as a receptionist in order to earn more money to pay for her hefty mortgage, thinking it would all be worth it when Sophia blossomed into a happy, independent spirit who didn't need a man to take care of her.

She remembered meeting Lisa so clearly. The meeting point was in the local park, near the coffee shop, and all of the other mothers were already there when Christina had turned up. It was a sticky day in July, the air soupy with humidity. As soon as she arrived, she realised that she stood out like a sore thumb in her tiny shorts and very tight white T-shirt that was sticking to her sweaty back. The other mums were in flowing dresses and sparkling sandals. Sophia had gripped onto Christina's leg, hiding behind her as the other kids played, still sulking from being forced to have sun cream applied to her tiny nose.

Lisa was the first to get up and approach Christina with a welcoming smile. She had invited her to come and join her on the other side of the group. Nerves took over and in her haste to follow Lisa, Christina had shoved Sophia towards the other kids, desperate for her to engage with them and make friends, but Sophia had tripped over the edge of a picnic blanket and fallen, then started to scream.

Christina was mortified and had scooped her up to see her lip was bleeding. The other mothers had looked on in what had felt like judgement, but Lisa had taken over, calmly gathering up Sophia, distracting her with a bag of Haribo as she dabbed at her bleeding lip with a tissue, and introducing her to her daughter, Emma.

Sally was also sitting among the mums spread out on the grass, but she had her hands full with her twin boys, who seemed to cause chaos everywhere they went, whether it was racing towards the pond, poking at each other with sharp sticks or pulling the legs off a small spider.

Lena was there too, sitting cross-legged in dignified silence while her son, Kai, sat in her lap eating raisins and watching the twins with detached interest.

As it turned out, Sophia and Emma were instant best friends once the blood and tears had been wiped away. The group had met again later in the week in the pub, with Christina having to park a sleeping Sophia in the corner of the pub in her pushchair since she didn't have a babysitter. Everyone had voiced sympathy of her situation and, although her and Sally clearly shared a love of wine, Lisa and Christina had giggled at everything and got along really well, while Lena merely sat quietly and watched them, mildly bemused, nursing a Diet Coke.

As she kept one foot on the pushchair, rocking Sophia gently while she slept through the noise of the pub, Christina had told Lisa that night how much the childcare was going to be for Sophia in the afternoons after school while she was at work and Lisa had offered to help her out. She had suggested that Christina pay her a much smaller amount to cover food and any arts and crafts, and Lisa would look after Sophia since she would be at home with Emma anyway.

It was the perfect set-up. Lisa would collect the girls from school, take them home for lunch, then they would play educational games or do arts and crafts in the afternoon. Lisa would then make them dinner and Christina would arrive to collect Sophia just as the dinner plates were being cleared away and would take Sophia home for bath time and bed. On Fridays, Christina finished earlier and would go straight from work to Lisa's house with a bottle of wine. They'd chat and drink while the girls finished their tea, sometimes letting the evening rumble on until Christina was carrying Sophia home already asleep in borrowed pyjamas. They lived close enough for her to do that.

Lisa then offered to continue during the school holidays because Emma and Sophia were such good friends. It had seemed that, after all the heartbreak and discord of the last few years, life couldn't have worked out better for Christina.

She sighed and leaned her forehead on the steering wheel.

But nothing is permanent, is it?

One afternoon, one impulsive moment, and that bubble had burst. And Lisa and Christina's friendship had come to a very abrupt end.

There'd been gossip, rumours, some of it going too far. Socially, the two women had been forced to share space since Lisa hadn't wanted to go quietly. They had circled each other in the playground like caged tigers, scowling and spitting, but the older the kids got, the harder it was to force themselves to be polite, especially since the girls were not the best of friends any longer. Christina had encouraged Sophia to find her friendships elsewhere and she had been delighted when Emma was no longer part of her squad.

But this? Sitting outside a hospital, too scared to go in and hear what had happened, who was hurt, how badly?

Christina wouldn't wish this on her worst enemy, even Lisa. She knew that her children meant everything to Lisa and the idea that any of them could end up in this situation was horrifying.

Christina felt like ice had been poured down her throat and into her chest.

With a deep breath, she opened the car door and strode into the hospital on legs that were not as stable as she was pretending.

5

Sophia

Six Weeks Ago

The teenagers sat in the lounge, spilling over the sides of the couches and onto the floor, passing drinks between them, bowls of crisps sitting untouched on the coffee table. This had become their weekend routine – gathering at someone's house with illegally bought bottles of vodka and listening to music while they scrolled absently on their phones. Often it ended up being at Sophia's house because her mother, Christina, was cool about it.

There were more of them in the kitchen. Someone had opened the back door despite the chill in the air. The twins, Carter and Leo, were ordering pizza using their mother's Domino's account. They insisted she wouldn't mind, so Sophia let them carry on. Her mother was very happy to hand her house over to them whenever Sophia asked, but she couldn't afford to feed them too. Sometimes Sophia only invited the twins because they brought a lot of the booze and always ended up paying for the food. Sally gave in to them so easily. The twins were always laughing about it behind her back, laughing about her too. Sophia found it sad that they had so little respect for Sally. Maybe it was because they were boys – but Kai wasn't like that about Lena.

Sophia walked out of the kitchen and sat down on the couch in the lounge. She leaned against her current boyfriend, Ollie. He reached out to stroke her hair. He'd taken to doing this, but she felt like a pet dog when he did. She twitched and swiped at his hand, hoping he would get the hint, but he carried on.

She watched Kai from across the room. He was quiet tonight, but that wasn't unusual. He had never been like the other boys she knew. He was thoughtful, considerate, always making sure the girls were ok and calling the other boys out on their behaviour, especially the twins who could get a bit handsy when they were drunk or high. He looked over at her and smiled.

Her stomach flipped over. She looked away.

The pungent smell of weed wafted through from the other room. She pushed Ollie's hand away and got up to see who had brought drugs, although she was pretty certain it was the twins. Her mother was ok with weed – she had a stash of her own in her artist's studio at the bottom of the garden – but Sophia wasn't interested in drugs and also wanted to make sure the twins hadn't been in the studio and stolen her mother's supply, because that would not go down well. The studio was strictly off limits.

She stepped over legs and bodies, and walked into the hallway just as the doorbell rang. Expecting the pizza delivery, she opened the door.

Emma stood on the front step.

'Oh, hi,' Sophia said in surprise. 'What are you doing here?'

'So I... er... saw on your Snap that you had people over and I was kinda bored, so wondered if you'd mind if I joined in?'

Sophia felt uncomfortable. She couldn't say no, but she knew most of the people in the house behind her would not want Emma here.

'Oh, right.'

But what could she say? It was one thing being mean behind her back, but another to look her in the face and tell her she wasn't welcome.

Although they still said hello to each other in the corridor and were polite on the surface, their friendship had cooled over the years, especially since their mums fell out. Emma was nice enough to Sophia, but she was a geek, always studying, didn't make an effort to hang out with anyone, and very condescending to everyone else. She did herself no favours. Her clothes were on the wrong side of a trend; she never bothered with make-up or anything; she didn't even play sport. She studied. That was it. And everyone sneered at her for it. There was also their history – Christina had warned Sophia about how toxic Lisa and her family could be.

So to see her here, on Sophia's doorstep – and swaying a little, Sophia noticed – was very unusual.

'Um, sure, come in.' She held the door open. Emma tripped on her way in. Sophia noticed that she was clutching a bottle of vodka in her hand. Half of it was gone. Emma had attempted to put on make-up, but the eyeliner was too heavy and smudged under her eyes.

'You ok, Emma?'

'Yeah.' She gave Sophia the fakest of smiles, swigged straight from the vodka bottle, and wandered down the hall towards the kitchen. Sophia followed her.

It was indeed Carter and Leo who were smoking the weed. The kitchen door was closed now and a heavy cloud of smoke hovered around their heads. She pushed past Emma. 'God, can you open the door again please? I don't want to get lung cancer thanks to you two idiots,' Sophia said with distaste. They pulled a face at her.

Sophia stormed over to the door herself and pushed it wide open. A blast of cold air swept into the room.

'God, it's freezing!' Leo complained as Carter started to giggle. Then Leo said, 'Emma.'

Carter frowned and turned to see her standing in the doorway, watching with interest. 'Emma. Hi,' Carter said.

'Carter – or Leo... I'm not sure which one...' Emma giggled and swigged from the bottle again.

'Can I get you some water, Emma?' Sophia asked in concern.

'No, why?'

Sophia shrugged. The doorbell rang again. She listened to hear if anyone else would answer. Moments passed. It chimed once more. Sophia sighed and went to answer it.

The pizza delivery guy shoved three large pizzas into her outstretched arms and sloped away. She kicked the door closed with her foot and went into the lounge, shouting, 'Pizza's here!'

Carter and Leo appeared in nanoseconds, followed more sedately by Emma.

'What's she doing here?' Sophia's friend, Max, said loudly.

Sophia shrugged. 'I said she could hang out with us. If you don't like it, you can do one.'

Max shrugged in reply.

Kai was the only one to look happy about Emma being there. He smiled and waved her over, pushing over on the couch so that there was space next to him for her. Emma stepped over everyone, ignoring the curious glances and sniggers.

Sophia plonked the pizza boxes on the coffee table and stepped back as they swooped in.

Sophia watched Emma and Kai talking. They had basically sat in the corner and ignored everyone else for the last hour. She didn't mind Emma coming over, but she did expect her to mix with everyone, get involved in other conversations maybe. Everyone was now playing Truth or Dare, a game Sophia hated, but the twins had started it and Leo was currently being dared to run up the street naked.

He stripped off in the hallway and the group followed en masse to watch him as he darted out into the cold night air and ran screaming up the middle of the street. Everyone except Emma and Kai.

They all piled back into the lounge, laughing at Leo. Emma and Kai hadn't moved. Emma was still swigging from her vodka bottle and Sophia hadn't seen her eat any of the pizza. Now there were just abandoned crusts in the boxes and the crisp bowls were empty too. No food left to soak up the vodka she had swallowed.

Sophia was distracted for a while by Ollie, who suggested

that the two of them should go upstairs. Ollie was nice enough, but not for that. He had an annoying habit of blinking like he had something in his eye or a twitch of some kind, and it was getting on her nerves – that and the fact that he followed her around like a puppy. The twitch had gone into overdrive while he'd made his proposition. She felt like she couldn't breathe. She pushed past him and went into the now quiet kitchen. The twins had left their spliff end smouldering on the kitchen table. She picked it up, stubbed it out on the side of an empty beer can and shoved it to the bottom of the bin.

Someone came up behind her. Hands snaked around her waist. Fury bloomed in her chest, red and spicy. She was furious that it was Ollie standing behind her, that he was paying her so much attention, that he was so needy.

That he wasn't Kai.

'Ollie, just leave me alone. Stop pawing at me like I'm a pet dog.'

He stepped back, visibly shocked at her outburst. 'Whoa, what's up with you?'

'I just… you know, I'm not feeling this, you and me. I think we're done.'

'What the fuck, Soph? Why?'

She shrugged – the eternal language of teenagers that could say so much and yet so little in one tiny movement.

He looked at her, baffled, then embarrassed. 'Yeah, well, whatever. You're not all that anyway.' He stormed out. She heard the front door slam moments later.

She felt like crying and wasn't sure why. She didn't really like Ollie. She just knew that if you wanted to fit in, you had to have the right kind of boyfriend, otherwise you were a loser, and he had fit the bill.

Look at Emma. She was actually quite pretty with perfectly straight, dark hair, but her teeth stuck out a little at the front and her nose was too prominent. None of this was a crime, but because she made no effort, she was subjected to plenty of abuse at school. People tripping her up in the canteen, posting stuff about her and her nose online, deliberately targeting her in dodge ball because she was so uncoordinated. Sophia thought she would die if she was suddenly the one in the crosshairs.

She wandered back into the lounge, pondering whether she could ask everyone to leave yet. Her mother was at the school quiz night and that was only due to end in about an hour. Even so, her friends knew that Christina often came home after being out and joined in the fun, laughing with the teenagers, maybe lending a shoulder to cry on if needed, and definitely helping the drunk ones to sober up before they made their way home.

Her friends loved Christina because she was like one of them and so different to their own parents. No judgement, she just held their hair back, cleaned up their mess, made sure they were safe and sent them on their way. Sophia knew she had lucked out when they handed out parents, even if Christina was doing it on her own and had to be both father and mother to her.

Kai and Emma were now sitting even closer together. Kai was leaning in to talk to her and Emma was giggling. Their hands were intertwined. Sophia felt that deep-seated fury burn through her again.

Kai got to his feet and held out his hand to help Emma up. She swayed and Sophia thought she would topple over, but she righted herself and smiled like Sophia had never seen before.

The fury blipped in Sophia's throat until she could taste it. She grabbed her phone and snapped a few photos of them as they left the lounge to a chorus of excited jeering that followed them upstairs. Sophia went after them, watching through narrowed eyes, the rage still burning. She stood at the foot of the stairs and took a few more photos as they stopped at the top of the stairs and Kai leaned in for a kiss.

She couldn't watch anymore. Her cheeks burned; her chest was on fire. She shoved her phone into her pocket and went back into the lounge.

'Right,' she said loudly. 'This is boring. Let's get some boat races going!'

6

Lisa

Now

The drive was the longest journey of her life. Ben sat beside her in stony silence, gripping the steering wheel so tightly that his knuckles were flaring red. He looked over at her and smiled thinly, saw her staring at his hands and forced them to relax. Then the tapping started, his ring clicking against the steering wheel in a way that set her teeth on edge and made her want to scream at him.

She looked away, out of the window into the night. There were still so many people about, walking along the streets, shouting, laughing, sirens blaring and horns hooting. Normal lives playing out loudly in public while Lisa felt like she was shrivelling up inside. Their car weaved through the late-night London traffic to a part of the city she didn't recognise. She watched faces pass them by, faces she would never see again, faces she now envied for their carefree existence.

They had left their fourteen-year-old daughter, Lucy, at home, not wanting to freak her out until they knew what they were dealing with. Lisa had thought about calling her mother, but it was a twenty-minute drive from her house to Lisa's and she would have been in bed for hours already. Instead, Lisa woke Lucy and explained that they had to go and fetch Emma from a gig. Lucy had merely nodded, rolled over and gone back to sleep. Lisa expected to get to the hospital, find that Emma was fine and they would be home within the hour. Lucy would be none the wiser. And if it took longer – maybe she had broken her arm and she needed a cast or something – then Ben could come back home and be with Lucy.

But if she was so sure it was just a broken arm, why did she have this gaping hole of emptiness in her chest?

Lisa forbade her mind to go to darker places. It was probably a broken arm. Maybe she had had too much to drink and had fallen – we all know what teenagers were like. That was it. Nothing serious. Christina was making a mountain out of a molehill.

And maybe it wasn't even Emma. It could be Sophia who had had the accident. Christina hadn't actually said who it was. Or had she? Had she tried to tell Lisa more and Lisa hadn't wanted to hear it? She couldn't remember anymore.

That was it. They would find Emma in the waiting room, waiting for a lift home, annoyed that Sophia had ruined their night.

Ben pulled into the drop-off zone outside the hospital. Lisa knew she had to get out, but couldn't get her feet to move, despite what she had spent the whole journey trying to convince herself of. Her brain screamed at her that she was wasting time, but her legs remained rooted to the dirty floormat of the car.

Ben looked over and gave her an encouraging smile. 'I'll be two minutes. Just need to park somewhere. I'll come and find you. She'll be ok, you'll see.' His tone was soft, paternal, but the sheer terror she was feeling was mirrored in his eyes and in the tight lines around his mouth. She smiled back weakly and mustered the strength to open the car door.

The fluorescent lights of the hospital blinded her as she walked through the automatic doors. She stopped just inside, the doors swishing shut behind her, then swishing open again as she stood in the way of the sensor. She looked around, unsure where to go, what to do. Then she saw Christina ahead of her, standing with her hands clasped in front of her, wringing at each other.

Lisa glared at her. Her feet moved her towards Christina. She could feel her teeth grinding.

'Where is she?'

'Listen, Lisa, I think you should sit down and listen first before I take you to her.' Christina put a hand on her arm, but Lisa snatched it away.

'Just tell me where my daughter is. What the hell have you done to her? You were supposed to be watching them.'

'I haven't done anything! They were at a gig. It's not my fault your daughter lied to you.' Christina exhaled and said in a calmer voice, 'This way.'

Lisa followed her along corridor after corridor, all the same, like an endless, sterile maze painted in mint green.

7

Lisa

Six Weeks Ago

They stumbled down the road, the cold air forming clouds around their heads. Ben had linked arms with Colin and they were singing as they weaved down the street like old school buddies, not two blokes that had just met at a school quiz. Christina and Sally walked a few paces behind, giggling, their voices reaching Lisa in stage whispers.

Lisa could feel a low hum of tension running through her body like an electric current. It wasn't just the unexpected and sudden intrusion of everyone in her home, bringing with it the worries about whether the girls had cleared away their pizza boxes or if she had emptied the pile of laundry that had been sitting in the kitchen all week. It was also the thought of this group of people in the same small space together for much longer. A school hall had barely managed to contain the friction. She felt like she was tiptoeing around an unexploded bomb.

Ben hadn't said a word to Lisa yet about why he had been

so late, nor apologised for that matter. He was too drunk for good manners. They had barely said two words to each other and now he was avoiding the inevitable altercation even more by inviting everyone back to their house. She hadn't seen him drink this much in a long time. As far as she knew, it had been a regular day at the office, so how had he ended up in such a state? Sure, he'd been distracted lately, spending more time at the gym, saying very little, coming home from work with his tie already loosened, as though he couldn't wait to release the pressure around his neck. Then falling asleep on the couch, having said very little to her. Lisa told herself it was stress at work, but there was a niggling whine in her ear about something else going on. She had tried to talk to him, but their conversations were snippy and curt.

She watched him as he staggered along with Colin, a pebble of unease sitting in the base of her throat.

'You ok, Lisa?' Owen asked. Lisa had almost forgotten that he was walking one pace behind her, his hand clasped tightly to Lena's, like she was clutching onto him. Lena towered over Lisa, statuesque in her flat shoes, making Lisa feel insignificant and small. Lena's usually smooth forehead had been knotted into a frown for most of the evening.

'Yes, thanks Owen. I'm fine, just wasn't really up for a long night tonight and I have a headache from the cheap school wine.'

'You can tell them all to go home, you know,' Owen said.

'I don't think the decision is up to me,' Lisa said with a thin smile. 'He's... I don't know, he's in a strange mood. Drunk way more than he should have.'

'Listen, I'll come back to your house with you – moral support. Christina is in a very disagreeable mood too.'

'But what about me? I don't want to stay out. I have a big run tomorrow and there's the babysitter to consider,' Lena said snippily.

'I can still walk you home, pay the babysitter, and then go back to Lisa's. I just think she needs my support. Besides, you'll be asleep soon anyway,' he replied.

Lisa watched the dynamic play out with interest. 'I don't want to cause any trouble,' she said quietly. She didn't want to admit how much she wanted Owen there.

'It's no trouble at all,' Owen answered, but Lena was making it clear that she was not pleased with the arrangement. 'I'll walk Lena home first, the come back to yours. Lena has a big run planned tomorrow.'

'Oh yes, there's not long to go now to the marathon, is there?' Lisa tried to lighten the mood, but Lena merely scowled.

Lena was running the London Marathon for the umpteenth time. Lord knew why. Lisa understood the need for health and fitness – she was a part-time yoga and pilates instructor, after all – but she didn't understand the desire to put your body under that kind of trauma and stress by running in a straight line for hours on end. There was a lot about Lena that Lisa found fascinating, alluring, often baffling, from her natural Scandinavian beauty to the fact that she could have three children and still look like she had walked off a film set with minimal effort every day while finding the time to run marathons and manage an online business selling gifts and jewellery. Some women just seemed to wake up on the right side of the bed every day, while Lisa felt like she was tumbling out of the wrong side more often than not, then putting her knickers on inside out and struggling through the day trying to work out why she felt off kilter.

Lena accelerated ahead.

'Are you sure this is ok?' Lisa said to Owen.

'Ben isn't the only one in a strange mood. I'll see you in a bit,' he replied and followed after Lena.

The rest of the group turned into Lisa's road as Lena and Owen carried on straight towards where they lived a few streets further along. Lisa followed at a distance. She could hear Sally cackling, loud in the quiet street, while Christina gripped onto her arm, teetering on those high, thin heels that looked more suited to a strip show than a school quiz. Lisa was uncomfortable in her wedges and had been looking forward to kicking them off as soon as she got home. Could she still do that? Surely they were all too drunk to notice if she was barefoot.

As they neared the house and she started to rummage in her handbag for her keys, Lisa wondered why she still made time to hang out with these people. This was the pure definition of a toxic environment.

It hadn't always been like this, but Lisa had realised recently that these were her only friends, if she could call them that. Ben had his colleagues at work and a few friends he was still in contact with from his university days, but she had put her career on hold for the kids years ago and didn't really have any hobbies through which she could meet new people.

So this was it.

Depressing.

Their motley crew reached the house, but before Lisa could push through them to open the door, Ben pulled his keys out. He seemed to be having a problem getting the key in the lock. Sally was giggling and hiccupping while leaning on Trevor, who was stumbling under the weight of her. Lisa thought she saw her neighbour's curtains flutter as their voices rose in merriment, taunting Ben for his lack of co-ordination.

Eventually, Lisa's impatience won out and she pushed through the bodies blocking the doorway to grab the key from Ben. 'I'll do it.'

'Oooooh, touchy,' said Christina.

Lisa resisted the urge to stab her in the throat with the key.

She pushed open the door. All of the lights were on. Today's teenagers were all about being eco-friendly and yet couldn't turn off a light when they left a room. It was 11 p.m. and she fully expected Lucy to at least be in bed, but the blue glare of the television flickered onto the white walls of the hallway. Lisa shrugged out of her coat and hung it on the hook just inside the door, leaving the rest of them to fall into the house of their own accord.

Jester, their cockapoo, barked twice, then rushed at her, his tail wagging his entire body. She patted him briefly before he moved onto the others.

Lisa walked into the lounge where Lucy was curled up under a blanket on the couch, watching old *Love Island* episodes.

'You're still up. And what are you watching that for? You know I've said you're too young.'

'Oh Mum, it's fine. It's teaching me about how stupid

some people can be,' Lucy replied with a grin and the wide eyes of someone who has watched too much television.

A pizza box was tossed onto the coffee table, along with an empty ice cream pot that pooled melted chocolate ice cream onto the wood, along with a dirty spoon and an empty can of Coke. Lisa frowned when she saw the Coke – no wonder Lucy was still awake.

'Your dad has invited everyone back here for another drink.'

'Oh, right, fun.' Lucy sat up a little straighter, but didn't seem too bothered.

'Where's Em?'

'She's been upstairs for most of the night. She said she wasn't feeling well and said not to disturb her.'

Lisa was annoyed to hear that. The least Emma could've done was hang out with her little sister for a bit.

The voices behind her grew louder as they all crowded into the lounge doorway, peering over Lisa, loudly greeting Jester. Lisa quickly gathered up Lucy's mess.

'Hello Lucy!' Sally shouted, while Ben pushed through to collapse on Lucy in what was meant to be a hug but ended up being a pile-on, with Sally collapsing on top of Ben.

Lucy laughed. 'Good quiz then?'

Christina walked straight past the lounge and disappeared into the kitchen at the other end of the hall, calling out, 'I'll find the wine!'

Lisa sighed and followed after her.

Christina had her head in the fridge already. 'The wine is in this fridge, Christina,' Lisa said frostily and indicated the wine fridge built under the kitchen island.

'Ooh, posh,' Christina said, despite knowing where the wine fridge was. There was no thank you as Lisa handed over a full bottle of white wine. Instead, Christina said, 'Crisps. We need crisps. I'm starving.'

The rest of the group had remained in the lounge and she could hear them teasing and quizzing Lucy in equal measure. She felt torn by the need to protect her daughter from the drunkenness on show in the other room and leaving Christina to her own devices in her kitchen. Lisa flung open a cupboard, grabbed a large bag of crisps and flung them at Christina. 'I'll bring the glasses.'

Christina flounced from the room, leaving Lisa alone. She leaned against the countertop, her head in her hands, the headache now firmly rooted behind her eyes. She could hear the television being turned off and someone asking for a speaker so that they could find a Spotify playlist. Sally was still cackling about nothing presumably, while Colin's gravelly voice was suggesting 'party songs to get us in the mood'.

'Mum?' She turned to see Lucy standing behind her, wrapped in her blanket. 'You ok?'

'Yes, just got a headache and could do without this tonight. Sorry, love, it was your dad's idea.'

'Oh, I don't mind. They're funny when they're drunk – and Dad could do with having some fun.'

Lisa frowned. She sometimes forgot how perceptive Lucy was, how she could pick up on a vibe or read a room better than anyone Lisa had ever met.

'I'm going to go upstairs – can I carry on watching *Love Island* on my laptop?' she said.

Lisa paused, then said, 'Sure, but just for tonight.'

Lucy kissed her on the cheek and bounced away.

Lisa grabbed glasses and a couple of bottles of beer, and headed back into the lounge.

8

Ben

Now

He had no idea how he had got here, sitting in his car in the dark in the A&E car park.

He had been fast asleep. These days it was like that. One minute he was sitting down to watch the football highlights and the next he was waking up and it was three in the morning. And then he would be wide awake, his mind turning everything over, his body exhausted and aching.

He hadn't had a proper conversation with Lisa in what felt like months. He knew she could sense him pulling away, but he couldn't find the words to vocalise what he wanted to say. Everything felt like an argument he wasn't going to win.

She had barrelled into the bedroom and turned on the light, which actually hadn't woken him. She had to shove him a few times and say his name loudly. He had heard it from a distance, calling through a fog, and had eventually sat up in bed, groggy, his eyes dry, his throat raspy.

All she had said was that there had been an accident

involving Sophia and Emma, but she didn't know what had happened or if they were hurt. She had been babbling at him, the words disjointed and tangled up. From what he could gather, she didn't know anything definitive, but was going off what Christina had said in a phone call.

Ben didn't even know Emma had gone out. That shamed him a little bit. But he had been so caught up in everything else going on in his life that he had been selfishly oblivious to those around him.

He was disgusted at himself, cowardly hiding in the dark while Lisa had gone straight into the hospital, her eyes focused and her back straight. Instead, he sat in the shadows, looking at the looming hospital building with a horrible sense of dread. People came here when they were sick or dying. Instead of rushing in after her to find out what had happened, he had found a parking space straight away and then just sat, cemented into the car seat.

He slowly unfurled his hands and grabbed his phone from the centre console. The locked screen showed the recent text message that he had avoided responding to, still there, a constant reminder of the mess he had got himself into.

He swiped away the message and got out of the car.

9

Emma

Six Weeks Ago

Emma's breath froze as she neared the house. She had expected it to be in darkness, her parents in bed already, but the fact that every room was illuminated and she could hear the dull thud of music meant an impromptu party had broken out.

Tonight was full of surprises.

She stepped back and leaned against a garden wall, deep in the shadows on the other side of the street, dizziness hitting her. She closed her eyes for a second, tried to still the seasick feeling in her stomach. She opened her eyes again and focused on the house.

This was very much unusual behaviour for her parents, who were possibly the most boring people she had ever encountered. They didn't even go out for dinner together anymore, let alone have parties. Not that she could talk. Tonight was probably the first night she had been out in ages – and she hadn't officially been invited.

She had just wanted to be a part of something for a

change. Trying to stop the horrible feeling that her life was being planned out for her and she had lost control of it. She had nearly chickened out, knowing that the reception was likely going to be less than friendly. She knew none of them liked her. That's why she had stolen the vodka from her parent's cupboard. Maybe if she pretended to be like them, they would let her in.

She could see heads bobbing through the bay window where the wooden shutters were still wide open to the street. Sophia's mum, Christina, was definitely there and was dancing with some bloke with a belly and more hair on his chin than on his head. They looked to be gyrating against each other from what Emma could see.

Emma pulled her fake leather jacket tighter to her body as the cold air penetrated her skin. She could see her dad dancing too, holding a bottle of beer in the air and singing to 'Mr Brightside'. The music had been turned up and was now clearly audible. Mr Schaeffer next door would be annoyed.

Emma looked up at the window on the second floor of her house. It was dark, but the curtains were still open and there was a bluish tinge to the light, which meant Lucy was still up and watching something on her laptop. Probably *Love Island*. She was obsessed with it.

Emma wondered where her mum was. Maybe she had gone to bed. Not likely though with the music blaring. More likely, she was sitting on the couch in the corner, scowling at everyone else having fun.

Neither of her parents had noticed she wasn't home clearly. But then she had made sure they wouldn't. She had padded her bed with old teddies and left some hair extensions on the pillow to make it look like it was her hair fanning out around her. If they had poked their head into her room, it would've looked like she was fast asleep. She pulled her phone from her back pocket and checked it. There were no panicked missed calls from either of them. Or from Lucy, who had followed her earlier instructions to leave her alone. All she had received was a Snapchat from Kai that she was ignoring.

She went to step out of the shadows, then jumped back again as someone walked up to their front door. A man, his head covered by a beanie hat, his coat padded and puffy. He paused, leaned backwards to look into the bay window, shook his head and knocked loudly on the door.

A few seconds passed while he shuffled from foot to foot in the cold. The door opened and the beam of light from the hallway spilled onto him. Owen, Kai's dad. He pulled the beanie from his head as he said something to whoever had opened the door. An arm came out and grabbed onto his hand, held onto it while they spoke. As he stepped inside, the person in the house moved to one side and Emma could see that it was her mother.

Emma instinctively pinned herself back against the wall again, even though she was dressed head to toe in black and there was no way her mother would see her from there.

The door closed again.

Emma stood for a little longer, watching the window thoughtfully, then she stepped out of the shadows and crossed the street silently. There was an alleyway down the side of their house, dark and overgrown with weeds. Her feet carried her along in the darkness. She paused when her foot kicked an empty bottle that had been lying discarded in the weeds, then she carried on down the alley. She halted again as she saw eyes peering back at her from the darkness ahead.

Her heart jumped.

The fox considered her for a moment, then strolled away to root in someone's bins.

Their house backed onto another alley leading to the railway station and there was a small gate cut into their back garden fence. It had a combination lock on it and she knew the code. As far as she knew, it had never been changed.

She punched in the code and pushed open the gate as quietly as she could. She didn't know why she was taking such care. There was no way they would be able to hear her over the music. If anything, it would be Jester that gave her away. She could see him now, standing behind the glass door of the kitchen, watching her as she crept through the garden, his tail wagging excitedly.

The kitchen and open-plan dining room beyond the door was lit up, but there was no one in there other than Jester. She paused, held her finger up to her mouth, said, 'Shhhhh' to Jester and carried on around the side of the house.

The ladder was still propped up where she had left it. Her father was not one for DIY, so hadn't noticed it had been relocated. She climbed the ladder and swung herself up onto the flat roof, feeling the excitement of it all ticking through her like live electricity, helping to sober her mind. For a moment, she felt like she was going to throw up, but she breathed through it and the nausea passed.

Emma looked down through the skylight. For a moment, she imagined herself stepping onto the glass, feeling it crack and groan beneath her weight like an icy lake, shifting slowly, bulging inwards before yielding and collapsing in on itself, taking her with it, gravity pulling her body down.

Then her eyes fell on Jester as he peered up at her. He gave one sharp bark, his eyes wide and confused.

She stepped away from the skylight, put her hands on the ledge of her bedroom window and pulled herself inside, making sure to close the window again behind her.

10

Christina

Now

'Now before we get ahead of ourselves, we need to understand what they have taken,' the doctor was saying to Lisa, who sat in a chair, bent over double, her face in her hands.

Christina couldn't sit. It felt like the mint-green walls were pulsating and throbbing. She had been pacing the corridor, keeping some distance between herself and Lisa, the movement helping to keep her from falling into full panic mode while she waited to hear about Sophia. She had drawn closer when the doctor had approached.

'Ask her! She will have given them whatever it was!' Lisa shouted suddenly, launching to her feet and making the doctor recoil. She was pointing a shaking finger at Christina.

Christina's mouth dropped open. What was she on about? 'Me? Why would I have given them anything?'

'Because you don't think drugs are dangerous! You think it's a laugh, that you need to be best friends with the kids, not a parent.' Lisa was advancing towards Christina as she flung the accusations around, suddenly looking so much taller than her five foot four and making Christina shrink away from her. The look on Lisa's face was pure hatred. 'This is your way of getting back at me, isn't it?'

'Lisa, stop. I know as much as you do about what has happened.'

'Do you remember that argument at the quiz night? Do you? When you said you wanted them to try drugs?' She cackled then, bitterly. It sounded like ice cracking. 'Of course you don't remember. You were drunk. Slut dropping and shoving your boobs in everyone's face.' She laughed hollowly again, shook her head.

'That is not what I said – and yes, I might have had a little too much to drink that night, but I do remember the... disagreement between us. You're taking it out of context.'

The doctor was watching them like he was at Wimbledon, his head swivelling from one to the other, one arm outstretched, as though that would do anything to keep them apart. 'Ladies—' he mumbled.

'Am I? Am I?' Lisa screeched. 'This is your fault and you know it. You gave them the drugs – I saw you!'

Confusion made Christina stutter. 'Wha—? I... when?'

'A few days ago. I saw her standing on your front doorstep and you handed her a packet. I saw you!'

'You have no idea what you're talking about, Lisa.'

'Look, ladies—' the doctor tried again.

'If you paid more attention, you would know why they were at my house in the first place,' Christina said in a low voice.

Lisa looked like she was going to launch herself at

Christina, but at just that moment, a tired and pale Ben strode up the corridor. 'Lisa! Enough!'

Lisa stopped, turned and looked like she was going to go off again, but crumpled into a seat instead and put her face in her hands again.

'Right, Doctor, please can you tell us what is going on here?' Ben said calmly.

11

Christina

Six Weeks Ago

Christina watched Lisa sit awkwardly in an armchair in the corner of her own living room, making it look like she was sitting in a gynaecologist's waiting room.

It was a predominantly beige room. There were the obligatory photo frames of the children, a smiles and teeth wedding photo, and a few carefully placed coffee table books, but no colour, no personality. Everything was carefully placed, easily forgettable, neat and contained.

Ben was dancing around, waving his arms in the air, sprinkling beer everywhere. Sweat pressed his shirt to his chest. Christina could see Lisa's eyes twitch with every sprinkle, like she was itching to get a mop out and clean up around his feet. Sally was singing loudly and out of tune, her round belly jiggling as she danced with Ben. They were at least having fun.

The pale fabric of the sofa Christina was sitting on was making her skin itchy. She drained her glass of wine and put the glass on the side table to the side of the coaster, hoping it would leave a ring. She was bored and more than a little drunk. The room was moving in and out like a kaleidoscope. She closed one eye to see if it would help, but that made her want to close the other one too and go to sleep, which she refused to do. She wasn't going to pass out on Lisa's scratchy sofa. How embarrassing.

She needed to move, to wake herself up. She swiped away Colin's hand where it sat, clammy, on her thigh and got to her feet, arching her back a little so that her best assets were on display. She swept over to where Ben and Sally were dancing. A look of disappointment flickered across Sally's red cheeks as Ben turned away from her when he saw Christina approach.

She knew Lisa was watching. Her eyes were laser pointers focused on Christina's back. Christina swayed up close to Ben, biting her lip. She stuck her chest out even more before moving over to the wall leading to the kitchen and leaning against it. She slid down the wall, flicking her hips from side to side, trying for a slut drop but also needing to use the wall to stop her from falling face-first onto the beige carpet. The studs on the pockets of her jeans scraped at the cream wall. Ben watched her with a curious mix of bemusement and mild fascination.

'Jeez, Christina, you'll leave marks on the paintwork,' Owen said loudly as he walked past her towards the kitchen, his lip curled in disgust. 'I think your pole-dancing days are behind you, don't you?'

Sally shrieked with laughter. Ben sniggered and Christina felt the heat of mortification flush her cheeks. She sashayed back over to Colin, feigning nonchalance while saying loudly, 'Another drink please, Colin.' Colin leapt to his feet to oblige. At least he seemed to have liked the show she had put on.

Owen returned from the kitchen with a low-alcohol beer for himself and a glass of water for Lisa. He sat back down next to her and gave her the glass, then leaned over and said something in her ear, clearly about Christina as they both looked over at her. Christina raised her hand and waved her fingers at them with a caustic smirk.

Sally plopped down onto the couch next to Christina, taking the space Colin had just vacated. Christina felt herself catapulted upwards. 'You two haven't let bygones be bygones then?' Sally said, out of breath. There were beads of sweat on her top lip and her cheeks were puce, like she had run five kilometres, not just danced a bit in someone's lounge. Sally was a walking heart attack waiting to happen. She had the bag of crisps in her hand. She ripped it open and offered it to Christina. The smell of cheese made Christina feel nauseous. She shook her head and pushed the open bag away from her. Sally shrugged and grabbed a fistful.

'What do you mean?' Christina replied, her eyes on Owen and Lisa as they talked quietly.

Ben had now disappeared into the kitchen with Colin. She could hear bottles clinking together.

'Well, that thing between you was years ago, but you've been glaring at each other all night. I can't remember the last time we all hung out and everyone was in a good mood. Why do we even invite her if you can't be in the same room?'

'I don't forgive easily, especially when it involves my child. Besides, you invited her, not me. You always invite her.'

'Because I like her and I want us all to get along, like we

did in the early days. I think she felt terrible about what happened and we certainly made her pay for it. All that talk and stuff.'

'Sally, you like everyone. That doesn't mean they are nice people; it means you are gullible.'

'There's nothing wrong with seeing the good in people, Christina – and in giving second chances.' She stood up and went to sit next to Trevor, who was asleep on the other couch, his head all but disappearing into the over-plumped cushion.

Christina scowled. It wasn't like Sally to stand up for herself like that. She was now engaged in a lively chat with Owen and Lisa, four of them (including the sleeping Trevor) squeezed onto the three-seater couch, Sally's hands gesticulating like she was conducting the London Philharmonic Orchestra. Lisa was smiling and looked like she might be thawing, which annoyed Christina even more. Trevor snored, woke himself up, looked around in confusion, then went back to sleep.

The truth was these were her only friends and, despite how annoying Sally was, she was fun to be around, if only because she acted as a foil to Christina since they were so different. Sally may be naïve and easily manipulated, but she was kind-hearted and just wanted to please those around her. Christina secretly wished she was a little bit more like Sally sometimes and it was good to have her around to remind herself of that.

But tonight, Christina was feeling salty and disagreeable. Blame it on the cheap wine. 'I know what this party needs. Does anyone have a joint?' she said over the music, which had moved into the 1990s.

'What the hell, Christina?' Owen said.

'What? Don't tell me a bit of weed is scandalous to you, Owen. You must have smoked a spliff or two in your time?'

'Not at our age, for God's sake.'

'Not at our age? Really? I'm not even fifty and I'm certainly not dead!'

'Drugs will certainly shorten your lifespan,' Lisa said in the tone of the high and mighty.

'Well, I'm not surprised you haven't tried anything, Lisa. Heaven forbid anyone should go against you, because we all know what the consequences would be.' Her tongue felt thick in her mouth and she still felt nauseous.

Lisa glared at her, but didn't rise to the bait. 'I don't want to try drugs. I have more sense than that.'

Christina sat forward. 'What would you do if you caught one of your girls smoking a joint?'

'Why?'

'I'm curious, that's all.'

'I'd advise them that weed is a gateway drug to harder stuff and that they are heading down a dangerous path.'

'Wow, so self-righteous. It must be a bundle of laughs in your house. And are you sure that's how you would react? You would talk to them calmly, would you? Not lose your temper just a little bit?'

'Yes, I would talk to them calmly. And I suppose you'd be alright with Sophia taking drugs. You were always so *relaxed* with her.'

'Sure, I think she should be allowed to experiment with it in a safe environment and make her own judgement call.'

'A safe environment – what, like your own house?'

Lisa had also sat forward and they glared at each other, the tension simmering like a pot on the boil.

'Well, you've always been a stickler for discipline, haven't you, Lisa? Particularly in *your* own home. At least my daughter talks to me.'

Lisa was interrupted from replying by Ben and Colin bursting into the room, carrying a bottle of something green and announcing there would be shots. Lisa launched to her feet.

'Enough, Ben!' she shouted.

Ben was too drunk to be embarrassed. 'Oh, come on Lisa. It's a bit of harmless fun.'

'No, Ben, no, it's not. Why does everyone here think that alcohol and drugs are just harmless fun? Ben, you are inebriated and the girls are upstairs. What kind of example are you setting?'

'What is your problem with fun, Lisa? Life is too short. Let your hair down a bit. You used to be fun. You used to take risks.' Ben sounded angry now, the words spitting from his lips.

'That's it, the party is over,' Owen said, looking more than a little embarrassed at the argument playing out in front of him.

Ben replied, 'I decide when the party is over, buddy. My house, my rules. And Lisa, I'm a big boy and you are not my mother.'

There was an audible gasp from Sally.

'Now I think we should all take a breath,' Owen said again, struggling a little with the saggy couch, but managing to get to his feet eventually. Trevor opened one eye, then closed it again.

Ben spun on Owen and said, 'You can fuck off home, Owen.'

Silence settled on them like a weighted blanket, broken only by the jarringly merry playlist that continued in the background.

Christina stood up too. 'Lisa, just chill. We are all adults having fun on a Friday evening. You're so worried about your girls seeing you have fun that it's pathetic. I'd rather that Sophia knew her mother could have a laugh and let her hair down – and yes, even smoke a spliff or two – than for her to think I was a self-righteous, stuck-up cow like you, looking down your nose at all of us. Colin, Ben, forget about these losers and pour me a shot!'

The cold air slapped her cheeks as Christina stumbled into the dark street, with Colin holding onto her arm. Her throat was raw and there was a horrible taste in her mouth. The door slammed behind them and she turned to look over her shoulder, but dizziness made her head spin and she sat down heavily on the footpath.

She laughed loudly as Colin tried to scoop her up by her armpits. He wasn't laughing anymore.

Christina's head was full of fluff and a buzzing noise that made forming thoughts difficult. She just wanted to sleep here, on the cold cement, because it was cool and steady, and if she lay down, everything would stop swaying, but Colin kept telling her they had to go home, that she couldn't sleep here. Then he started getting annoyed, saying she could sleep there for all he cared.

Which is it, Colin? Can I sleep here or not?

The next thing she remembered, she was unlocking her front door and collapsing onto the couch, fully clothed, face down into the cushion. She couldn't remember where Colin had gone. He was there – and then he wasn't. Had he even come home with her?

She didn't really care. She closed her eyes and passed out.

12

Lisa

Now

This was all too much. The lights were too bright, the doctors too brisk. Lisa felt confused, dizzy, like the air was pulsating, advancing and retreating in disinfected waves. She sat heavily, hoping the chair would be there to catch her. It was. She put her head in her hands, trying to stop the feeling of being on a lurching boat.

She could hear Ben's voice, but it was like it was coming from afar. Then another voice that sounded like Christina's, before she felt someone lifting her up. She wanted to say that her legs wouldn't hold her, that she couldn't stand because she would fall over, but her tongue had swollen in her mouth and she couldn't articulate any words.

Her heart was racing, her pulse erratic. She wondered if perhaps she was having a heart attack or some sort of seizure.

Then she was being led down the garishly mint-painted corridor and everything was swaying away from her, turning grey.

*

She opened her eyes to see Ben staring down at her in concern. She blinked, confused. She was in a small room on a hospital gurney. She felt like she had run a marathon, her legs weak, her heart hammering. She tried to sit up.

'Take your time,' Ben was saying, but he pushed her gently back onto the bed.

She lay still, then remembered what she had heard before the room dissolved away. She sat up sharply, felt the room tilt again, but managed to force out, 'What's going on? Where's Emma?'

'You passed out, Lisa. You need to take it easy.'

There was a blood pressure clip on her finger. She pulled it off and swung her legs off the gurney. 'I need to see her.'

'Ok, ok, but take it slowly.'

A nurse was hovering. She came over and said, 'Your husband is right. You've had a bit of a shock, so you need to take it slowly or you'll be no good to your daughter.' She smiled gently and Lisa wanted to slap that silly smile off her face. What did she know? Who the hell was she, telling her to take it easy? And where the hell was Emma?

Her daughter needed her and these two were smiling at her, telling her to take it easy? She needed to see Emma, hold her hand, tell her everything would be ok, just like she had when she had had nightmares as a toddler.

But would Emma wake up from this nightmare? Or would she be trapped in it, running and trying to escape, every turn in the maze a dead end, every step a stumble as the ground fell away, a monster around every corner as she tried to claw her way back to the present, but feeling like invisible hands were pushing her further down into the dark.

Lisa could feel the panic building again, waves of it threatening to engulf her. Was that really what it felt like to Emma? That's how Lisa imagined it to be. She needed to see Emma's face – if she looked to be resting peacefully, then Lisa could breathe again herself.

And what if she's not peaceful? What can I do about it? This is something I cannot control.

What if she is stuck in the dark in this nightmare forever?

13

Lisa

Six Weeks Ago

Lisa peeled back the Marigolds and flung them onto the kitchen counter. The smell of vomit clung to her like a vapour. Thank God she wasn't hungover or that clean-up task would've been unbearable. The fact that she hadn't found the putrid mess until this morning meant it was crusty and difficult to shift without a bit of elbow grease. Even now, there was a lingering smell and the pale-grey paint on the wall was stained.

The thought that Christina would be suffering this morning brought her a moment of smug joy.

She was also still finding glasses in peculiar places. She had just retrieved a shot glass from inside the money plant next to the fireplace. She sighed and looked out of the kitchen window into the garden at the depressingly bare branches and patchy lawn. Jester was rummaging in the far corner, his paws digging at something in the dirt, but she had neither the heart nor the energy to shout at him. She would need to get the garden sorted before summer came.

Add that to the mental list that ran like ticker tape through her head constantly.

She heard footsteps coming down the stairs. Her back stiffened. She kept her eyes on Jester and didn't turn around.

Ben sloped in wearing a dressing gown, his hair on end, his eyes bloodshot.

'Where were you last night?' she said to the window. The words were heavy with accusation.

'I was here with you. How much did you have to drink?' He chuckled at his own joke. She heard the fridge open. She spun around. He reached for the orange juice, took off the plastic lid and drank deeply, straight from the carton.

'You know what I mean, Ben. You were hours late for the quiz. It was embarrassing.'

'It's not a big deal. I was working late, then went off to the pub for a few to unwind. I got there eventually, didn't I? Do we have any paracetamol?' He put the lid back on the carton and shoved it back in the fridge. Lisa noted with annoyance that he had put it back on the wrong shelf and at an angle that meant it could easily fall out when the door was opened again.

Couldn't he do anything right?

'Then inviting everyone back here? Why? Why would you do that?'

He looked at her full in the face for the first time that morning. 'Because we never do anything fun anymore. Anything spontaneous. And it was fun – well, I had a good time anyway,' he added in a mumble. 'You never want to have people over anymore. When was the last time we did that?'

'But *those* people?'

'Who else do we know, Lisa? Who else do you even socialise with?'

'She was goading me all night. You heard what she was saying. You did nothing. In fact, you made it worse, took her side.' Her voice was rising in frustration. He wouldn't understand. He never even tried to. Why couldn't he see where she was coming from, recognise what she had been through? It was like he wanted to punish her for what happened as much as Christina did.

He paused, looked a little confused, probably couldn't even remember the conversation, then said, 'Since when do you need me to fight your battles?' It was clear he had no idea what she was talking about. He fumbled with the coffee machine, dropped the spoon, nearly knocked over the bottle of milk that was standing next to his elbow.

'She threw up all over the downstairs loo. I've just finished cleaning it up. I can still see the marks on the wall.'

He looked at her blankly. 'I'm going back to bed.'

He left just as Lucy bounced in, still wearing her pyjamas, her eyes glued to her phone. There was a tinny sound of cheering and music coming from it.

'What are you watching?' Lisa asked out of politeness rather than curiosity.

'Oh my God, Mum, you have to see what was going on at Sophia's house last night,' she declared with glee. She turned the screen to Lisa. The TikTok app was open and Lisa recognised Christina's kitchen in the video, crammed with teenagers. There were bottles of alcohol spread across the kitchen table and two lines of shot glasses filled with clear liquid. Sophia was standing at one end of the table while a boy stood at the other, with everyone around them counting down in loud shrieks. Sophia and the boy began at the end and moved down the line of glasses, downing the shots one after the other until they were all gone. Sophia was the clear winner, then the video showed her doubling over, her face scrunched up, before it cut out.

'I bet she threw up afterwards,' Lucy said with a laugh.

'You know that's not sensible, right? She could get alcohol poisoning or black out, choke on her own vomit, anything,' Lisa said.

Lucy rolled her eyes. 'There's another one where someone else looks completely out of it. It's hilarious.' Lucy flicked through more posts as she said, 'Don't tell Christina, ok? Sophia will kill me if she knows you've seen that.' Then her fingers stilled on one post. She zoomed in, paled and left, her eyes still glued to the screen.

Lisa called after her to have some breakfast, but the plea fell on deaf ears.

No matter what her feelings for Christina, Lisa had always liked Sophia as a kid, but she looked to be going off the rails. Lisa had heard some of the gossip from Lucy about drinking, boyfriends that seemed to only last a minute, parties at the house. Lisa's own daughter was doing everything she possible could to get into Oxford University and make something of her life while Sophia was throwing her future away, more interested in booze and boys than a degree. No doubt Sophia would turn out just like her mother, aimless, living from one commission to the next, from one boyfriend to the next.

Lisa turned to stare out of the kitchen window again,

then saw a reflection in the glass. Someone was standing right behind her. She spun around, startled.

'Em! You frightened me!'

'Sorry, I thought you heard me.' Emma opened the fridge and stuck her head inside. The orange juice carton tilted and fell, just as Lisa had predicted. She waited to see if Emma would pick it up, but instead she pulled out another bottle of milk, left the fridge door open and moved towards the cupboards on the hunt for cereal, a bowl and a spoon.

Lisa felt annoyance ticking at her. 'There is an open milk out already.'

Emma flicked her a withering glare. 'I have a headache,' she said, as if that justified anything.

So do I, Emma, so do I.

Sighing, she took the open bottle of milk over to Emma, swapped it for the new bottle, bent to pick up the orange juice, put both back in the fridge and closed the door just as the alarm started beeping in protest. She wanted to tell her that it had taken all of ten seconds to do it, but bit her lip instead.

'You were all really loud last night,' Emma said.

'Oh, sorry, your dad's fault. He invited everyone back here and I couldn't get them to leave.'

'It's fine, they just woke me up, that's all. Then I couldn't get back to sleep for ages.'

'Yeah, they were quite drunk. Christina was, anyway. That woman is awful when she's drunk.'

'She's funny,' Emma replied.

'When have you seen her drunk?'

'Oh, well, just from what I could hear last night, that's all. If it was her singing, that is.'

'It may have been Sally.'

'Hmmm, maybe.' Emma began to spoon cereal into her mouth mechanically. Lisa thought she looked pale.

'Did you get much revision done last night?' Lisa asked.

'Some, but I struggled to concentrate a bit, you know, the noise.'

'I really need you to do well, Em. Your first round of mocks are just around the corner. So try and find a way to focus, yeah?'

'Then try and keep the noise down!' she snapped back.

'Excuse me?'

'You constantly telling me how important these exams are is not really helping me right now. I am doing my best.' She banged her spoon down, pushed back her chair and stalked from the kitchen, leaving her cereal half eaten.

Lisa sighed again. She hated this feeling of helplessness, of not being in control of her daughter's life anymore. She used to make every decision for her – what she ate, when she ate, what she wore, where they went. Now she had to sit by and watch, hoping that everything she had done until now had made the right impression, sent the right message, been heard and understood.

She heard herself telling Emma to not make the same mistakes she had, to put her studies before everything else, to keep her distance from girls like Sophia, but it was her own fear that she was giving voice to, not Sophia's. And when did any teenager ever do anything because they were told to? Lisa knew what she sounded like, but she couldn't help herself in the moment.

Only time would tell if Sophia had heard her too.

Lisa sat at the table with a feeling of gnawing anxiety in her stomach, letting it inch up into her chest, not liking it but not knowing how to stop it.

14

Christina

Now

Christina almost sympathised with Lisa. This was all too much to comprehend. People rushed around, some in scrubs, others in uniform; there was constant noise from machines, talking, squeaking linoleum, policemen arriving, asking questions, doctors giving sparse updates, tears, raised voices.

A&E wasn't for the faint-hearted.

She had been pleased when someone had moved her to a family waiting area further away from the main A&E, just to escape the volume of stress, pain and anxiety that seemed to be the soundtrack of every A&E department, but it meant that she was now forced to wait in a smaller room with Lisa and Ben, now that Lisa had recovered from her rather melodramatic fainting episode. Even when she was collapsing onto the linoleum, she managed to look rigid and controlled.

She looked at them now, sitting on the other side of the

room. They had each other, even if they didn't seem to be talking.

Christina was here alone.

Ben looked like he was struggling to breathe, his face tight and pale. He had lost weight. Could someone have lost weight in one night? Enough for him to look hollow-cheeked? Is that what worry and panic could do? Or had he lost the weight since she had last seen him, all those weeks ago at the school quiz?

Either way, he looked haunted now as he sat beside Lisa.

Who would hold Christina's hand if her legs gave way? She would probably drop like a stone, nothing graceful about it, a heap on the floor, knickers on show. She had no one here to catch her – and her legs did feel weak, trembly, unsteady. She needed coffee. Strong coffee. And to be away from Lisa and Ben, to take stock, process what had happened, maybe get some answers.

She felt like she had been holding her breath for the last half an hour, scared to inhale in case something changed for the worst, but also aware that the worst could have already happened.

'I think we all need a coffee, don't you?' Christina said out loud, although she didn't think anyone heard her.

She walked down the corridor and turned left, then right, unsure where she was going, but moving felt good. Then she panicked that she wouldn't be where she was supposed to be if they came looking for her with news about Sophia. She looked around in confusion. There were rooms and beds, patients and nurses. She retraced her steps and saw a nurse's station ahead of her.

A young woman in scrubs that strained across her boobs looked up as she approached. She smiled the distanced, polite smile of someone who did not want to be bothered.

'You ok, love?'

'Erm, I'm looking for coffee – and an update on my daughter and her friends.'

'Coffee I can help with – if you go down this corridor and take your second left, you will find some vending machines. Now then, what's your daughter's name and I'll see what else I can find out for you.'

15

Sophia

Six Weeks Ago

Sophia stood in the kitchen doorway and watched her mother blow a stream of smoke from her red-wine-stained lips into the frigid morning air. Christina stood in the garden wearing ridiculously large sunglasses and a red, satin kimono. She had an astonishing green tinge to her skin and the remnants of last night's mascara under her eyes.

Sophia had heard them come in last night, doors banging, thumping as they climbed the stairs, lights going on and off again. Then she had heard her mother retching and throwing up in the bathroom. That was when Sophia had put her AirPods in and focused on her music because drunk nights meant her mother and her boyfriend would be inappropriately loud when they eventually got into bed. And she couldn't deal with that tonight. Not after what had gone down earlier.

Sophia herself was finally feeling more sober. Those boat races had been a bad idea, a reflex in response to seeing Emma and Kai disappear upstairs together. She was still annoyed at that. She knew Emma didn't know about how she felt about Kai, but that didn't mean she could just turn up out of the blue and go off with him like that.

Thankfully, everyone had left by the time Christina and Colin came home much later than Sophia expected. That was fine, though. Sometimes, much as her friends thought Christina was cool and fun, Sophia was actually embarrassed by her mother, with her skin-tight clothes, drunken antics and revolving door of boyfriends. Last night would've been just one more disappointment to add to the list if her mother had rattled in drunk and started partying with her friends.

She flicked on the kettle. There were no clean mugs; dirty ones were strewn around the house. Colin seemed to be allergic to using the same mug twice. He was also allergic to any form of tidying up or cleaning from what Sophia could see. Why her mother liked him was beyond her.

She stared at the photos from last night, zoomed in on Kai's face as he followed Emma up the stairs. He was smiling, pleased with himself. Then she zoomed in on Emma's face. She was frowning, her brow knotted together. She looked like she was walking the plank. That annoyed Sophia even more.

What the hell, Emma?

She opened Snapchat and created a story using the photo. As soon as she posted it, she felt better.

The back door opened and Christina staggered in on a cloud of nicotine.

'Hey, honey,' Christina said, her voice cracking. 'Ooh, make me one, would you? I'm gasping.' She thumped down into a kitchen chair.

Sophia turned her back on her. She wanted her mother to

ask her about last night, maybe say thank you for tidying up all the mess – but that wasn't Christina's style. She didn't notice stuff like that – or care, for that matter. Sometimes, Sophia went around with the vacuum cleaner herself, just because she couldn't stand the feeling of the carpet under her bare feet any longer. Or she would clean the bathrooms and straighten up the brightly coloured blankets on the couch when she knew her friends were coming over, but only because she didn't want to be judged when they all lived in immaculately clean houses while Christina's hadn't seen a duster in months. Sophia liked tidiness and routine, perhaps because Christina did not.

Order out of chaos. Taking control when there was none.

'Everything ok?' Christina mumbled. She sat with her head in her hands. There was a faint, rancid smell of vomit and stale alcohol about her.

'Yeah, just… I dunno…'

'How was last night?'

'S'ok.'

'How many came in the end?'

'Maybe fifteen of us. More than normal, I guess. Ollie brought a few friends I didn't know. They were ok, though.'

The spoon clattered against the mug, the bin swallowed up the squeezed teabag with a clang, the milk bottle rattled into the recycling bin, empty of its contents.

'Keep it down, would you? Headache. You're a right misery this morning – and I thought I felt horrible. You hungover too?' Christina snapped.

'No, I'm not actually,' she lied.

'Well, that's disappointing. You didn't try hard enough then.'

Sophia was used to her mother encouraging her to have fun, as though her misbehaviour was something Christina was proud of. Not her grades at school or her university ambitions. The litmus test was how many bevs she could get through without passing out and how many boys wanted to hang with her.

'We were drinking,' she said eventually. 'Quite a lot, actually.'

'Glad I wasn't the only one,' Christina replied. 'I started on white wine, then we went back to – you'll never guess whose house – only Ben and Lisa's! I got stuck into the red wine there...' She paused and looked like she was going to retch at the memory of it.

Sophia waited to see if she would run off to the toilet, but the moment seemed to pass. Her mother remained in her chair, a faint sheen of sweat on her upper lip.

'Yeah, we were drinking a lot,' Sophia said. 'It started with the usual stuff, you know, cider, beer, bit of vodka. Then one of the boys brought out this bottle of something, I don't know, a shot of some kind, and it... got a bit out of hand.' Her words were like pebbles, small and hard, and she was feeling her way around them carefully. There were things she wanted to tell her mother, wanted to hear herself say them out loud so that she could process them, but there was also so much she didn't want to share. She was conflicted about Kai and Emma – and could feel the annoyance building again. But she knew what Christina would say. She knew how much her mother hated Emma's family. Christina wouldn't understand – or wouldn't listen to the important bits, anyway. Sophia had learned over the years that her mother only heard what she wanted to hear, selectively ignoring the parts that she didn't find relevant.

'So what happened?' Christina looked around her kitchen, as if looking for evidence of some sort of crime or catastrophe. There were no sticky rings on the countertops, no discarded glasses lying around, no empty crisp packets or bowl with crumbs in them. No blood, no vomit, no signs of a struggle or a dead body.

No teenage carnage whatsoever.

The only carnage was in Sophia's head.

Sophia pulled out a chair and sat at the table, pulling her foot up to her bum and resting her head on her knee. She had dinosaurs on her pyjamas and a similar shadow of leftover make-up under her eyes as her mother.

'I was in a mood and someone suggested boat races. You know? When you race each other to drink a line of shots?'

Christina nodded, then held her head at the temples after clashing her brain against her skull. Christina looked like everything was painful, even concentrating on what her daughter was saying.

'Me and this guy Simon started them – my party, so I had to do the first one.' She shrugged. No point arguing with the laws of society. 'It was fine; I beat him.'

'Nice.'

Sophia sipped at her tea. Christina rubbed at her eyes and stared into her tea as if it was poison.

'It's just that I was quite drunk after that. Simon's mate, Finn, videoed me doing the boat races and put it on his stories, that's all. I mean I don't mind too much. Whatever. It makes Simon look worse anyway because he lost to a girl. Then afterwards I kind of threw up and they filmed that too.' She scrunched up her face. 'It's bound to be doing the rounds already.'

Christina laughed out loud. 'Oh well! Like mother, like daughter! I threw up last night too – according to Colin, anyway. I don't actually remember it. Bloody Ben and Colin found a bottle of something – I don't even remember what – and it's all a bit vague after that. But Colin says we had to leave because I had an argument with Lisa that happened before the shots and then I threw up all over her downstairs loo. I would love to see her face when she goes in there this morning! I'd been drinking red wine for a bit too, so it would've been quite a colour.' She chuckled again.

Sophia sighed. 'Yeah, but there's no video evidence of you, no chance of it being posted all over everyone's socials.'

This wasn't a competition. She didn't care if her mother had drunk more than her, thrown up more dramatically, behaved worse. She wanted her to listen to the stuff Sophia wasn't telling her, maybe notice there was more to say, but Christina was getting to her feet, pulling her kimono around herself, muttering about 'feeling like shit, need more sleep'. Conversation over.

So Sophia let her go back to bed where Colin was still snoring in his stained boxer shorts.

She didn't tell her about breaking up with Ollie. Christina had liked him, thought he was 'cute'. She didn't tell her about Emma turning up or Kai disappearing upstairs with her. She didn't tell her about sending the Snaps this morning to make herself feel better, what she had started to divert attention.

She picked up her phone and began scrolling again, sipping at her tea while the drama exploded in the palm of her hand.

16

Lisa

Now

'This place is something, isn't it?' Ben said.

Lisa scowled at him. What kind of conversation was he trying to start? He hadn't spoken to her in weeks and now he was trying to pass small talk.

She ignored him. He started to pace, his feet squeaking on the linoleum, setting her teeth on edge.

'Why is she here?' she said instead.

'Who?'

'Christina. Why is she here?'

Ben looked confused. 'Because of Sophia.'

'But why is she *here*, sitting with us? Is she here for you?'

'I don't understand.'

'Did you ask her to come? Is she here to support you?'

'Sometimes I don't know what goes on in your head, Lisa,' he said and walked away from her, his head bowed.

Lisa watched him go with some relief. He was making her feel claustrophobic as he hovered and said stupid things.

And Christina. Well, there was a time when she would've

been the first person Lisa would call in a crisis. But then one moment of instinct, one instance of sheer panic, and that all ended.

She sometimes wondered what could've happened if they had talked about it afterwards calmly, rationally, but when it came to your kids, there was no sense of calm when you thought they had been wronged. Christina had seen it one way and Lisa another. It was as simple and as complicated as that. Lisa was protecting her child, as was Christina, and what happened afterwards changed their relationship, and that of their girls, forever.

She remembered that day so clearly, the feeling of panic and then later, of shame. She had meant to phone Christina the next day, talk to her, take her for coffee maybe, but Christina's reaction had been so vehement, so heated, that by the time she got to the school drop-off point the next morning, they were all already whispering.

And those whispers grew in volume until they were a steady rumble over the next few weeks and months. All she could do was make herself as small and as invisible as possible, hoping that the volume would dial down eventually.

And it did. But by then the damage had been done.

However, at no point had Christina come to her and asked her about it, asked for an explanation, given her a chance to apologise. She had latched onto what she thought she had seen and she had run with it, straight into the playground and the ears of the other mothers.

And here they were now. Thrown together on what was easily the worst night of Lisa's life and once more there were questions about how they parented their children. But who was wrong this time?

She felt a prickle of anguish. What if she had brought this on herself? What if Christina had been right all along?

No, she couldn't start down that road.

It was in times like these that you could drive yourself mad with *what ifs*.

And she felt like she was going mad.

17

Lisa

Six Weeks Ago

They sat around the table on Sunday evening like strangers.

It wasn't the food. Lisa could proudly contest to the fact that the roast dinner was excellent as always. There were even extra Yorkshire puddings, which would've thrilled Lucy when she was younger. Back then, it was all about the Yorkshire puddings. Now she stuck to one, disciplined and controlled about her eating. Teenagers these days were such a juxtaposition of extreme control and wild excess. It made Lisa's head spin as she tried to navigate through all the rules: don't eat this because of palm oil; you can't use that because of excess plastic; that term is offensive and using it risks being cancelled. And yet, they undermined each other and exploited moments of weakness with apparent relish, the technology that was meant to help them being used as a weapon. At once wanting to save the world and also setting fire to each other at every opportunity.

Lucy had just been telling a story about a girl at school

who was now identifying as a cat or a rabbit or something or other, and Lisa had to bite her tongue to stop herself from saying what she really thought.

How were these kids supposed to get through life if they were constantly being told they were saying the wrong things, labelling themselves incorrectly, labelling themselves at all, eating too much, then eating too little, being too selfish, not being selfish enough?

It exhausted her, so she kept quiet because silence was safer when it came to the dinner table.

Ben was no help. After trying to talk to him again yesterday once he had crawled out of bed for the second time, he had sloped off to the golf club and stayed there until well after the sun had gone down. He came home smelling of beer with a pizza box in his hands and fell asleep in an armchair, the box reeking cheese and threatening to slide off his lap. Jester sat at his feet, waiting to clean up if it did. Lisa had watched him snuffle and snore his way through the highlights of some football game or other, then had taken herself off to her own room, closing the door, turning on the television and letting her eyes watch the images on the screen without taking in what she was seeing either.

Her phone had buzzed numerous times while Jennifer Aniston and Reese Witherspoon argued onscreen. Owen was sending her messages, checking in to make sure she was ok after her run-in with Christina and Ben. She ignored the texts for now, couldn't think about it yet. She was ok – she had handled worse than that from Christina in recent years – but she was mortified that she had argued with Ben in front of Owen, in front of all of them.

Sunday morning came and Lisa had taken Lucy to her

hockey training session. When she returned home, Ben had taken Jester out for a walk and Emma was sitting in the family room with her AirPods in and her hoodie pulled up over her head, her laptop open in front of her. She had said very little all weekend, but that wasn't unusual anymore. Lisa put it down to her working hard – they had talked about her going to Oxford or Cambridge and her upcoming mock A Level exams would be very important for the early entry applications in a few months' time, so Lisa was pleased she was working so hard. It was bound to take its toll, but it would be worth it.

Now the four of them sat with their eyes on their food and their mouths closed to talking. Lisa looked at each of them in turn. Emma was eating slowly, making sure each forkful had a little bit of everything on it. Her skin was pale and there were dark rings under eyes, but the hoodie wasn't pulled up to hide her face at least. Lucy was playing with her food, pushing a carrot around with disinterest. She had arranged her plate so that nothing was touching. Ben was mechanically shovelling his food in one-handed with his fork, the knife discarded on the tablecloth and his other arm flung out in front of him like a stabiliser. He was also flaunting the 'no phones at the table' rule by positioning his phone next to his abandoned knife. It was thankfully set to silent, but she caught him looking at it every time it buzzed. He seemed to be getting quite a few messages and she ached to ask who they were from.

Annoyance bubbled inside her. 'Ben, must you have that on the table when we are eating?'

He sighed, but didn't move it.

'Lucy, please stop playing with your food and just eat it,'

she snapped again, then stopped as she heard herself. She exhaled. 'So did everyone have a good weekend?'

Lucy shrugged, still playing with the carrot. Ben kept his eyes on his plate.

'Anyone up to anything interesting this week?'

Barely noticeable shakes of the head.

'What about you, Ben? Are you around this week?'

'Why do you want to know?'

'So I can plan meals? So that I know what to expect?'

He didn't offer any other information.

Lisa willed someone to make a joke, do something silly, laugh like they used to. Instead, they sat like strangers in a train station, tolerating each other's existence until they could move on to a better destination.

Lucy looked from one parent to the other. 'We should do something next weekend – as a family. A film night or something. We never do that anymore.' She pushed her plate away from her.

'That's a great idea, Lucy,' Lisa said, relieved someone else was trying for a change, even if it was the youngest member of the family.

'Em, are you busy next weekend? Can we watch a film together?' Lucy's voice was timid.

'Where would I be going? I've got mocks coming up. I need to revise,' Emma snapped.

Lucy shrugged. 'Oh, sorry.'

'Besides, we can never agree on what to watch.' Emma looked sulky. 'And Dad always falls asleep, so what's the point?'

'The point is that we should at least try to spend some

time together, Emma. And don't snap at your sister.' Lisa's patience was wearing thin underneath a layer of panic at what was happening to her family.

'Why? You snap at all of us all the time.' She got to her feet and stomped from the room.

Lisa looked at Ben for support, hoping he'd say something or tell her off, but he merely sighed, grabbed his phone and followed Emma.

Lisa stood at the sink rinsing plates and stacking them slowly in the dishwasher. The dinner had disbanded with her and Lucy silently clearing the table while the other two had closed themselves into separate rooms. Lisa had been avoiding thoughts about Christina all day, but now the mundanity of the task at hand pulled her mind towards their altercation and what had been said.

Christina's goading, aired in slurred words dipped in alcohol. Ben belittling her in front of everyone, leaving Owen to dilute the tension. The awkward silence that fell, drowning out even the music that still blared, tinny and discordant, from the speaker. The shots downed in defiance by both Ben and Christina, suddenly in solidarity against her. The smell of Trevor's body odour as he shifted position next to her, now wide awake and uncomfortable.

Lisa had left the room then, disappearing upstairs in mortification. She had heard the front door close moments later and a peek through her bedroom blinds showed Owen walking away from her house, his head down, his beanie pulled low. She wasn't sure when Sally, Trevor, Christina or Colin left. She had gone to bed, tried to put the night behind her.

Lisa flushed with mortification now, wondering what had been going through Owen's head. He knew a version of what happened between her and Christina, but she didn't think any of them knew the real truth. They knew the narrative Christina had constructed through whispered comments into idle ears in the playground. No one had ever asked Lisa for her side. The whole episode, created from a huge difference in opinion on how to raise children effectively, still clearly sat between them like an icy glacier that refused to melt.

She closed the dishwasher door with an angry shove and reached for her phone, which lay in a soapy puddle next to the sink. She wiped the screen on her jumper and opened Owen's texts from earlier.

He was asking if she was ok, reminding her that it had happened a long time ago, that Christina needed to let it go, that Ben and Christina were out of order. Four texts spread out over thirty minutes a few hours ago, then nothing after she aired him.

The air in the room was thick with the lingering smells of the roast dinner that no one had enjoyed. She sat heavily in a chair and typed a reply that she was fine, that she was over it already, but her fingers shook as she typed and she had to go back and correct her spelling a few times. She wanted to call him, talk to him, talk to anyone really, but she couldn't bring herself to admit that it felt like she was unravelling. Her marriage was hanging by a thin thread; her younger daughter was interested in everything but school; her older daughter was so stressed about her exams and university applications that she was mute; her husband looked like he wanted to be anywhere but here; and Lisa herself felt like a ghost walking the halls of the house, unseen, unheard, trying to reach out but not making contact.

But nothing was permanent, right? Lucy would see Emma make a success of her exams and would want to emulate her. Emma would go on to great things. And Ben? She was drawing a blank there. The question was, did she love him enough to want to reconnect? Or would her life be easier if she was on her own?

She walked out of the kitchen and straight past the lounge where Ben was lying on the couch, feet up, mouth open, eyes closed, his phone clutched to his chest. Upstairs, she paused outside Emma's room, thought about knocking, going to tuck her in like she used to. She could hear music playing and glimpsed a dull glow of light in the gap beneath the door. She walked on, past Lucy's room where she could hear a video playing and a narrator's voice droning through the wall, to her own room where she climbed into bed and pulled the covers over her head.

18

Ben

Now

Ben was worried about Lisa. She looked like she was about to crumble – and he didn't know if he had any strength left to hold her up.

There was so much he wanted to say to her, so much he needed to admit about what had been going on lately. He had been trying to talk to her for what felt like weeks, but every time he started, they ended up talking about Emma and her exams or university applications, or about Lucy and how Lisa thought she wasn't working hard enough, how she may not get into university (which for Lisa was a cardinal sin), so he backed off, knowing she had enough to deal with.

It was a battleground. Every time they spoke, he felt like she was attacking him, blaming him for leaving it all to her, but also knowing that whatever he did to try and help was never going to be good enough in her eyes and he would be disappointing her either way. So he defended himself, which then sounded like he was attacking her, that she had failed.

And so they went on, around and around, getting nowhere except further apart.

And now, with Emma in the hospital, his chance to talk to Lisa about what was going on with him had passed. Just another way in which he had failed.

Lisa was now pacing up and down as they waited for an update from the doctors.

It was funny how everyone dealt with stress differently.

Lisa liked to pace and demand answers and glare at people, the tiger mum in her wanting to fight for her cubs. Christina wanted to be useful, offering to get coffee and phone people and organise things, clearly trying to distract herself from processing what was going on. It was awkward that they'd been asked to wait in the same area and certainly wasn't helping his stress levels. He knew Sophia had gone for x-rays. A doctor had come to update Christina and the relief that flooded through her was visceral. He envied her at that moment. Now, though, she was hovering on the edge of their peripheral vision and putting herself in the firing line of Lisa's wrath.

And yet, he was surprised to find that he was glad she was here. It wasn't only Lisa who had lost a friend when everything imploded. He had enjoyed coming home to a house full of laughter on a Friday evening, with Lisa and Christina most of the way through a bottle of wine and music playing. Lisa had been happy too.

And him? How did he deal with stuff? He pretended the bad stuff didn't happen, tucked his head well and truly in the sand and hoped it would all go away. Of course, it didn't. If he had learned anything from recent events, it was that you couldn't avoid a problem forever. Eventually it would grow, taking up all available space until it demanded your attention.

Christina walked towards him, carrying a cardboard tray with three cups stuck into the circular holders. She gave him a weak smile and said, 'Coffee? It might help.'

He smiled back, reached out and accepted the coffee. 'Thanks, Chris. God, how did this happen, eh? They're good kids! What were they thinking? But that's the thing with teenagers, isn't it? They don't think. They believe that they are invincible and that everything will be a laugh. We were probably the same.'

'Maybe – but I think they've just been unlucky. They were having fun – that isn't a crime. Teenagers are supposed to have fun, experiment, live recklessly because they can.'

He sighed. 'Maybe you're right – but Emma? I just didn't think she'd...'

'Maybe you don't know her as well as you think.'

Before he could reply, Christina walked towards Lisa and offered her a coffee.

'I don't drink coffee,' was the terse reply.

'Since when?' Christina asked. 'You used to always have a coffee in your hand.'

'Yeah, well, people change.' She turned away, dismissing Christina in no uncertain terms.

Ben watched Christina's shoulders slump. He was about to say something to Lisa when Christina's eyes narrowed. She walked towards him, then past him and said hello to someone behind him.

Ben turned to see who it was, felt the skin across his body tighten and said, 'What the fuck are you doing here?'

19

Emma

Four Weeks Ago

Emma made her way to class like a dead man walking, her feet dragging and her shoulders slumped, the weight of her phone heavy in her backpack. She could feel it shudder with every alert that pinged through. Cutting it fine, she had timed it so that she was at the tail end of the stream of students. She kept her eyes downcast, her chin dipped, the volume on her music turned up beyond what was probably considered safe.

They shoved past her in the hallway with sharp elbows. She shut out the volume of their voices with the music, letting herself be jostled and jabbed. She entered the classroom seconds before the teacher closed the door, ignoring his disapproving glare, and settled into a seat at the back. Only then did she open her bag, take out her phone and silence the music without looking at her notifications.

There was nothing in them she wanted to see or hear. The party at Sophia's house had been two weeks ago, but it was still an ever-present threat, poking itself into her daily business. The trolling since that night had been relentless. Name-calling, whispering, direct messages that were thinly veiled threats. The worst of it was that she deserved it, all of it. She was everything they were saying. They were right to hate her.

At least today there were no nasty surprises waiting for her in her locker. That constituted a good day so far.

Sophia sat a few rows ahead of her, her back straight, her neck long beneath an eye-wateringly tight ponytail. She turned and looked at Emma, but Emma avoided making eye contact. The twins sat in the row ahead of Sophia. They rocked backwards on their chair legs, in sync, kicking at the table in front of them and making the girl next to them scowl while they smirked.

Emma flicked her eyes over to the far end of the row and saw Kai looking at her, his brow knotted. He nodded his head at her, but she looked back down, making a show of rummaging in her backpack and pulling out her books.

The lesson was a muted blur of words and assignments. The test that the teacher returned to her was marked with a 'U', shouting at her from the page in green ink. She crumpled it up and shoved it to the bottom of her bag along with the others she'd received lately.

When the lesson was over, she took her time packing up, ignoring the glances as the rest filed past. She emerged into the corridor to find Kai waiting for her.

'You haven't answered my Snaps,' he said.

'I haven't read your Snaps.'

'Why? What's going on with you? Why won't you talk to me?'

'Don't act like you don't know.'

'Um, I don't, actually.'

She shrugged, ignored the hurt that rippled across his face. He continued to stare at her, expectations high but ultimately let down. She began to walk away, knowing she was heading in the opposite direction to where they should be going.

'Where are you going?' he called after her.

'Away from you.'

She kept walking, didn't look back, despite wanting to. She could feel the tears prickling, difficult to avoid. Everyone thought he was so nice, so sweet. But he had told them. No one else would've said anything, so it had to have been him telling his mates what they did, who then passed it around, all of them probably laughing at her, and before she even got home that night, she had been labelled. No longer the no-mates nerd; now a slut.

How quickly they circled their prey.

She walked around the school buildings, sticking to the shadows against the walls so that she wasn't noticed, until she reached the metal fire escape that ran down the side of the drama block. She climbed the metal stairs, then hoisted herself up onto the flat roof and carefully made her way to the patch of weak sun that spread across the far edge of the roof. She had discovered this place by accident that first day back at school after the party when she was desperately trying to escape the voices and nudging, rumours and name-calling, when the trolling was just taking off and she had realised just how quickly pack mentality could take over. She'd wanted to run and hide. She'd seen the metal fire escape, followed the urge to get higher and higher, away from all of them, until she'd collapsed onto the roof, where she had remained hidden for hours. Only later, after finding her way there every day for moments of solace, did she realise that if she lay on her front with her chin in her hands, she could see them scurrying below her like insects. She could imagine stepping out with one huge, powerful foot and squashing them all into a mush of blood and bone.

It was now her place to escape. She hadn't left the school grounds, so she wasn't breaking any rules technically. For all they knew, she was in the study base or the library between classes. The perfect student, working hard to get into Oxford. The perfect example of a balanced teenager.

You learned all sorts of things from up here. Things people didn't want you to see. Like the biology teacher who claimed to be vegan and an advocate of only putting good things in your body, who hid behind the sports block for a sneaky smoke break every day; or the two teachers, both married to other people, who she saw snogging in the shadows. Like Liv, one of Sophia's posse, who regularly ducked behind the storage shed to self-harm. She had a tin that she buried deep in her schoolbag, containing all the bits and pieces she needed to patch herself up afterwards.

Emma lay on her back, ignoring the dead leaves crunching into her hair and the smell of damp rot, and finally looked at her phone properly. She pulled the screen across enough to glimpse some of the messages, then let it ping back, leaving them unread. She read Kai's messages, but didn't reply. At least his showed concern rather than vitriol, but she didn't want his concern.

This was all his fault.

She opened SnapChat, saw the stories, and closed it straight away.

She lay with her eyes open, watching the clouds amble past. The sounds of the world below washed over her: the shouts and laughter, the bell ringing, the traffic on the road on the other side of the wall, a siren in the distance. The air was warm, carrying with it the faint smell of cut grass, the sky a periwinkle blue. It should be lifting her soul, but she felt detached from it, unmoved.

She pulled the bottle from her backpack and unscrewed the cap, letting the warm vodka burn down her throat. She needed it to blot everything out, to numb it all while she figured out what to do. Rather that than cutting herself to shreds like Liv, though.

She was angry all of the time. At herself mostly, but also her mother, her so-called friends, her life. She wanted to cry out, to scream for help, but there was no one there to hear it. She felt like she was trapped behind a clear glass wall and could see everyone she cared about on the other side, but she couldn't reach them or make them hear without breaking the glass.

And the only way to break the glass was to blow it all up.

She stood up then, stepped right up to the edge of the flat roof. She shuffled her filthy Converses forward until the toes were over the edge and looked down onto the tarmac below, covered in leaves and dirt, empty crisp packets and crumpled Coke cans. The bottle hung loosely at her side. She shuffled forward some more, felt her weight teeter forwards, her pulse inch up ever so slightly.

She heard a cough behind her and turned to look over her shoulder.

Sophia was standing behind her, looking pale, her back rigid.

'What the fuck are you doing here?' Emma said, furious that her moment of solitude had been shattered.

'I could ask the same question,' Sophia said.

'How did you find me?'

Sophia just shrugged. 'I saw you earlier and, I dunno, you looked worn out, I guess, and then I saw you were going in completely the wrong direction to everyone else, so I followed you.'

There was silence for a moment. Emma turned and looked back down to the ground below.

'How often do you come here?' Sophia asked.

'Enough. It's quiet – at least it used to be. Gives me headspace.' There was an isolation to everything up here. The sounds of the school were muffled, the sky was vast above them, and it felt freeing and safe at the same time. It was weirdly peaceful. Emma stared up at the clouds, tracked a bird as it made its way across her line of vision.

'You're... um... not, like, thinking of jumping or anything, are you?'

'Dunno, maybe. That would shut everyone up.'

'Maybe don't, though?'

'What do you care?'

'I'm sorry.'

Emma spun around and glared at Sophia, whose eyes fell on the vodka bottle, worry fusing her forehead into lines. She looked like she wanted to say something else. Emma could see the indecision on her face. 'Really? That's all you've got? You've been posting as much as anyone else.'

'I... didn't think.' She shrugged, looked like she might cry. 'Can you step away from the edge please?'

She made her wait, the seconds lengthened and weighted.

Then she stepped towards Sophia and dropped down to sit cross-legged, putting the bottle in her lap. Then she lay all the way down, squinting into the sky. After a moment, Sophia came to lie next to her.

They lay in silence until Emma said, 'You won't tell anyone about this place, will you?' There was an edge of desperation in her tone now.

'No.'

Emma held out the bottle. 'Want some?'

Sophia paused, unsure if she wanted to say yes or not. It wasn't even lunchtime yet. 'Um, ok, I guess?'

'You don't have to. I don't give a shit if you do or not. More for me, frankly.'

'This isn't like you.'

'How do you know?' Emma said, then added, quieter, 'It helps my brain shut off.'

'Fair enough,' Sophia said and took the bottle. She coughed a little as the vodka hit the back of her throat, then handed it back.

'I wasn't going to, you know. I just come up here to clear my head, get away from the noise down there.'

Sophia nodded and looked away, out over the playing fields. She didn't say anything for a while, then said, 'Does it bother you then? What they're saying? Can you not just ignore it?' She looked like she was working out a complicated puzzle, the cogs and wheels turning behind her eyes.

'Oh, yeah! Why didn't I think of that?' Emma snapped.

They lay for some time, not speaking, each caught in their own thoughts, with Emma taking regular sips from the bottle but Sophia shaking her head when she was next offered, until Sophia said, 'We used to be really good friends, you and me, didn't we?'

'Yeah, I guess we did.'

'What happened?'

'You turned into a bitch. Our mothers fell out. I dunno.' Emma shrugged, feigning a nonchalance she didn't feel.

'Wow, tell me what you really think.'

'You were my best friend and then our mothers fell out and by the time we got to secondary school, you had all these new, popular, plastic friends and I didn't fit in with the cool crowd,' Emma said.

Sophia knew it was true. She knew she had pulled away from Emma when it became more important to hang out with the popular ones, but to hear it spelled out plainly and dispassionately was brutal in its honesty. 'I'm sorry. I just thought it became harder to be friends when our mums weren't speaking.'

'That didn't help, I guess, but we see each other every day. We would've worked around that. And since when do I care about what my mother thinks?'

'I thought you did.'

'You were, like, my only friend then, but you just dropped me. Looks like you hang out with some right bitches now, though – and the boys are no better.'

'Ok, but at least I have friends.'

This time the silence was weighted, the anger giving it volume. This had escalated quickly.

'Sorry, I shouldn't have said that,' Sophia mumbled.

Emma sat up. 'Why did you follow me up here, Sophia? To get more material for them down there? More ammunition to bully me?' Her voice was taut with hatred. 'A video of the slut dangling off the edge of the roof? That would get the views, wouldn't it?'

Sophia rolled onto her side and propped her head up on her elbow. She paused, took in the dark rings under Emma's eyes, the splattering of spots on her chin and the greasy lines in her hair. 'I was worried about you, saw you on the edge. It made me think, made me realise the effect it might be having, I suppose. Kai is worried about you too. I didn't realise that what they were saying was getting to you, but then I saw you come up here and... I panicked, I guess. Especially since there was a rumour going around that you were high the other day.'

'Oh please! That is the least of what has been going around about Emma Marco! Some of it straight from you, let's not forget. I have every reason to push you off this roof. But mostly from Kai. He must've started it, the rumours, but I know you've all been spreading it.'

Like a virus carried in the air, the talk had spread far and wide until Emma's name was on everyone's lips. The only one who still wanted to be nice to her was Kai, but Emma was batting him away like a fly.

Emma wasn't about to lie back quietly and take it, though. Despite what she had said to Sophia, she was not going to fling herself off a building in defeat, but it was hard not to give in to such intrusive thoughts.

Sophia started talking again. 'This thing has caught fire and it's out of control. I've seen the posts, how it's escalated, what they are saying now and I'm sorry. I guess I never thought about how it would affect you. But you can't let it break you.' She paused, hoping Emma would say something. 'The truth is, I really liked you as a friend. You were genuine and actually quite funny when you weren't being so uptight.' She paused, picked at a weed growing through the vinyl. 'You can talk to me, you know? We could be friends again.'

Emma looked at her, really looked, her eyes burning into Sophia's, which were deep pools of guilt.

She got to her feet, stashed the bottle back in her bag and said, 'Fuck you,' before leaving.

20

Lisa

Now

It was all such a nightmare. Doctors were talking to them, at them. Words that strung together to make phrases that she wanted to swat away like stinging wasps: class A drugs, medically induced comas, a long road ahead, intensive care.

And now, not only did she have to put up with Christina invading her space, but Owen was here too. Kai had apparently been at the gig as well.

Now Ben was squaring up to Owen, asking if Kai was the reason they were in this state, where had they got the drugs from, who was responsible. Voices were rising, Ben and Owen shouting, and Lisa couldn't make sense of it all.

And all the while, Christina was standing there with a cardboard tray of coffee held in front of her. Like any of them could think of drinking coffee right now.

These were their children. Their babies.

Something awful had happened, something terrifying and life changing and incomprehensible, and she was standing there offering everyone coffee.

Lisa was swinging between the urge to scream at them all and a need to run away, let someone else deal with this.

Christina was talking in a low voice to Ben, her free hand on his arm, putting herself between him and Owen. Lisa was aware that it should be her talking Ben down, getting between them, pouring warm water on his anger. Her eyes zoned in on that hand on the arm, the red fingernails polished and shaped into claws, the ringless finger.

Then it occurred to her that perhaps the answer had been here, right in front of her, all along.

How many times had Ben tried to convince her that Christina and her just needed to talk, to listen to each other's point of view, in order to put it all behind them? How he had tried to convince her that Christina was only thinking of her daughter, that Lisa needed a friend and Christina had been a good one once?

Was it her? Had she just been blind to what was going on under her very nose?

She shook her head, trying to dislodge the thoughts.

This was not the time. She was sitting in a hospital, being told her daughter was in a critical condition, fighting for her life, and this is what she was focusing on.

There were police hovering too, approaching Ben and Owen, talking in low, calming tones. Owen responded and led them out of the family room, saying he would answer whatever questions he was able to but that he didn't know very much at all. Just hearing him say that as he walked away terrified Lisa – because it meant she had to admit, like they all did, that perhaps they didn't know their children very well after all.

Perhaps all that hard work making sure they were clothed and fed and safe and capable of making the right choices had been for nothing.

Perhaps they were all terrible people and this was down to them.

21

Lisa

Four Weeks Ago

L isa rummaged through his pockets one more time, convinced she had missed something, but there were no receipts, no ticket stubs, no evidence at all of him having an affair.

Her morning yoga class was finished and she had been sitting in the kitchen, Jester lying at her feet, when the thought had hopped into her brain and settled in for the long haul. There was definitely something going on with Ben and an affair was the only explanation.

She had rushed upstairs and gone through his suit jacket pocket, his trousers, even the receipts flung onto the bedside table beside his cufflinks and golf tees. But if it was true, then he was being very careful because there was nothing to find, no evidence whatsoever.

No, she was just latching onto the obvious. A cliché. It was probably nothing like that at all.

But what if he was having an affair? Would she blame him?

Would she care?

She went into Lucy's room to collect the laundry basket and spent a moment looking around the immaculate space. Lucy liked everything to have a place. Even her pens on her desk were lined up like toy soldiers. Not an empty glass or dirty plate to be found. The duvet on the bed was wrinkle-free, her pyjamas folded and placed neatly under the pillow, a teddy bear sitting politely in the exact middle, his dark eyes watching her as she inspected the space.

She closed the bedroom door and opened the one next to it. In contrast, Emma's room was in darkness, the curtains still closed, the bed unmade, a stale smell in the air. There were clothes scattered on every surface and her desk was a jumble of make-up, dirty glasses and hair ties. Empty crisp packets were discarded on her dressing table and there were pairs of dirty knickers in the corner, some distance away from the laundry basket.

Lisa flung open the curtains and spent some time making the bed and gathering up some of the dirty dishes. She tried to make out what was dirty and what was clean from the jumble of clothes on the floor and others tossed over the desk chair. With her arms full, she made her way back towards the door, but tripped over a discarded Converse high-top and dropped one of the glasses she was juggling. It bounced on the fluffy carpet and rolled under the bed.

Lisa flung the dirty clothes into the washing basket, balanced the dirty dishes on top and returned to retrieve the glass. She had to get onto all fours and crouch right down to reach it from where it had rolled quite far under the bed. As she grabbed the glass, her eyes fell on a bottle lying next to it. She pulled it out. An empty vodka bottle. Not unusual in a seventeen year old's bedroom, she supposed, but definitely unusual in Emma's room. Emma had never shown any sign of breaking the rules.

She didn't even go out with friends very often.

She put the bottle on top of the pile of dishes, meaning to talk to her about it later.

As she turned to leave, she noticed the wastepaper bin was full too. She tucked it under her arm and managed to juggle everything back downstairs.

Once the washing was sorted and a load was running, she put all of Emma's dishes in the dishwasher and went to empty the bin.

Curiosity perhaps – or some would say nosiness – but something made her look closely at one of the crumpled papers. It was an essay from the looks of it, written in Emma's handwriting, but there were notes and crossing out throughout in bright-red pen. It was an assignment for one of her classes and the mark that had been given at the top constituted a fail.

Lisa was momentarily shocked. She didn't think Emma had failed at anything before. Her last report had been exemplary as always. A hard-working student, conscientious, likely to go on to great things. Of course, everyone was allowed to make a mistake.

Lisa unfolded another piece of paper. Another assignment, another fail.

There were three more like it.

Lisa didn't know what to think. Why was Emma suddenly failing her courses?

Because it wasn't just one subject. It was all of them.

*

Lisa sat heavily at the table, thinking hard about her daughter, her demeanour and how quiet she had been of late. A temporary blip, that's all. Just the pressure getting to her ahead of her exams, maybe being overwhelmed at trying to decide how to shape her future. Lisa refused to think about the vodka, about whether her daughter was so stressed that she needed alcohol. Or worse. Drugs? You heard stories sometimes. She needed to be calm when she spoke to her.

She had smoothed out some of the crumbled papers and they sat on the table in front of her, documents ready to be entered into evidence. The vodka bottle sat next to the papers.

The key sounded in the front door. Footsteps in the hallway. The thud of a backpack being flung to the floor.

At first, Emma didn't notice Lisa sitting so still at the table. Jester was bouncing around her and she fussed over him as he weaved between her legs. She went straight over to the fridge, flung open the door and stared at the contents for a few moments, then slammed the door shut. She did the same with the cupboard, finally settling on a big bag of popcorn. It gave Lisa a moment to watch her, really look at her. She had lost weight, her arms looked almost frail, and there were dark rings under her eyes and spots on her face that were angry and red against her translucent skin. Her hair was lank and dull.

Emma turned around to see Lisa sitting quietly, her legs crossed, her tea cold in front of her.

'Oh, Mum, you scared me.'

'How was school?'

'S'ok. Got revision to do.'

Emma started to leave the room, but stopped as Lisa said, 'We need to talk.'

She had her back to Lisa still when she replied, 'About what?'

'Come and sit down. Please.' Lisa's voice was like stone.

Emma didn't react immediately and Lisa had the sudden thought that she was going to ignore her and walk away. Lisa held her breath, panicked at the idea of how she would handle it if she did.

Emma turned slowly and came to sit opposite her. Her back was straight, her glare challenging, and Lisa faltered. She took a deep breath. 'What's going on with you?'

'What do you mean?' Emma was on the defence immediately. Her eyes flicked to the bottle, then back to Lisa.

'You just don't seem yourself. You look pale, like you're not sleeping – and I found this in your room.'

'How would you know how I am? And why are you going through my stuff?'

'Um, well, I watch you and I don't seem to see as much revision going on as there used to be. You spend your time glued to your phone now or in your room with the door closed, doing God knows what.' She nodded at the bottle. Lisa hadn't wanted it to sound accusatory, but every word was stacked.

'For all you know, I could be studying in my bedroom. You can't see through walls.'

'Ok, then explain these to me.' Lisa pushed the crumbled papers across the table. Emma flicked her eyes at them, looked away quickly and removed her hands from the table, tucking them under her legs.

'So I've had a couple of bad tests lately. So what? It happens.'

'Not to you and not at this stage. If you want to get into Oxford—'

'What if I don't?'

Lisa went cold in the very bottom of her stomach. 'Pardon?'

'What if I don't want to go to Oxford or Cambridge or St Andrew's or any of those stupid places? What if I don't want to go to university at all?'

'But... you've always talked about university, about Oxford.'

'No, *you* have. You and Dad. That's all you've talked about for the last two years. But I don't think either of you have actually asked me what *I* want.'

Lisa exhaled slowly, tried to control the panic that was creating a wormhole in her chest. 'You know how important university is for your future and we just want you to succeed. We would never force you into anything you don't want to do, though.'

'Don't kid yourself, Mother.' Her words were ice chips. 'You bang on about how hard I must work, how I don't want to let myself down, how important university is, but it's only because you never went, you never did anything with your life, so you want to live it through me. Or is it so that you can use it to throw in Christina's face? How I got into a top university and Sophia didn't? Is that it? Christina lets Sophia be herself, who she wants to be, not some sad version of what she wishes she had become.'

A shockwave of silence rolled over them. Emma had high spots of redness in her cheeks and lightning in her blue eyes.

'How dare you.' Lisa said finally. 'Your father and I have only ever wanted the best for you. And I know that if you waste this opportunity, you will regret it for the rest of your life.'

'Like you did, you mean?'

Emma was challenging her now and the anger was biting at Lisa's throat.

'From now on, you will sit at this table and revise in front of me, where I can see you. I will monitor how much you are doing and I will say when you can get up from the table and take a break. I will not let you ruin your life. I understand that it is hard, but this for your own good. You are so close. Don't ruin it now.'

Tears had sprung up in Emma's eyes. They hovered on the edges of her eyelashes, stubbornly refusing to fall.

Then one did, followed by another. Emma did not make a sound, though. Her face was impassive except for the two fat tears that worked their way slowly down each cheek.

The anger in Lisa's throat began to dissolve away in the wake of Emma's tears. She said in a softer voice, 'I understand how hard it is, how hard everything is when you are seventeen, but this is important. Far more important than anything else that you might have going on. So I am serious about this. It starts today. Go and get your bag. You can have half an hour to relax, but then you bring your books and start.'

Emma glared for a moment longer, then rose to her feet stiffly and left the room as though she was heading to the gallows.

Lisa exhaled, but felt a tightness in her chest. So that hadn't gone like she had intended it to. She slumped in her seat and put her forehead in her hands.

She heard footfall behind her and sat up, an apology already jumping onto her tongue, expecting to see a contrite Emma, but it was Lucy, who must've come home while she was shouting at Emma.

'You ok, Mum?'

'Yes, yes, I'm fine,' she said hurriedly.

'Do you need a hug?'

Lisa wanted to weep at the innocence of the question and knew she would crumble if she accepted.

'That's sweet, but I'm fine, really. How was school?'

Lucy looked hurt. 'It was ok. I'm going to my room.' She left in much the same manner as her older sister had minutes before.

Lisa sat in the quiet, feeling the weight of the air pressing down on her shoulders, burning into her lungs, clouding her brain.

It was all going wrong. Why was it all going wrong?

Her phone buzzed across the table and she glanced at it unenthusiastically. A text from Ben, telling her he was working late again.

She looked down at the pieces of evidence on the table in front of her. She picked each one up and tore it into tiny confetti, letting it litter the table like ash.

22

Christina

Now

People never react as you expect in a crisis. Christina was bewildered. Lisa was by all accounts falling apart in front of them, slumped in the hard, plastic chair, her eyes wide but glassy, confused by everything going on around her, while Ben puffed out his chest and threw his weight around, demanding answers from whoever was in his crosshairs at any given moment.

Maybe it was because she had no one to prop her up or hold her hand, but now that she was here, Christina felt strangely calm and in control. It wasn't that she was in denial about what was going on here. They had all heard the horror stories of what could happen when the wrong pill was taken on a night out, but in this moment of shock and panic, she stood calmly and watched everything playing out in front of her, listened to what the doctors were saying with a level head and prepared to put Sophia first in whatever was required of her.

Lisa had always come across as a bit of a tiger mum. The

first one to write an email to the school when grades slipped or teachers made mistakes. The first one to volunteer for PTAs and cake sales. The first to sign up for every single extracurricular class when the girls were younger. Talk about overcompensating for being a bad parent behind closed doors. She had made it so easy to hate her.

The falling out hadn't been about Emma. Christina had always liked her, felt a little sorry for her to be honest, even all those years ago when Lisa had regulated how much sugar she was eating and how much time she spent in the sun. Christina had wanted to tell Lisa to relax, to let her be, to let her make mistakes so that she could learn from them. Emma had had a serious side, certainly, but she was so light and happy when she was playing with Sophia.

Even now, in pushing Emma to apply to Oxford, it felt a bit like Lisa's ambition and need to control outstripped any of her daughter's dreams. And yet, when it came to the crunch, when everything was crumbling around them and the kids needed them all to step up, be strong and help them through this nightmare, Lisa was a quivering, sobbing mess, clinging onto Ben like he was a life preserver. She had buried her face in Ben's shoulder. He was pale, his previous bluster having blown itself out, and now he was staring emptily at the wall, his face tight.

They could scoff at Christina all they wanted – the single mum who never quite lived up to their high standards – but right now, she was holding it together. Ok, so she didn't have a child in a drug-induced coma, but still, she had no idea if Sophia had taken anything. Maybe she got lucky. Maybe she could've been in the bed next to Emma.

Or worse.

But she wasn't and Christina agonised over the relief she felt at someone else's expense.

Karma had a way of coming back around. What if this wasn't ever over? What if life was irreversibly altered from this point on? What if their lives were never going to be the same again?

What if somehow this was down to Sophia?

Now Christina could feel the panic inching up the back of her calves, behind her knees, the back of her thighs, weakening her legs until they felt like they might buckle. She sat down in the nearest chair as a cold sweat broke out on her forehead. Everything felt fuzzy around the edges, but there was no way she was going to faint or collapse now. She needed to be right here when Sophia came back from the x-rays. She needed to smile, say the right words to her, give her a hug and leave this place.

Christina realised she was still holding the damn tray of coffee cups. She set it down on the seat next to her without spilling a drop, despite the tremor she could feel in her fingers.

She closed her eyes, put her hands between her legs and let her head drop, breathing in deeply for a few moments and willing the sudden surge of panic to recede.

After a few deep inhales and exhales, she could feel control start to creep back. She sat back up and opened her eyes.

A doctor was striding towards her, concern all over his face.

Ice settled into her veins.

23

Sophia

Three Weeks Ago

The doorbell rang once, twice.

'Soph, can you get that please?' Christina called from the lounge where she was doing nothing more interesting than watching *Come Dine with Me* with Colin, the two of them laughing loudly while they slurped tea and dunked digestive biscuits.

Sophia sighed and pushed away from the dining room table where she had spread out her history textbooks.

She flung open the door and found Emma standing on her front step with Jester next to her on a lead. He wagged his tail enthusiastically and tried to surge into the house, but Emma held him back.

'Is your mum home?' Emma said without greeting her.

'Um, yeah. Why? Do you want to see her?'

'No, I don't want her to know I'm here. Duh.'

'Oh, ok. Come around the back then and I'll meet you by the shed.'

'Who is it, Soph?' Christina called.

Sophia closed the door on Emma as her mother's head poked out of the front room.

'Someone raising money for Battersea. I told them we already donate monthly.'

'Ah, I like dogs,' Christina said before disappearing again.

Sophia made her way past the lounge, flinching at a glimpse of Colin's hairy toes and yellowing toenails from where they were propped up on the coffee table. She made her way quietly through the kitchen and out into the garden towards Christina's studio. Christina liked to refer to it as the 'posh shed', but it was more than a shed. The studio stretched across the width of the garden. It had been built for Christina by an ex-boyfriend who loved DIY. Sophia had liked him, thought he was going to stick around, but none of them did for long. One side of the shed housed Christina's studio with everything she needed for her sculptures and art. There was a large window on one side that caught the light for most of the day and the space was dominated by paint, clay and dust. The other side of the building resembled a mini spa retreat, complete with an in-built sound system, wine fridge and a corner bar that Pat Butcher would've been proud of, with purple, velvet bar stools and old album cover artwork on the walls. Just outside the glass doors was a hot tub, in which Christina and Colin spent many hours, sipping on gin and tonics in the frothy, warm water.

Sophia walked around the side of the shed to the back gate and let Emma and Jester into the garden.

'In here,' she said and pulled open the shed door. 'Are you ok?'

The online abuse had tapered off a little in the last week

or so, mostly engineered by Sophia as she redirected the attention elsewhere. Seeing Emma standing on the edge of that roof, a dark energy crackling around her, looking nowhere near as scared as she should've been, had rattled Sophia to the core. Emma's expression of calm resignation still haunted her and she often wondered what could've happened if she hadn't followed her up there that day.

Emma sat on a bar stool. She looked pale, her eyes like marbles. Jester settled at her feet. She said nothing at first, just looked down at her hands. Then she said, 'Did you mean what you said? About being here for me if I need to talk?'

'Of course I did.' Sophia plonked down on the stool next to her.

'Can I have some of that?' Emma nodded at the bottles of alcohol behind the bar.

Sophia shrugged. 'Sure, take your pick.'

Emma pointed at the vodka and Sophia poured them each a shot. Emma didn't hesitate, just knocked it back and winced. Sophia let hers sit in front of her.

Still Emma said nothing more and Sophia started to get impatient. She still had so much to get through before her history test tomorrow. 'Em, what is it?' Her voice was sharper than she had intended.

'Ok,' said Emma, 'what I am about to tell you, you have to promise me you will never breathe a word of it to anyone. Swear on your mum's life.'

'Gees, Em, you're scaring me. What have you done?'

Emma had a skittishness about her, like she was high on something that was making her twitch and jerk. Her foot tapped against the leg of the bar stool and her fingers fidgeted with the now empty shot glass. The skin around her fingernails was red raw. She reached out and grabbed Sophia's glass, knocking it back without wincing this time.

'Swear it, Soph!'

'Ok, I swear!' Sophia could feel her pulse tapping in her neck like a drum roll.

'I think I'm pregnant.'

The silence stretched on like an elastic band. Sophia didn't know what to say. This was the last thing she had expected to hear.

Eventually, Sophia said, 'How? When?'

Emma rolled her eyes. 'Surely you know how by now. The when? At your house.'

Sophia flinched. Images of Emma following Kai upstairs, both of them quite drunk, laughing, flirting. Sophia had watched her go, said nothing, just stood by, letting jealousy fester inside her. She remembered the anger that had bubbled and popped like gas in her throat, born of the fact that it was Emma who was going upstairs with him and not Sophia, that he had picked her of all people over Sophia. How that jealousy had twisted her insides until the only thing that made her feel better was sending the first message to the group and then watching it catch fire.

Emma sighed. 'I'm late, like, a week late. And I'm never late.'

'Um, how do you feel?'

'How do I feel? How do I feel?' Her voice raised incrementally. 'I feel fucking terrified.'

'I meant, like, you know, sick or whatever,' Sophia mumbled.

Emma exhaled, said in a calmer voice, 'I'm angry, confused, I guess.'

'Sorry, I... it's just a shock, that's all. Are you sure it was then?'

'I don't make a habit of sleeping around, Soph.' Her voice was scalpel sharp. 'That was my first time.'

'So what are you going to do?'

'I don't know.'

'Have you told him?'

'No! I haven't told anyone – apart from you.' She picked at her nail.

'Shit, Em. I don't know what to say.'

'Those bitches at school are going to love this. You've seen the stuff that's been going around about me already.' Then she added, 'I swear if you tell anyone, I will end you.'

The look in her eyes convinced Sophia that this was not an exaggeration.

'I won't, ok?' Sophia looked down at Jester, now napping at their feet. 'Ok, so you and Kai made a mistake, fine. We just have to figure out what to do, I guess.'

'Wait, what?'

Sophia frowned. How had that been the wrong thing to say?

'Kai must never know, first of all, and second of all, it was more than a mistake.'

'What do you mean?'

'I mean it shouldn't have happened at all.' Her eyes were almost feverish, matching the colour that had sprung up on her cheekbones. 'The thing is... I don't remember it.'

Sophia looked up sharply. 'What?'

'Well, I have flashbacks, like little snips of things, of being in the room, of putting my jeans back on, but the actual *thing* I don't remember. I was drunk. It's like I can remember the final destination, but not how we got there. It's just a blank. Maybe... maybe it didn't happen? Maybe I blacked out and nothing more happened.' She sounded very much like someone convincing themselves of the truth. 'I don't know.'

'Well, you need to take a test first, I think?'

'Yes, but if I am pregnant and I can't remember what happened...' Her voice trailed off. She watched Sophia closely.

Sophia felt cold. She couldn't believe what Emma was insinuating. 'If it happened but you can't remember, are you sure you wanted it to?'

Oh my God, Kai, what did you do?

How many times had teachers drummed the concept of consent into them at school? How many times had the teachers told them to think of it like a cup of tea that you may or may not want and how important it was to make sure? How you were allowed to change your mind about wanting that cup of tea? How many times had they sniggered in class, all thinking they would know the rules if it came down to it?

She thought about that moment, watching Kai and Emma climb the stairs. Emma had been drunk. That was obvious. But had her anger made Sophia blind to what was actually happening?

And Kai? Surely he wasn't one of those boys. He was always the first to tell the twins when they were being inappropriate. Was it all an act? Did she even know him at all?

'Right, you have to do a test.' Sophia said, finding a calm in her voice she certainly didn't feel. 'Let's make sure first. You're right, you might not have done it, in which case you are panicking about nothing. Besides, we know Kai. He's not like that, is he? He wouldn't without, you know…'

'Isn't he?'

The question fell flat in the space between them.

'Ok, first things first. I will come to your house tomorrow and we can do the test. I'll get one from the chemist and bring it with me,' Sophia said.

'My mum will be home.'

'Tell her I'm coming to revise. Tell her you're tutoring me – she'll believe that.'

'Ok.'

Sophia reached out and took Emma's hands in hers. They were ice cold. 'It will be ok. We will figure this out.'

Tears sprung into Emma's eyes and Sophia heard her breath catch in her throat, but Emma held it together, didn't say another word, just dropped down from the vulgar bar stool, grabbed Jester's lead and left through the back gate.

Sophia felt a bit sick herself when she rang the doorbell on time at four o'clock the next day. She'd gone past Superdrug on the high street after school, praying she wouldn't see anyone she knew. If she'd been clever about it, she would've gone to the small chemist at the other end of town, but that would've meant an extra ten-minute bus ride and she just wanted to get on with this, prove the test was negative and forget about the possible ramifications of what a positive result would mean.

Superdrug was a high-risk environment though, full of people from school buying highlighter and colour palettes that were no different to the other five they already owned. However, Sophia figured that if she acted confidently and styled it out, no one would question what she was buying. They'd probably think she was buying tampons.

She had kept her head down and left without taking too much notice of anyone around her, hoping they would do the same.

It was Lisa who opened the front door, just as Emma had warned. She was dressed in Sweaty Betty Lycra with her hair pulled into a loose ponytail, no make-up. She looked fresh-faced and youthful, despite being a similar age to Sophia's mum, who seemed to wear more lines on her face with every passing day, lines that were often filled with foundation, but Christina said that that was what a face that wasn't botoxed to death was supposed to look like. Sophia looked at Lisa now and figured the botox was worth it if it meant you looked this unmarked by time.

Christina had small lines around her mouth from where she sucked on cigarettes all day and skin that carried a grey hue from alcoholic overindulgence. She had little crinkly lines around her eyes where they folded in on themselves when she laughed her throaty laugh, which was often. Lisa had none of that. Sophia knew from Emma that Lisa didn't smoke or drink very much. Apparently, she didn't smile much either.

She was smiling at Sophia now, but with a vagueness that carried the impression of looking *through* Sophia rather than at her.

'Sophia. Lovely to see you. Ems said you would be coming over. Always good to know when to ask for help when it comes to revision, isn't it? I'm sure you'll find it useful.'

Sophia smiled thinly and said, 'Hi, Mrs Marco. Nice to see you.' She bent down to make a fuss of a wriggling Jester, trying to make it look like she hadn't just seen him yesterday. That was the thing with dogs. No matter when they saw you, the next time was always the first time.

Lisa stepped just far enough aside for Sophia to squeeze past. After closing the door, she called up the stairs, 'Ems! Sophia is here for her tutoring session! Jester, enough now – to your bed.' She turned and shooed Jester away.

Sophia pulled a face behind her back, just as Lucy emerged from the lounge. Sophia blushed, but Lucy just grinned and disappeared back into the lounge.

Lisa said, 'Go on up, Sophia. You remember where Emma's room is?'

'I'm here, Mum.' Emma stood at the top of the stairs, her arms folded tightly across her chest.

Sophia followed Emma into her surprisingly messy bedroom. It had been some years since she had been in here. Back then, it had been decorated in lilac with a Laura Ashley duvet cover and flowered curtains. Now the room was painted a stark white, with very little other decoration to be seen. The old duvet cover was still there, but there were no more throw pillows, tassels or fairy lights. It was a bland room with only a few black and white posters on the wall to indicate any sense of Emma's personality. It was also an absolute mess.

'Did you get one?' she said as Sophia tossed her backpack onto a pile of clothes that lined the far side of the double bed. There was just enough empty space on the bed for Emma to sleep.

'I got two, just in case.' She hadn't been sure how these things work – was it like a Covid test where the first try could be a dud?

Emma was pacing, stepping over clothes and kicking out at shoes lying abandoned on the floor. 'You'll wear a hole in the carpet,' Sophia said.

'What?'

'Nothing, just something my mum says,' Sophia mumbled back. She opened her backpack and brought out the Superdrug bag.

'Nobody saw you, did they?'

'I don't think so, but if they did, they would never think it was for you.'

No, they'd think it was for Sophia, the one who doesn't work hard, parties with boys and will probably not amount to much in life. Unlike Emma: all-star student, heading to Oxford, the whole world at her feet. Oh, the irony. She tried to ignore a small flicker of delight at that. No, she shouldn't be enjoying this at all.

They sat facing each other, the tests on the bed between them. Sophia waited for Emma to pick one up, but she just stared at it like it was a petri dish of nastiness.

'Ok, let's see,' Sophia said in the end, trying not to vocalise her impatience. Why had this become her problem?

She opened the box and unfolded the instructions. 'I think you just pee on it, if the TV programmes are true.' She read the instructions anyway, just to be sure. 'Yes, you just pee on the end and wait.'

'I've been drinking water all afternoon just in case and five minutes ago, I really needed the loo, but now I don't,' Emma said.

'That's just nerves. Here.' She handed Emma the stick. 'Off you go.'

Emma took the stick with quivering fingers, inhaled deeply and left the room, her feet dragging.

While she was gone, Sophia looked around the room, at the bareness of the walls, the mess. One of her cupboard doors stood open, clothes spilling out like the stuffing of a teddy. Make-up was scattered across her desk, leaving foundation smears. There was a pile of school books on the floor next to the bed and a novel on her bedside table, the corner of a page turned down, the spine cracked. Looking around, Sophia was reminded that they hadn't been real friends for years and that maybe she didn't know her very well at all now. She knew five-year-old Emma really well, the summer-hazy memories still fresh, but her knowledge of 17-year-old Emma was based on assumption and gossip. Sophia picked up the book. It was about a group of friends at university in the nineties. As she read the back of it, a photograph fell from between the pages. Two smiling girls in frilly, neon swimming costumes, sitting in a half-full paddling pool and holding melting ice lollies. Emma and Sophia when Lisa used to look after them after school.

The bedroom door swung open. Sophia quickly shoved

the photo back into the book and set it back on the bedside table.

Emma was ashen. She closed the door and sat on the bed, the stick wrapped in tissue paper and clenched in her hand like dynamite.

'Ok, time it,' she said.

Sophia pulled her phone from her back pocket and set the timer for two minutes, then made it three. 'Just to make sure,' she said. 'You can put it down, you know.' Emma was still gripping the stick, her knuckles white.

'Right, yeah.' She leaned over and put it on top of the book.

'Did you pee on that hand? Hope you washed it,' Sophia said.

Emma looked at her, then at her hand.

'I'm joking,' Sophia said with a careful smile.

It took a few seconds, but then Emma leaned over and rubbed her hand on Sophia's cheek. 'No, I didn't wash it.'

They both started to laugh.

The laughter petered out until they were quiet again, just watching the time tick down. Sophia gave Emma a shaky smile. 'Not sure what we talk about. It's weird, isn't it?'

Emma nodded.

'Music, maybe we need music to distract us.' Sophia pulled her phone out and searched through Spotify for a playlist.

'Nothing with babies or anything in it, though,' Emma said.

Sophia kept scrolling, but nothing seemed appropriate for waiting to hear if your friend had ruined her life – and possibly the life of your other friend too. She set her phone down again, defeated.

'How's your revision going?' Sophia said instead.

'Non-existent, really. Just can't concentrate on anything.'

'You'll be ok though – your predicted grades are good enough as they are?'

'Maybe. I just don't care, to be honest. It's her – *she* wants me to go to Oxford.'

'Who? Your mum? So you don't want to go?' Sophia found this surprising. She thought it was Emma's dream, not Lisa's.

She shrugged. 'I really like art – well, drawing comic books, actually – and there's this idea I've been working on… it's nothing, but I just find it, I dunno, calming I guess? And if it's good enough, maybe it could be something, you know? Like a career.' She shrugged again. That one movement could say so much. Sophia could tell this was something she was serious about.

'Wow, I had no idea. Show me.'

'No, you'll laugh. It's really not that good.'

'It probably is good, knowing you. Please show me?'

Emma ran her eyes over Sophia's face, trying to work out if she was taking the piss or not. She looked at the timer again, slowly winding down, seemingly getting no closer. There was a small chest of drawers on the other side of the double bed. She reached over and opened the top drawer. It was filled with notebooks, one stacked on top of another. Emma took out the top one and handed it to Sophia.

Sophia was suddenly nervous as she took the notebook. What if Emma wasn't that good? Could she hold a poker face? If she was going to be honest with herself, there was a part of her that really hoped the drawings were bad. Sophia didn't know why, especially after feeling so guilty about the damage she had inflicted recently. Perhaps it had to do with the look on her mother's face when she asked how Emma was doing and Sophia had to admit that she was so clever and applying to Oxford. She knew her mother still compared herself to Lisa, so maybe Sophia wanted to see Emma fail so that her mother felt better.

You keep telling yourself that.

Emma set her face into a neutral mask, not ready to betray her inner thoughts. She opened the notebook and began to page through it. The A5 pages were filled with small, detailed boxes of drawings in black ink, all adding up to the story of a girl and her dog, lost in the woods and having to fend for themselves. The drawings were better than good. Sophia could make out every facial expression, every nuance of location.

Emma sat quietly, watching Sophia's face, chewing on her bottom lip. Sophia got to the last page and set the notebook aside.

'Fuck me, Ems, these are brilliant! I had no idea. I mean, you were good at art back in Year 7 – I remember you did this chalk drawing of a thistle and the teacher held it up and showed the class – but I had no idea you were into comics. You should do something with these, send them off to a publisher or whatever it is you have to do.'

Emma shrugged again, but her face had filled with colour and she smiled, just a little bit.

'My dad used to read comics,' Sophia said out of the blue.

'Really?'

'Yeah, I found a box of them once in the loft. I was putting a box of old school stuff up there and I came across these old copies of Marvel comics, *Spiderman* and stuff like that.'

'That's really cool. Do you still have them?'

'No. I asked my mum about them and she got really mad, didn't know they were still up there and then when I looked again, they were gone.'

'What was the deal with them anyway?'

'I dunno. He left when I was about one and my mum never speaks about him. I heard her once talking to Sally when they'd had a few too many glasses of wine. I heard her say she threw him out and he never looked back.'

The buzzer on Sophia's phone trilled and they both jumped. Emma grabbed the notebook and shoved it back in the drawer with the rest.

'Ok, here we go.' Emma reached for the test and slowly peeled back the toilet paper.

24

Lisa

Now

Lisa watched the doctor talking to Christina. Christina had stood up instantly and was almost eye to eye with him as he talked in a low tone, but Lisa was too far away to hear what he was saying. There was a fair bit of gesticulating from him, and plenty of supportive smiles in between whatever word bombs he was dropping.

Lisa watched Christina's face, looking for signs. What was he saying? Was he giving her the worst news of all? Or was she getting a reprieve from this horror? Why was she hoping that their places had been swapped suddenly?

Christina was saying something to him now, her forehead caught in a tight frown. The doctor replied in low tones. He reached out a hand and placed it on Christina's arm, patted it fatherly and gave her one of those pity smiles that were so hard to read.

Christina sat down heavily again. Then she started to cry. Quietly, shoulders hunched but shaking, her face in her hands.

Lisa frowned. She didn't think she had ever seen Christina cry. Angry, yes; drunk, certainly. But not crying. She looked vulnerable, almost child-like. Interestingly, Lisa had expected ugly crying from her – wailing and thrashing – but Christina was silent. Lisa had a moment of annoyance at that. It would've felt better if Christina had caused a scene.

The doctor patted Christina's shoulder once more and walked away.

What had he told her? Lisa got to her feet and noticed Ben watching Christina too. His face was a picture of concern. She looked from him to Christina and back again. Ben caught her watching and nodded in Christina's direction, then shrugged and returned to looking at his hands. He didn't get up or go to speak to Christina. Lisa wasn't sure what to make of it all.

If they were having an affair, surely Ben would have gone over to comfort her? Or was he deliberately keeping his distance so as not to draw attention?

She wished Owen was here because he could find out what Christina had been told, but he hadn't come back since he went to talk to the police.

Lisa started walking towards Christina, but Ben leapt to his feet and intercepted her. 'Where are you going?'

'I'm just going to check on Christina. She's upset.'

'Really?'

'Yes, really. Why? Why shouldn't I?'

'It's just...'

Christina looked up, saw them talking. Mascara had pooled under her eyes. She swiped at the tears, smeared some of the mascara, and said, 'I can hear you talking about me, you know.'

'Is… is everything ok?' Ben said.

Her reaction was immediate and heated. 'Oh, so now you're asking if I'm ok? Right, I see.' She narrowed her eyes.

Lisa looked from one to the other. She opened her mouth, ready to ask the question that was burning a hole through the floor of her mouth, but before she could, Christina launched to her feet, relief making her body pliable and loose.

'Baby! Oh, thank God!'

Sophia was walking down the corridor, escorted by a nurse. Her arm was in fresh plaster, a sling holding it in place.

Christina pulled her into a tight embrace. They stood that way for some time.

Every second of watching Christina hug her daughter was torture for Lisa.

25

Lisa

Three Weeks Ago

'I don't know anymore. It feels like I'm living with a lodger in my house sometimes. Last night, he came home late again, dumped his gym bag in the hallway. It's still there, stinking out the place. The girls and I had eaten our dinner already. He grabbed the plate I had left out for him, sat in front of the television to eat it, complained that there wasn't a salad on the side – seriously, a salad! – then put the plate on the countertop *above* the dishwasher. Not in it, where I had already loaded the rest of the dinner dishes, but above it! Why do that?'

Lisa knew how nagging she sounded, but her levels of frustration were overpowering everything else. The phone sat heavily in her hand. She could see the gym bag, spilling onto the carpet, from her seat in the kitchen.

'That is annoying,' Owen replied, his voice oozing sympathy into her ear.

'I bet you load the dishwasher, don't you?'

'Well, the difference for me is that I work from home,

so I do most of the housework while Lena is at work,' Owen replied, then added quickly, 'Not that I'm justifying it, though. It should not be just one person's job. You are a team, a partnership. You need to have respect for each other first and foremost.'

'I know I don't work full time and he is overworked, but still, he can put a plate in the dishwasher, can't he? I do everything else. Do you know how soulless it is trying to decide what meals to cook every night? Only to have him complain about the choices I am making.'

'I know – and half the time, they turn their noses up and say they don't fancy that tonight. Oh, Lisa, I hear you. I really do. But maybe there's something going on with him. You say he's hitting the gym hard, requesting salads, cutting back on coffee and drinking smoothies...'

'You mean an affair.'

Owen cleared his throat. 'Not necessarily, but he's a fool if he is. Look, you know Ben and I aren't the best of friends, but if I was married to you, I wouldn't need to go looking for someone else.'

Lisa giggled at the compliment, felt her cheeks flush. 'Oh shush.' Suddenly uncomfortably warm, she switched the phone to her other ear.

'Maybe you're right. He's taken to going to the gym a lot. He works late a lot, he's watching what he eats suddenly. He has nothing to say to me most days, like he's all talked out, and he's tired all the time. It's all just so clichéd, isn't it?'

'Yeah, it is, but we all know men are not the smartest sometimes.'

'I don't know. It just seems so unlike him.'

'Said every woman whose husband has ever cheated on them,' Owen said. 'You're my friend, Lisa, and I worry about you. I don't think he knows what he's got right in front of him.'

There was a pause in their telephone conversation as she struggled with what to say. Sometimes Owen had a way of being so direct that it made her squirm a little. She could imagine him and Lena discussing their feelings of a Friday evening, how she was *invalidating his feelings*, how she needed to be her *authentic self*, while they drank green tea and ate acai bowls. Sometimes, she felt like a philistine around him.

Owen carried on. 'Have you asked him outright?'

'What? Straight out? "Darling, are you shagging someone else?" No, I haven't asked him.' She felt cold at that idea, but it wasn't from fear of the truth; rather, fear of what the truth would mean. 'This is going to sound odd, but I don't think I would mind if he was having an affair. A worse scenario for me would be him telling me he was moving out.'

'Why?' Owen seemed baffled and Lisa could understand why.

'Because then I would be on my own with the girls and with exams coming up and everything... I mean, what if it derails Emma's chances for a place at Oxford? At this stage in their lives, they need stability, not divorcing parents and two houses to shuffle between. No, I think despite him being an absolute arse to live with at the moment, I think it's best if things stay as they are. Even if it means burying my head in the sand and ignoring what is going on.'

'Oh, Lisa, but that sounds so sad for you. You deserve to have someone take care of you for a change. You've done everything for those girls – and him.'

'Oh, but I've done it willingly.'

'That doesn't matter. Now you're invalidating yourself. He doesn't deserve you, it's as simple as that. Listen, why don't I come over for a bit? Have a cup of tea? You sound like you need a hug.'

At that moment in time, listening to him flatter her and tell her what she deserved, what she needed, rather than what she got, his deep, coffee-smooth voice repeating the thoughts in her head, all she really wanted was for him to turn up on her front doorstep.

She heard a thump through the ceiling, coming from Emma's room, like a full stop on her racing thoughts.

'I can't – Sophia is here with Emma,' she said.

'Oh, right.' He sounded disappointed, even a little annoyed that his flattery had been rejected.

'Apparently, Emma is tutoring her,' Lisa went on quickly, hoping to steer the conversation back onto firmer ground, not wanting him to say goodbye just yet. 'Goodness knows that girl could use all the help she can get. I can't imagine Christina is much good to her with the exams coming up.'

'She's a good kid. They all are.'

'Hmmmm, well, our kids might be, but I think Sophia is going off the rails a bit. From what I've heard from Lucy, there's a lot of partying, drinking and boys, and not much else. But what do you expect, I guess? That's how Christina lives too. What did you make of Colin?'

'I thought he seemed a nice bloke. Quite a laugh, really.'

'I guess – a little rough around the edges.'

'Careful, Lisa, or you'll sound like a snob.' He still sounded piqued.

'Ouch, you're right, Owen. I can always count on you to tell me what I need to hear. I apologise. I just worry that it must be unsettling for Sophia to have loads of men in and out of the house all the time. How many boyfriends has Christina had over the years? I've lost count.'

'A few, I agree, but most seem harmless. Do you remember the one she nearly moved in with, was going to move Sophia to Hertfordshire or somewhere? What was his name? Alan or Adam?'

'Oh yes! Then it turned out he was still married. See what I mean? A terrible judge of character when it comes to men.'

The line went quiet then. Lisa felt panic pinch at her chest – had she just said the wrong thing? 'Of course, if it's meant to be and all that... the point is, Sophia could do a lot worse than my Ems helping her through her exams. How's Kai doing with his revision?'

'He seems fine. Lena is really good at sitting with him in the evenings and going over everything he has done that day. She does that with all of the kids. It makes her feel in control and gives him a chance to consolidate what he has revised.'

'Oh, right. Every night? Wow. How does she find the time?' Lisa didn't even know what Emma was revising. She had been forcing Emma to sit at the table and work where Lisa could check on her at any point and she was always there, books open, AirPods in for music, but Lisa never actually helped her to revise, didn't ask any questions.

What if she wasn't doing enough? Should she be sitting with her, questioning her, going over it all? If Emma didn't get the right marks, it would be down to her, wouldn't it?

'I should do that with Emma – and definitely Lucy as she needs more help than Emma. She's not as academic at all.'

'Really? I thought she was doing well?'

'She's getting Bs and the odd A here and there, mostly for English, which seems to be her favourite subject, but by this stage, Emma was getting A*s.'

'Lisa, don't make the mistake of expecting the same from both of them. They are very different people who need different kinds of motivation. But that isn't to say one is better than the other – and Bs are very good in my opinion. We live in a very strange, high-achieving bubble around here.'

'Yes, sorry, you're right,' she said quickly. She felt inadequate again, like she was always saying the wrong thing to him. What must he think of her? 'I know Lucy is bright; she just sometimes needs a push to apply herself.' She thought she heard him sigh. 'But they will all do things at their own pace and will turn out fine in the end. Like you say, they are all good kids. We're doing our best.'

'Yes, yes we are. None of it came with a manual, did it?'

Some of us are doing better than others, though.

Lisa couldn't help thinking Christina was not doing right by Sophia. She'd known that all those years ago and she had tried to help, but it wasn't her problem now. Her days of taking Sophia under her wing and shaping her were long gone.

'True, but you have to admit that if you think of the effort we are putting in compared to Christina, then Sophia has no chance. She's a lost cause if she's anything like her mother. I don't even know if she was ever that bright. I guess we will see when the exam results are in, but there's no parental guidance, no sense of discipline from what I can see. Christina treats that girl more like her best mate than a daughter that needs a firm hand. Christina should—' She heard a noise behind her and turned to look over her shoulder.

Sophia was standing behind her, her backpack and coat on. 'Bye, Mrs Marco. Nice to see you again.' The words were scalpel sharp and cut straight through Lisa.

An uncomfortable heat flooded through her body. 'Um, bye Sophia.'

She watched as Sophia walked away towards the front door, her head high, her back straight.

'Oh God,' Lisa said into the phone as the front door closed.

'Are you ok? Lisa? What is it?' Despite how wretched she felt, the note of concern in Owen's voice did not go unnoticed.

'Sophia – she was standing right behind me.' Lisa sunk her forehead into her hands. 'I hope she didn't hear me.' She knew perfectly well she had, though.

'I'm sure she didn't. You're not talking loudly.'

'Yes, maybe. I better go anyway. Time to start getting on with dinner – Ben should be home soon, I think. Unless he's working late again or going to the gym.'

'Well, you know where I am if you need to talk. And I am happy to come over – any time. You know that, right? Just pick up the phone or send me a text.'

'I know, thank you.'

She sat at the table for some time after she had hung up, not worrying about Sophia. If she had heard her, there was nothing Lisa could do about it now. Instead, she was thinking about what Owen had meant by coming over. She *thought* she knew what he meant, but wasn't sure. Not 100 per cent. She could be reading it all wrong – he did have Lena at home, who was beautiful and smart and successful – but all of that didn't make her perfect. He had said a few times that Lena could be just as inattentive as Ben was, treating him like a glorified babysitter and dismissing his job as inconsequential compared to hers.

And if he was suggesting what she thought he was? Well, what was apparently good for Ben was surely good for her too, right?

She picked up her phone and composed a text to Owen, thanking him for listening to her moan on. She waited with suspended breath for the reply and exhaled with a delicious rush when he replied with a love-heart emoji.

26

Christina

Now

The relief at seeing Sophia was palpable, like a metallic rust in her mouth. All she wanted to do was hold her close, tell her this was all a horrible nightmare that she would wake up from, that everything was going to be ok. So she clutched onto her like a life preserver, until Sophia said, 'Mum, I'm ok.'

Of course, she didn't know if that was true at this point.

She wanted it to be true, so much that it was causing a gaping hole in her chest that ached, but wanting and knowing were often streets apart from each other. She had a hundred and one questions about what had happened, how she had injured herself, but she held her tongue as they walked away, down the corridor, putting distance between them and Lisa.

Then she felt faint. Maybe the rush of it all hitting her, the shock and fear. There was a public bathroom ahead of her. 'Just need the loo,' she said.

She leaned over the basin and ran the cold tap as hard as

it would go. The water was icy and ran down the backs of the hands as she scooped it into her open palms, wetting the sleeves of her jumper. She splashed her face repeatedly, then scrabbled around for some tissue to dry herself.

She stared at her reflection in the mirror on the wall. She looked haunted. She wiped at the mascara that was still staining the underneath of her eyes, tried to pull herself together a little bit. She felt wobbly, shaky on the inside in the very pit of her stomach, like there was a coldness in there that refused to thaw. But Sophia would need her to be calm and composed now, not a physical and emotional wreck. There were so many questions to be asked and the answers may well be difficult to hear.

She was pleased to be away from Lisa and Ben though. Somehow, she knew this would be made out to be her fault. Lisa had already accused her of various things. But the ice-cold fear in her stomach was at hearing the answers to some of those questions because what if this was down to Sophia?

Christina knew what kind of girl she thought she had raised, but what if she was wrong? What if Sophia had made a mistake so serious that it had put Emma into a critical condition? What if she had to find the strength to support her daughter despite her actions? As a parent, she had said before that she would love her daughter no matter what and that she could never disappoint her, but was that actually true? What if there were some things that could not be forgiven?

Christina thought back to that day all those years ago when she had turned up to collect Sophia from Lisa's house and she had seen the searing red marks on Sophia's legs, could see the dried tears on her cheeks and the way she flinched when Lisa came towards her. She remembered the story Lisa had told her, how just for a tiny moment, Christina had doubted Sophia. That tiny flicker of time when a seed of doubt had been planted in her head about a side of Sophia's personality that she may have inherited from her father. Since then, Christina had been on the lookout for any more signs, any further indication she could be like him.

Was this it? Was this the evidence she needed?

She had never told anyone about the day he had hit her. She had thrown him out then and there, fearing that he would raise a hand to Sophia if he stayed, and he hadn't looked back. Thankfully, she hadn't heard from him since. Good riddance.

So, to see those marks inflicted on her daughter by her best friend?

She had vowed then that Sophia would never be in Lisa's care again and that she would never forgive Lisa, but it wasn't just about how Lisa had reacted. It was also about that seed of doubt that Lisa had planted in her own head. Their friendship died that day and Christina has never regretted the rash decisions she made in the hours and days afterwards – quitting her well-paid job; starting her own business as a sculptor; putting Sophia and her needs first before a career, money, everything; doing everything she possibly could to make sure Sophia was raised in her own likeness and not his.

But now it was all in jeopardy. Her sacrifice may have been for nothing.

She may have failed after all. A simple twist of genes.

No, she couldn't think like that. She needed to believe

that everything was going to be ok. Emma would come out of this and Sophia would go on to do great things.

Christina took a deep breath, pulled open the bathroom door and stepped into the artificially illuminated corridor where her daughter was waiting for her.

27

Christina

Three Weeks Ago

The front door slammed hard enough to ripple the surface of the coffee in Christina's mug.

'Woah! Steady on!' she called out as Sophia stormed into the lounge and flung her backpack to the ground. Sophia paced in front of Christina, her face dark, her eyes like marbles. 'What's going on?'

Sophia paced some more, her feet slapping the wooden floor.

'Soph, come on, what's happened? Is it someone at school?'

'Bloody Lisa!'

Not what Christina had expected to hear.

'Lisa? When did you see Lisa?'

'Just now. I went over to help Emma with... something.'

'Ok, and what did she do?'

'It's not what she did. It's what I overheard her saying.' Sophia spat the words out.

'Come on, sit, stop pacing. Tell me what happened.'

Sophia glared at her for a moment, then the bluster in her dropped away and she collapsed onto the couch.

'I overheard her on the phone talking to someone, I don't know who, but she was talking about me and you.' She now looked like she was going to cry. 'I think I'm upset because she's right.'

'Right about what?' Christina sat forward, on high alert, feeling the tiger blood in her veins bubbling and spitting.

'She said that she didn't think I had much of a chance of doing anything with my life and that I had never been that bright.'

'She what?'

Sophia shrugged. 'She's not wrong though, is she?'

'How dare she! Of course she's wrong! You can do anything you want to do. Give me my phone – I'm going to tell her exactly what I think of the nosy, opinionated cow.'

'No, Mum, don't. I'm just... I don't know. I'm stressed about the exams and doubt is creeping in, so now I'm thinking that she's right. I won't amount to much. I'm not smart like Emma. I have to work hard for everything. It all comes so easily to her. School, anyway.'

'Hey,' Christina said, leaning forward and pulling her into her chest. 'First of all, you don't know that. For all you know, she is working all hours to get the marks for Oxford, but in the process, she is missing out on all the fun stuff. Does she look happy to you? She doesn't to me. But you? You are happy, having fun, living your best life, you've got friends. That's what's really important. Forget good grades and university and sticking your head in books. What is important is finding what you are passionate about and following that dream. Living every day out in the sunlight.

There's a lot to be said for being successful, sure, but enjoying what you do enough to get out of bed every day is much more important. Having good friends to share it with, even more important.'

'Is it though, Mum? I don't know what I'm passionate about! I don't know what I want to do. Emma – she has dreams and ambitions and talent. I don't think I have anything special about me. I don't know what I'm good at. And these people I hang out with – are they my friends? Any one of them would cut my throat and film it if it meant they got likes. They are temporary and in a year's time, we will have all gone our separate ways.' She started to cry big gulps of tears.

'Oh baby, it takes time to meet your tribe.'

'And what about you? You have no real friends – you barely tolerate Sally because she is so annoying, you cut Lisa out of your life – yes, I know you had a good reason, but still – and you go from one boyfriend to another. Your only real friend is me. But you're supposed to be my mother, not my friend.'

The words slapped Christina's cheeks, but she tried to ignore it, knowing that Sophia was spiralling as the tears fell faster. 'Soph, sometimes our passions show later, but trust me, you are special and kind and generous. You youngsters have so much pressure on you. I wish you could take your time, slow down, see that everything doesn't have to be immediate. Good friends will come; your reason for being will present itself. And sometimes, the best friend you can have is yourself.' She pulled Sophia into a tight hug and let her cry into her chest, feeling every sob in her own gut.

Christina heard a key in the front door. 'Hola, señoritas!'

Colin burst into the lounge with a wide smile and a bottle of tequila in his hand. He pulled up short at seeing Sophia and Christina on the couch. Christina subtly shook her head at him.

'I'll just go and...' He retreated to the kitchen with his bottle.

Sophia sat up straight and swiped at her face. 'I didn't realise he was coming over again.' Her voice was flat.

'I didn't either, to be honest. A shame as maybe we could've had a girl's night in tonight. All you can eat pizza and ice cream. Wish I hadn't given him that key now.' She chuckled apologetically. 'I can tell him to go if you want?'

'No, it's fine. I have some work to do for tomorrow anyway.'

Clearly, from the look on her face, it was not fine.

'Take a night off, baby. Hang out with us. We can still order in pizza, and you and I can take the mickey out of Colin all night. What do you say?'

Sophia sighed. 'No, Mum, I can't take the night off. Unlike you, I actually want to prove Lisa wrong and make a success of my life.'

Christina tried to ignore how much the comment stung as Sophia swept past her.

'Soph, don't be like that. Soph!'

Sophia ignored her as she grabbed her backpack.

'Anyway, why were you at Lisa's? What did you have to help Emma with?'

But Sophia was already walking up the stairs and seconds later, the slamming of her bedroom door rattled the foundations once more.

Christina sat for a moment, digesting what Sophia had

said with difficulty, but certain phrases kept repeating on her.

Is that what Sophia thought of her? A failure because she didn't have some fancy career or loads of money? Was she really that transparent when it came to her friends, or lack thereof? She knew she liked to tell Sophia all about Sally and the stupid things she said or Lisa and her patronising, self-righteous ways, but she hadn't actually thought about what Sophia made of it all, what Sophia was learning from it.

They did alright, the two of them, didn't they? Sophia had never gone without anything. Sure, they didn't do fancy holidays or posh restaurants, but that wasn't everything in life. They were close, had a solid and good, open, honest relationship that many of her friends envied – that was what was important. Surely Sophia appreciated Christina's honesty and was just as honest in return? Christina might not have gone to university to become a doctor or a lawyer or an architect, but her sculptures did alright. And she loved it, the feel of the clay under her fingertips, the joy at seeing something emerge from nothing. That was the lesson she was trying to teach Sophia – that money wasn't everything. Being happy was all that mattered. And to be happy, you had to find your passion.

Colin startled her as he poked his head around the door and said, 'Safe to come in?'

She nodded, annoyed that he was here again, in her space. She had wanted to go and work on something in her studio later, but that wouldn't happen now. He seemed to be everywhere all at once now and she had a feeling the novelty of Colin was rapidly wearing off.

'So, what was that about? Boys, I reckon?' he said, plopping down into the space Sophia had vacated.

'No. Lisa.'

'What? The stuck-up one from the quiz night? What has she done?'

'Soph overheard her being rude about her.'

'And you're going to let it go? I'd be going straight over there, telling her what I think.'

Christina sat with this for a moment. He was right. Why the hell did she need Colin to tell her that? Why wasn't she defending Sophia, standing up for her?

'You're right, that's exactly what I'm going to do.'

Sweat ran between her shoulder blades as she pressed hard on the doorbell. She had covered the distance between their two houses in next to no time, outrage pushing up her pace. It took a while for the door to open, but when it did, she bit back on the words she had been rehearsing because it wasn't Lisa standing in front of her but Emma.

'Emma, is your mother in? I need a word right now.'

Emma looked like she was going to pass out. 'Um, why?'

Christina opened her mouth to say more, then heard the raised voices filtering through from deeper in the house. Angry words, each one poking like an accusing finger. Lisa and Ben were obviously having a domestic about something.

'Is everything ok in there?'

'Yes, they're just arguing again.' Emma looked nervous, scared almost. She was blinking fast and her fingers were pulling at the cords hanging from the neck of her hoodie.

'Are you ok, Emma?'

'What do you want to talk to her about?'

'Just something Sophia told me.'

'She told you? Fuck. You won't tell my mother, will you? Please.'

'Tell her what?'

Emma looked at her then, really looked at her, then said, 'Nothing, it's nothing. What did Sophia tell you?'

'It was something she overheard that upset her, that's all.' Christina had the distinct feeling something else was going on here. She reached out and touched Emma on the arm gently. 'Is there something you want to talk about?'

Emma opened her mouth, closed it, opened it again, as though she was trying to form the words in her mouth, feeling the weight of them on her tongue.

But before she could say anything, Lucy appeared behind Emma, her pale-blonde hair pulled back into a tight ponytail. She stared at the two of them curiously.

'Hi, how are you? Here to see Mum?'

'Er, no, it's fine. Now's not a good time, obviously. I'll give her a call instead.' Christina turned to go, then turned back to Emma and said in a low voice as Lucy walked away, 'You know you can always come and talk to me if you need to. I know your mum and I aren't friends anymore, but that doesn't mean I don't care about you – and sometimes talking to a grown-up who isn't part of the family can help. Sophia will tell you that I don't judge anyone. Ok?' She reached out and rubbed Emma's arm again.

Emma threw a quick glance over her shoulder and said, 'Thanks, but everything is fine.'

'Ok, well, no need to tell your mother I was here then. It's all forgotten.'

Emma looked relieved. 'Thanks.' She closed the door hurriedly as a voice came from inside, 'Emma, who are you talking to? Who's at the door?'

Christina walked away from the house as quickly as she had arrived. There was clearly a lot going on in that house that Christina knew nothing about.

And frankly, she didn't want to.

28

Ben

Now

Lisa wasn't coping. He wasn't surprised, though. He had known her since she was twenty-one and she had never handled stressful situations well in his opinion. She was prone to lashing out, usually verbally, at anyone around her and wanted to blame someone, anyone. Except herself.

She had never understood that sometimes things just happen, that there are things that are out of our control and cannot be planned for, expected, foreseen. And that sometimes, we all make mistakes.

Of course, spontaneity had never been her thing. It made her anxious when she hadn't had time to plan every minute. Holidays had to come with an itinerary; events needed to be timetabled. She was a creature of habit and routine, of extreme control.

So this, with all of its uncertainty, was a nightmare for all sorts of reasons other than the obvious.

He was trying to stay calm for both of them, but his own levels of panic were at an all-time high and he wanted to scream at her to pull herself together, to stop looking for someone to blame. That could come later when they knew what was happening with Emma. But right now, they needed to focus on her and not on anything else.

Lisa had watched Christina clutching onto Sophia and he could see it tearing strips off her, peeling away her composure, leaving her raw and exposed. She had crumbled as she watched them walk away, Sophia cradling her broken wrist and Christina cradling her broken daughter.

Now he was holding Lisa up, her legs apparently not working anymore, and she was a dead weight in his arms. He felt like he had a nest of wasps in his head, the buzzing noise deafening, the stings coming thick and fast. What he really wanted to do was run away, just for a few minutes, maybe just to sit in the car again. Could he get away with telling her that he needed to check on the parking ticket?

No, he couldn't leave her, not when she was in this state. And he also knew that if he left now, he probably wouldn't come back.

He lowered her into the tall-backed, easy to clean, but ultimately stiff and uncomfortable NHS-issue chair and wondered how many other parents had sat in this very chair, waiting to hear news on their child. If furniture could talk, then the furniture in an NHS A&E would have far too many tragedies to share.

The urge to run was building. He stayed standing, swayed from one foot to the other. He looked down the corridor and saw Christina emerge from the bathroom. Out of all of them, she was the calmest. Then he looked at Lisa, pale face, lips sucked in, red eyes.

This was why he hadn't told her what was going on with

him. He knew she had all sorts of suspicions, was jumping to conclusions, but he didn't think she could handle the truth for what it was. Especially now. And there was always someone to blame.

Christina looked up and made eye contact with him before walking away.

29

Emma

Two Weeks Ago

Emma paced across her bedroom floor, trampling everything in her path. The skin around her nails was bloody and sore. She picked at her thumb as she stared at her phone, willing it to ring. She checked the ringer was on and that she hadn't missed the call.

Should she call her? No, best to wait. She threw the phone down on her unmade bed, paced some more.

She heard a familiar creak outside her room – the fifth stair from the top. Probably her mother coming to check on her, make sure she was revising. She had ramped up the surveillance in the last few days, peppering her with questions about what she was reading, what she studying. It was tedious, especially since exams started in two days, but Emma couldn't concentrate on anything. Every time she sat down at her desk, her mind started hurtling towards a different kind of test result, what it meant, where she went from here. She had taken another three tests, all with the same outcome. There was no denying it.

So she had hatched a plan with Sophia. She knew what she had to do. Revising would have to wait until it was done. Everyone told her she was smart. She would have to count on that.

She flung herself onto her bed and pulled her books towards her, opened her notebook and picked up her pen. She held the pose for a minute, then another. When her bedroom door didn't open, she dropped the pen.

She listened hard, could hear her mother's voice. Pushing everything aside, she got up and walked over to the door, pressed her ear against it and listened. Lucy and her mother talking – or rather her mother talking at Lucy. She opened the door a crack and peered out. Her mother was standing in the doorway to Lucy's room.

'It won't do to sit in bed all day with your head in a sci-fi novel, Lucy. I'm worried. If you don't get into the habit of revising every day now, then you will struggle when it comes to your GCSEs. I know it feels like they are a long way away, but they aren't. Look at how dedicated your sister has always been – and look how well she did in her GCSEs. Take a leaf out of her book. Don't waste your life,' her mother said. She could imagine Lucy rolling her eyes at her, turning away, burying herself back in the story she was reading.

That's what Lucy did when the noise got too loud. She read a book, immersing herself in another world, another time. Piles of books were stacked on the floor beside her bed and on her bedside table, an unstable tower that Emma sometimes worried would fall on Lucy and crush her in the night like a tiny bug. That wouldn't happen, of course, but sometimes random thoughts like that would keep Emma awake and she would sneak into Lucy's room and check on her. She was always asleep, lying on her front with her head twisted at an unnatural angle, one foot poking out, her face relaxed. She slept like someone unbothered by pressure and expectation. But these weren't the books her mother wanted her to read. Lisa wanted her to be consuming the facts that were forced down their throats at school, while Lucy preferred make-believe and escapism.

Emma understood Lucy's need to drown in books because she did the same with her drawings. That was why she had so many notebooks in her drawer. There had been a cacophony of noise lately, so she had flung herself into telling her truth through her images, seeing the characters fight against all odds across the page. Sophia had seemed really taken by what she had seen, which had made Emma start to think about maybe doing something with the notebooks.

Her mother was still lecturing Lucy. Something about the amount of time Lucy spent in her room on her own, with the curtains closed and the room darkened. Emma wanted to tell her to shut up, to leave Lucy alone, but knew she wouldn't. She loved her sister, but they weren't close, not now anyway. She would never tell Lucy that she loved her, of course, but she kept an eye on her from a distance. Lucy had friends, genuine friends, from what Emma could see, so she was already miles ahead of Emma in her opinion. Still, things could change in an instant and before you knew it, you were alone and the laughing stock of the school.

The argument was still playing out in front of her, her mother pushing while Lucy retreated, until her mother finally sighed in frustration and turned away. Lucy took the opportunity to close the bedroom door in her face. Lisa stood for a moment, then walked back down the hallway. Only then did Emma notice Lisa was holding a plate with a sandwich on it. The plate hung limply in her hand, the sandwich on it looking like it would slide to the floor.

Emma ducked back into her room and got back into position.

Her mum came into her room without knocking. 'Ems, are you hungry? I made this for you. It's important you eat properly when you're revising so that you can maintain focus.'

Emma was about to say no, but the look on her mother's face burned into her. She looked like a woman desperately trying to make a difference, so Emma said, 'Yeah, great, thank you,' with a false smile and reached out to take the plate. Her mother balanced the plate on Emma's bedside table. Emma noticed the tightness of her lips when she then took a look around the room.

Emma could feel her phone vibrating from where she had tossed it on the bed. She needed her mother to leave so that she could answer it. She looked down at her books again, hoping her mother would take the hint.

Instead, Lisa hovered, still surveying the mess, and said, 'How's your revision going?'

'Ok, still lots to do, though.'

'I don't know how you concentrate in all this mess.'

Emma just shrugged. The phone stopped vibrating, then started up again almost immediately.

Just go already.

'Can I tidy up for you? Just a little bit? Straighten a few things up – it will help to organise your mind, help you to feel calmer.'

'No, Mum, it's fine as it is. I don't need tidiness and order to help me concentrate. I just need quiet and my own space.'

'Yes, but you know how important these exams are, so if a tidy room will help, then I think I should. Oxford is quite a feat, you know, so you will need every weapon in your arsenal.' She was throwing all the clichés out today.

She moved around the room, folding clothes and putting them in a neat pile on the chair, gathering up books and notepaper.

'Mum, please, I know where everything is. If you start moving stuff around, I won't be able to find my notes and flashcards.'

'Darling, trust me, this will help. It used to help me when I was writing exams. Your Uncle Robbie always had a messy room and look how he turned out – or didn't, as the case may be.'

'That's because he has a tendency for gambling, Mum, not because he had a messy bedroom as a child.'

'Still, if it worked for me, then it will work for you.' She worked her way over to Emma's desk. Emma felt her heart rate increase. Sitting on top of the wastepaper bin under her desk was the most recent pregnancy test. She had intended to empty the bin herself later. Her eyes zoned in on it, already imagining how things would implode if it was spotted.

'Mum, really, please leave it. Enough already.' Her voice was sharp, the words pointy, but her mother ignored her, started shuffling papers together from the desk and picking up used tissues. If Emma was lucky, she would just toss the tissues on top of the bin and not look any further, wouldn't notice it. She grabbed the used tissues with a tutting sound and tossed them into the bin.

Emma exhaled, then watched in slow motion, the air around her soupy and thick, as her mother picked up the bin and tilted it to push the tissues further down. The white plastic wand with the blue handle slid out and clattered onto the desk.

The room swayed.

'What's—' Lisa picked up the stick and turned to look at Emma, confusion wrinkling her forehead. 'What's this, Emma?'

Emma thought about denying everything, but there was no way of plausibly getting out of this since her mother was physically holding the evidence in her hand. Instead, she said, 'It's... nothing.' Inside her head, she berated herself. Was that the best she could've come up with? Really?

Circles of heat rushed into her mother's cheeks. 'Of course it's not *nothing*. Whose is it?'

Her mouth seemed to take over where her brain had let her down seconds before. 'Well, you can hardly think it's mine! I can't believe you would think that of me! You have so little faith in me that it's offensive.' The words were delivered with very convincing outrage.

Emma held her breath, then saw a flicker of doubt in Lisa's eyes.

'So whose is it?'

'It's Sophia's.'

Her mother audibly exhaled. 'I knew that girl would amount to nothing! It's all Christina's fault, you know. Like mother, like daughter. She takes absolutely no interest in that girl. Well, she's ruined her life now.'

The phone started to vibrate again. 'That's a bit harsh, Mum. It's not exactly something she asked for. It happens sometimes. She's really upset – and you can't say anything to Christina.'

'Christina doesn't know?'

'No, she doesn't know.' Emma looked down at the phone again.

'Is that her? Why is she calling you? Why is the test even here?'

'Because she had no one else to talk to. I've been helping her as a friend because she needed one.'

'Don't let her drama affect what you are trying to do, Ems. These exams are so important. You don't need anything to distract you. You don't have time for this.'

'I wasn't about to turn my back on her. She needed my help. I would hope you would do the same if someone you knew was in trouble.'

'That's Christina's job, not yours. This is a lot to heap on top of you, especially now. I can't believe she hasn't told her mother. Just shows you, doesn't it? This is why I am so grateful for the honest and open relationship we have. You would've told me straight away.'

Emma said nothing. The phone stopped buzzing.

They both stared at it as it lay still.

Lisa threw the stick in the wastepaper basket and carried it to the door.

'Please, Mum, promise me you won't tell anyone about

this. She needs time to get her head around it and to decide what she is going to do.'

Lisa paused, then said, 'Fine, I won't say anything, but I don't want you hanging out with her anymore.'

Emma nodded weakly.

Lisa looked like she had more to say, but instead nodded back and took the wastepaper basket out of the room.

Emma took some shallow breaths, trying to quell the nausea that clawed up her throat. She couldn't rush to the bathroom to throw up now, not until her mother had gone back downstairs, not until she had heard the tell-tale creak of the fifth stair.

Sweat broke out on her upper lip and she tried to breathe through the bilious wave.

As soon as she heard the stair creak, she rushed from her room, locked the bathroom door behind her, turned on the tap as full as it would go and threw up the very little that was in her stomach. She lay on the cold tile floor and began to cry silently. Despair gripped her by the shoulders.

Then she remembered the phone calls, remembered that someone wanted to help her. She staggered back to her room, her throat raw, and closed the door behind her. Sophia had called one more time since she had rushed to the bathroom. Emma pressed the call button.

'Emma! Why aren't you answering?'

'Sorry.' She was still crying, couldn't seem to stop.

'Oh my God, what's happened? Oh no, have you... lost it?'

'What? No, I wish. It's my mother. She found the test.'

'Fuck. What did she say? What did *you* say?'

'I told her it was yours.' The line was silent for so long

that Emma said, 'Soph?' to check she was still there. 'Soph, I'm sorry. I panicked. I didn't know what else to say.'

'Well, she probably wasn't surprised,' Sophia said eventually. 'It's fine. Let's just stick to the plan and it will all be over soon. If that's still what you want?'

'Yes, definitely.'

'I've made the assessment appointment for next Monday morning. Tell your mother you have an early exam, then come here, you can do it here and be back in school for the afternoon exam with time to spare. The pills will arrive through the post in an unmarked box a day or so later. You'll need money though – it's not cheap.'

'I have money. I've been saving up – for a car or something – but I can use it for this.'

'Ok, then. That's sorted.'

For the first time in days, Emma felt a little calmer, coming from a mix of Sophia's surprising attention to detail and relief at thinking she had managed to put her mother off the scent long enough for it to be sorted before she ever discovered the truth. It was Sophia's idea that she make the booking and handle everything in case her mother looked at Emma's laptop history. Not that Emma thought she would, but lately, her mother was being so strict about her revision that the idea of her looking at her browser history to see if she was spending time doing something else wasn't that crazy an idea.

'Thank you, Sophia. I mean it. I don't think I would've coped with all of this without you.'

'That's what friends are for, right?'

'If that's the case, I need you to do something else for me.

Think of it as a way of making up for what you did, you know, the posts and stuff.'

Sophia flinched. 'Sure, anything. What is it?'

'I need you to spread the word that I was drunk and that I didn't consent to it.'

30

Lisa

Now

Lisa didn't understand why they wouldn't let her see Emma. Seeing Christina walk away with Sophia nearly finished her. How come she got to walk away from this with just a broken bone, but Emma, her perfect, well-behaved, conscientious Emma, may not make it through this at all?

It wasn't fair.

She felt like she was going mad. All those arguments in the last few weeks about revision and now she realised that none of it was important, not if Emma was hurt. Her last conversation with Emma had been another argument – and for what?

Oh God, was it that argument that had pushed Emma to do something stupid?

No, she was a smart girl, sensible. She was the one Lisa could rely on to do the right thing, work hard, plan for the future, not throw it all away on a good time and a boy.

Not like Sophia, for instance. Abortions and drinking and parties.

Ben was watching her closely, like he thought she was going to implode. He had put his arm around her shoulder as they sat in these ridiculous chairs built for much bigger people than them. The weight of it felt like it was crushing her and she was being squished into the seat, disappearing into the padded cushion.

When Christina emerged from the bathroom, their eyes had locked. Ben was carrying a wariness about him. The look of a man who wanted to be anywhere but here. Was that because Christina was here too? Did that make him nervous, both of them in the same confined space? Or was it because he had to step up for a change?

Well, guess what, Ben? This is what being the parent is. The worrying, the constant indecision, questioning whether you said the right thing, did the right thing. She could feel anger building when she thought about how all he had to do was go to work every day, focus on himself, then come home to a cooked dinner and some downtime in front of the television, while she agonised, analysed and supervised everything else. If he was questioning his choices, then she was pleased. She wasn't the only one who could make mistakes.

She suddenly wished Owen was here. He would say the right things, make her feel less alone.

As if she'd conjured him from thin air, she looked past Ben to see Owen walking towards her, his face a picture of concern and anguish, his eyes glued to her, seeing only her.

Ben must've noticed the look of relief on her face because he looked over his shoulder and launched to his feet, saying, 'What the fuck does he want now?'

31

Lisa

Two Weeks Ago

'I need to see you.'

'Sure, when?'

'This afternoon if you can?'

'I can be over there in half an hour.'

Lisa hung up the phone and sat for a moment, enjoying the quiet, as she thought about everything that had happened in the last few days. She needed someone to talk to, to help her process it, but she also recognised the bottom of her stomach flipping like a pancake when she thought about Owen being here with her in an empty house in the middle of the afternoon.

Is this what Ben felt when he met whoever he was spending time with? The nervous energy? The fidgeting anticipation? The sense that it was wrong, but the thrill of doing it anyway?

Perfectly on time, there was a gentle knock on the front door. She shot to her feet and rushed to answer it, pausing briefly in front of the mirror in the hallway to smooth down her hair and exhale.

Owen was dressed casually in a T-shirt and loose-fitting jeans, with a smile on his face and a bakery box in his hand.

'Hey,' he said, handing her the box. 'For you – for our… coffee and catch-up.'

He somehow managed to load a heap full of innuendo into those simple words and she giggled.

Inexplicably, she looked up and down the street. Surely it was perfectly normal for two friends to get together for a coffee in the afternoon while their kids were at school? Wasn't it? If they were both women, it would be normal, so why should it matter that he was a man? Why did she feel so clandestine about it?

'Come in,' she said and led the way to the kitchen. She had opened the French doors to let in the weak sunlight that had finally graced them with its presence after a number of days of drizzly rain and the breeze was pleasantly cool and fresh. Lisa hoped it would take some of the heat out of her cheeks.

'Coffee?' she said. 'Or tea – whatever you prefer.' Why was she so nervous? He was here as someone she could talk to. A friend. Nothing else.

Who are you trying to convince, Lisa? You've matched your knickers to your bra today.

'A green tea, if that's ok?'

She turned on the kettle and peeked inside the bakery box. 'Oh, yummy, thank you.'

He shrugged. 'I was passing.' She knew he wasn't. There was no bakery between his house and hers. He would've had to have gone out of his way to get them, but that made her feel warm in her toes rather than awkward at knowing he had brought her an unsolicited gift.

'Are they custard doughnuts? My favourite!'

'Oh, no, that one's mine,' he said flatly.

'Oh, right.'

'Only kidding – they are both custard as it's my favourite too.' He grinned. She blushed. God, she was acting like a teenager.

'So what's the drama? You sounded like you needed a good chat earlier.'

'Oh, everything and nothing, I suppose. Ben and I had a huge fight the other day about Lucy and Emma. He thinks I'm not handling the teenager stuff properly, says I'm not keeping a close enough eye on them, questioning what I'm making them for dinner – too carb-heavy, apparently – but it's easy for him to criticise when he's not even here. He doesn't have to manage it in person day after day.'

The anger that had bubbled away like a geyser in the pit of her stomach began to spit and gurgle inside her. The words were rushed, like she was trying to expel them from her before they took root in her stomach. If they were out there, then maybe it wouldn't all be her responsibility anymore. But then the control would be lost and she didn't like that idea at all.

'That's frustrating. I'm sure you're doing a brilliant job. Have you found out where's he going yet, what he's been doing?' Owen asked, his face a perfect mask of concern and interest.

'No. I've checked his pockets, his bank account, his emails. There's nothing apart from a few transactions at Boots that

I haven't made – so he's either incredibly careful and set up duplicates or there's nothing to find. But something is definitely going on. He is so distant, so disengaged with all of us, and I can't get through to him. It's like he's a ghost. So I end up getting angry and defensive, which sets him off even more.'

'Oh, Lisa, that is so hard on you.' He stood up and came to stand behind her as she squeezed out the teabag in his mug. She felt his hands rest on her shoulders, kneading them like she was bread dough. It felt weird, intimate, awkward. She was afraid to turn around, felt trapped in the corner by the knowledge that how she reacted now would determine where they went from here. She poured milk into her cup with a quivering hand, stirred the tea, ignored the pressure on her shoulders. He stopped then and stepped back. She turned towards him, putting the mugs between them.

'Here you go,' she said without looking directly at him.

'Can I get more water than that please?'

'Oh, sorry, I just made it strong the way Ben likes it.'

'He drinks green tea?'

'Only lately. He's trying to cut back on caffeine.'

'Interesting.'

'Is it?'

'Well, just that it sounds like he's really taking care of himself lately, that's all.' He shrugged, smiled, took the tea from her and sat down, spreading his legs wide. Lisa took some plates from the cupboard and came to sit one chair away from him, putting a suitable buffer in the way.

'You're very patient with Ben, but at some point, you have to tackle this head-on,' Owen continued. 'I have to say it doesn't sound good from where I'm standing.'

'What do you mean? Why?'

'Well, it's classic mid-life male clichés, isn't it? Going to the gym, withdrawing from the family, working late. Soon he'll be going on shopping trips for trendy clothes and taking business trips over the weekends.'

'Do I have to tackle it, though? I could just ignore it?'

'Well, he's not making you very happy, is he? You're miserable. It's like the light has gone from your beautiful eyes. Is that really how you want to live?'

He was staring into her eyes earnestly as he spoke. She looked away, flushed, awkward. Had he always talked to her this way? Or was it just today when they were here alone?

'Yes, but with everything going on with Emma and her exams, I don't want anything to destabilise her.'

'Have you thought that maybe the girls already know? I find kids are very intuitive to their surroundings.'

The world stopped for a second then, the weighty revelation landing heavily on Lisa. She hadn't thought about what they were seeing, picking up on and talking about together.

'No, I don't think they've noticed.'

He shrugged. 'Ok, but if you and him are arguing a lot or he's absent, then they will pick up that something is going on between you. Then they'll start acting out of character, find something they can control rather than this that they can't. I'm no psychologist, but it makes sense to me. Has their behaviour changed at all? And if it has, is it better to stay together unhappily or is it time to admit defeat and move on so that everyone can be happier?'

Lisa thought about Lucy, closed in her room all day and

defiantly refusing to open a school book, and Emma, who barely said two words anymore.

Then she felt annoyed. How dare he come into her house and psychoanalyse her family? He didn't know them, was making sweeping assumptions about her and Ben, their relationship. Owen was the last person she would expect to make her feel judged, unworthy, below par as a parent, but he was making her and Ben sound incredibly selfish when the truth was the girls were always front and centre for them.

And let's not forget that Owen was sitting here in her kitchen while his beautiful wife was at work. A bit hypocritical. Quick on the heels of the heat of annoyance came a cold, white shame that she hadn't seen the issues herself, that it needed an outsider to point out what was playing out in her own house. And then the heat again. This was Ben's fault. No one else. He was the selfish one. He had done this.

Lisa played with her mug, turning it around in her hands as she turned the thoughts around in her head, feeling the anger bubble and recede, to be replaced by guilt. 'One of them would've said something to me. I have a good relationship with both of my girls.' Her voice was thin.

'Would they, though? We all have this firm belief that we know our children so well, that they would talk to us about anything, but in reality, they are now individuals who are starting to realise that their parents have been winging it all this time and actually don't know what they're doing. I would like to think Kai would talk to me about anything, but the truth is, I don't really know what he is thinking anymore. All I can hope is that some of what I have told him over the years has been heard and that he will make the right choice when it comes down to it – and be there to support him if he doesn't, I suppose.'

She was thoughtful for a moment, the realisation sitting uncomfortably. 'True. Do we know them as well as we think? I told my own mother practically nothing about what I was actually thinking or feeling when I was a teenager. I'd like to think I have a better relationship with my own children, but do I really? I mean, I found something out from Emma yesterday about... someone else... a friend of hers... and the girl has confided in Emma but not her own mother, even though I'm sure her mother also thinks she knows her daughter inside and out.'

'Found what out?' He leaned forward. She wasn't used to a man taking this much interest in what she was saying. Ben looked through her, but Owen looked *at* her. He was hanging on her every word. She felt like she could tell him anything and he would make it make sense, make *her* see sense, even if she didn't want to hear the truth.

His fingers were millimetres from hers on the table. It was distracting.

Lisa wanted to tell him about Sophia's pregnancy test, if not just to distract herself from the need to reach out and touch his hand. She wanted advice too. The knowledge was sitting heavily on her, like she had a bomb that she could detonate at any moment. He would know whether it was now her responsibility to tell Christina. But she had promised Emma she would keep it to herself. If Emma found out she had betrayed that trust, she wouldn't tell her anything ever again. Teenagers were that black and white about everything that Emma wouldn't understand. Just like

Emma's generation had this insatiable need to share every moment of their lives with hundreds of random connections on social media, so Lisa sometimes needed to vent, process, discuss in order to understand.

Part of her also needed Owen to be her conscience. She needed him to tell her that smugly letting Christina know that she had been right all along about Christina's relaxed approach to parenting was not in Sophia's best interests. It was taking every ounce of self-control that Lisa had not to have already knocked on Christina's door with the news, gloating, saying *I told you so.*

'Ok, I'll tell you, but you can't say anything to anyone. It stays between us, ok?' She felt and sounded like a rumour-spreading teenager herself, and wondered for a split second if she was about to make a mistake. But only for a second before the delicious need to gossip, especially about Christina, overtook everything else.

'Sure,' he said, helping himself to a doughnut. He took a large bite and came away with sugar on his nose. Without thinking, she reached over and dusted the sugar from his nose with the lightest of touch, then caught herself, her hand hovering awkwardly, millimetres from his face. Instead of the discomfort she expected to see in reaction, he laughed a deep, throaty sound of sheer pleasure. She dropped her hand. 'Sorry, instinct from years of wiping sugar from children's noses.'

'You can wipe the sugar from my nose anytime,' he said in a low voice and she clenched her teeth against a cringe.

More to divert from the awkward cheesiness of the moment than anything else, she carried on. 'So anyway, yesterday I went into Emma's room. She was revising, as she always is. She's so good and I'm just relieved I don't have to worry about her. Anyway, I was tidying up in her room a bit – you know, tidy room, tidy mind and all that – and I found a pregnancy test. It was positive.'

Owen gasped. 'I was not expecting that! How far gone is she? And more importantly, how are you?' He reached out and placed a slightly sugary hand over hers.

'It's not Emma's!' She sounded indignant at the suggestion, despite that having been her own first response too. She tried not to focus too much on the weight of his hand on hers.

'No, of course.'

'She's covering for someone, helping her, someone we know well.' She paused dramatically. 'Sophia.'

'Sophia Valdecchi? Oh, wow.'

'But according to Emma, she hasn't told Christina yet. I think it must be early days and she's still processing it, but now I sit with the responsibility of knowing. What do I do with that?'

'Hmmm.' He lifted his hand away from where it had rested to pick up his tea and she immediately felt its absence. He sipped thoughtfully, dusted more sugar from his chin and the countertop. 'I guess if it was my daughter, I would want you to tell me so that I could help her through it, you know? She shouldn't have to go through that alone. The same if it was Kai's problem. I'd want to talk to him, discuss his options, let him know he was supported. But good on Emma to try and help her.'

'I know, but I promised Emma I wouldn't say anything. If I do, then Emma may not trust me with anything else. You know how reactive teenagers can be.'

'Maybe you need to make Emma see that telling Christina is the best thing for Sophia from a safeguarding point of view. Bring her around to your point of view. Christina should know. Not a conversation I would relish having with any parent, though. Do you know who the father is?'

'Emma didn't say anything about that, but I know some of the things Sophia gets up to, so I'd be surprised if there weren't a few names in the running, if you know what I mean. You know, after everything that happened between us, I'd quite like to be the one to tell Christina. Does that make me a bitch? She spent years spreading those rumours about me, saying that I was a bad parent, had a violent temper. Now who's the bad parent between the two of us?'

A flicker of distaste crossed Owen's face. 'Women love to tear each other down, don't they?'

'Sorry, you're right. That was bitchy of me. I shouldn't even be considering rubbing her nose in this. It's just I think I'm still raw from when she started that hate campaign against me. I'm not thinking straight and I'm all over the place. Stress, you know.'

'No, it's understandable that you have conflicting emotions about this one. I mean, I wouldn't call it a *hate campaign* as such, but she has been awful to you over the years and this is a chance at retribution for you, I guess,' he said, but he wasn't looking at her now. He was staring into his mug.

She felt a blip of panic that she had upset him in her bluntness. They sat for a moment in silence as she searched for what to say next. Owen petted Jester distractedly under the table where he had rested his head on Owen's leg, hoping for sugar crystals to fall his way.

'You have to feel sorry for Sophia, though,' Owen said eventually. 'It's a lot for a girl her age.'

'Yes, it is. She used to be such a lovely little thing.'

'So, what are you going to do?'

'I don't know. I'm torn between wanting what's best for Sophia, not wanting to betray Emma and this awful feeling of self-righteousness, I guess, that her parenting model of letting them have independence to make mistakes isn't the right approach after all.'

'It's called *schadenfreude*.'

'What is?' she said, feeling like the conversation had spiralled out of her control. She reached for a doughnut, despite not wanting to eat in front of him in case he found it unattractive. Was anyone ever alluring when eating a fat doughnut?

'That feeling you have – the pleasure you feel from Christina's ultimate misfortune. It's a German word and a common response. An understandable reaction if you think about what she put you through.'

'Oh, right. I've never heard of it.' She chewed slowly, the doughnut cloying.

'But there's a difference between thinking about these things and acting on them. I think what's important is how you handle this. She deserves to know, but ultimately you should bring Emma around to the idea that you are telling Christina, so that you don't betray her in the process because if she thinks you have gone behind her back, it could ruin the trust between you, especially if you two have such a close bond as you say.'

'Yes, that is exactly my dilemma. You understand me so well, Owen.'

He reached out and put his hand over hers again. She felt his fingers begin to stroke her skin. She tried to remember if she had used hand cream after she had last washed her hands. Were they soft and smooth or like wrinkled crêpe paper? She struggled to swallow the last bite of the doughnut. It was as though her throat had closed up.

She removed her hand from under his in order to dust off the sugar that was sticking to her chin. 'Um, thank you for that, it was delicious.'

His voice was little above a whisper as he said, 'You have... er...' He brushed her cheek very gently with his fingertips. 'Sugar.'

She reached out and placed her hand next to his on the table, quietly giving him permission to hold it again. She felt like she had forgotten how to breathe.

Two sharp chords sounded, cutting into the moment. For a second, she was disoriented, then she realised what they were. The video doorbell. Someone was on their front step.

She glanced at the alert on her phone and saw a familiar figure rummaging in his bag for his keys.

'Shit, Ben is home!' She yanked her hand back.

'What?' Owen said in confusion.

'He's at the front door. The doorbell camera! He's looking for his keys. Quick, go out the back.'

'But we're just having coffee, nothing else.'

'I just don't want to have to explain. Please, Owen – go out the back.'

'He can see me arriving on the camera himself if he checks.'

'He never checks. He can't remember the log-in. Please,

Owen, I don't want to have another argument with him tonight.'

'Ok, fine.'

Lisa grabbed his arm and pulled him through the French doors into the garden and on towards the back gate. Jester started to bound after them, then turned sharply and ran back into the house as he heard the front door open.

Lisa opened the gate and shoved Owen through, then followed him out into the alleyway along the side of the house.

'I'm sorry, I just...'

'Hey, no need to explain. I prefer our friendship like this anyway, like a secret only you and I know. It's exciting. You are very compelling, you know.'

Lisa was panting a little as she led him towards the mouth of the alleyway into the street. She stopped and turned back to him. 'Thank you – for today.'

'Anytime,' he said.

Then he grabbed her by the tops of her arms and pushed her against the wall of her house. She gasped in surprise. He leaned in slowly, his face magnifying. She was weirdly aware of the fact that Ben would be on the other side of that very wall, saying hello to his dog, perhaps calling out her name in greeting. And here she was, a few bricks away from him, about to kiss another man.

She didn't notice the figure across the street who watched them, feeling like her heart had cracked open ever so slightly as her mother clawed at the shirt of the man who was not her father, as she pulled him into a kiss that seemed to begin tentatively but then gathered pace. She didn't know that the heat of it reached right across the street to the other side, where she had stopped to tie her lace after dropping her bag to the floor and crouching down by the tree. If she had been just a few minutes later, she wouldn't have seen them. Then it wouldn't feel like everything had changed instantly, like a fault line had appeared, a crack down the middle.

Lisa and Owen were still clenched into each other, no air between them. A car raced past and they pulled away at the noise. The figure moved behind a tree as Lisa looked around nervously.

'I need to go,' she said to Owen, but the smile told him she didn't want to. He smiled back, stroked her face gently.

'This was unexpected, but to be continued,' he said.

Lisa watched him as he walked away up the street in the direction of his own house. She looked over at Ben's car in the driveway, then turned and hurried back along the alleyway.

Emma stood up slowly from her crouched position and crossed the road to her front door, each step heavy, like she was walking through mud.

32

Ben

Now

Owen's face was tight like the skin of a drum. Crying out to be punched, in Ben's opinion. He stalked into the room and straight over to Lisa. Ben had been held back from punching him before, but this time he didn't think even The Rock himself would be able to stop him as Owen held out his arms and Ben watched Lisa fold into them with an affection that looked far more natural than any emotion she had been showing towards him for quite some time.

'I swear to God, Owen...' he growled.

Owen pulled away from Lisa. 'Ben, I just came to check on Lisa, to make sure she is ok and to see how the girls are.'

'Is Kai ok?' Lisa said, ignoring Ben completely.

'Yes, he's ok. Shook up a bit, naturally, but ok. He's with Christina and Sophia. They are in the waiting area down the corridor. They want to stay in case there's more news about Emma.'

'Right, you've checked on her. Now you can go,' Ben said.

Owen's voice was firm. 'I will go when I am sure Lisa is ok.'

'She's fine. She has me.'

'Does she?'

Ben could hear himself breathing, shallow, through his mouth, making his lips dry. He swallowed painfully and looked from Owen to Lisa and back again. Everything about them suggested a familiarity that he hadn't noticed before – the way she was pointing her shoulders towards Owen instead of him, her head tilted ever so slightly towards him too, like he was a point on her compass.

He tried to level his voice. 'Listen, *mate*.' He took a step towards Owen. 'I don't know what's been going on between you and *my wife*, but you can jog on now.'

'If you paid her more attention, then she wouldn't need to look elsewhere.'

They were now nose to nose, then Ben grabbed at Owen's shirt and pushed him back against the wall. 'What do you mean, *look elsewhere*? What the f—'

'Ben! Ben, not here!'

The two men glowered at each other. Bizarrely Ben noticed how neat Owen's eyebrows were, like they were drawn on in pencil. Why had he never noticed that before? It crossed his mind that Owen probably looked after himself, watched what he ate, went to CrossFit, moisturised daily. He was hit with a wave of self-pity, self-shame. Of course Owen was better for Lisa than Ben. It was plainly obvious.

Ben felt his spine concertina in defeat and he released Owen's shirt. Returning to his chair, he put his face in his hands. His shoulders began to shake. He couldn't seem to stop them. He hadn't even noticed the tears. He felt Lisa sit down next to him and he folded himself into her, like she was a cloak he needed to wear, as he cried silently.

A look of distaste passed over Owen's face. He turned to walk away, then paused, turned back. 'Look, I just want to say that I hope Emma is ok. We all do. With everything that has happened, I just think it's important that you know we are all thinking of you. Kai in particular. He's really worried. I told him and Sophia that they can stay until we hear more about Emma. I thought you would be ok with that. Anyway, despite everything, he's really worried about her.'

Ben looked up, got to his feet. He took a step towards Owen, his face calm now but his cheeks still wet.

He pulled his arm back and punched Owen in the face.

33

Sophia

Two Weeks Ago

'Mum, I need to talk to you.'

Christina and Colin were getting into the hot tub. Christina was wearing a bikini that would look more suitable in the Bahamas than suburban Teddington and Sophia was alarmed to see Colin was wearing a tiny pair of Speedos that were barely visible below his protruding stomach. He had his leg cocked over the rim of the tub and a bottle of prosecco in his hand.

'Right now, baby? We're just relaxing, enjoying the sunshine.'

'There is no sunshine. And this is important.'

Colin sighed loudly. 'Give your mother a break. She's having some me time.'

Sophia looked at Colin with such disdain that he recoiled.

She turned and walked back into the house. Emma's request rebounded around her head like a pinball. She didn't even mind that Sophia had lied to Lisa about whose test it was. She was a little worried about what Lisa would do with that information, though. It was no secret how much she hated Christina. Sophia had a horrible feeling that by this time tomorrow, she was going to be the talk of the school for all the wrong reasons – and none of it would be true.

Oh, the irony.

Karma is a bitch.

However, if she did what Emma asked her to do, it wouldn't be Sophia everyone was talking about.

It would be Kai.

Sophia figured she could take it – the whispering, the shoves, the notes in her locker and kicks in the canteen queue. She liked to think she was tougher than Emma and wouldn't necessarily find herself standing on the edge of a flat roof with a bottle of vodka in her hand. She would sit back and take it, nod and wave as adults told her how they expected nothing less from her, how no one was surprised at how she could blow up her life, just when she had a chance to get something right for a change.

But Kai was different. He was gentle and quiet. They'd eat him alive.

But maybe she didn't know him as well as she thought. If what Emma was saying was true, then he deserved everything he got. In fact, he was probably getting off lightly with a little bit of bullying when Emma should really be talking to the police.

And yet something had felt off when Emma had told her. There was a note to her voice that almost sounded like she was *excited*.

Sophia slammed her bedroom door and felt a little better

for about a second – until her brain set off again, chasing itself around and getting nowhere.

She flung herself on her bed and wrapped her arms around her old teddy, who was still a faithful companion after sixteen years, the one she cuddled into when her mother assumed she was on her phone but she was actually studying late into the night. The teddy her dad had given her just before he left when she was one – after her mother had driven him away, thinking it was better that it was just the two of them than if they were to keep him in their family unit. Her mother hated that bear, kept trying to sneak it into the charity donation bags. Sophia loved it. It was the only thing she had from him now, apart from her brown eyes and the weird slope of her nose.

Christina claimed her father was a waste of space, but had never elaborated, choosing instead to not talk about him at all or to change the subject. From Sophia's point of view, she had experienced first-hand how fickle Christina could be when it came to men. There had been more than a few trampling through the house over the years, all starting hot and feverish, then fizzling out into ambivalence and eventually being unceremoniously expelled, only for a new one to take their place soon after. Christina was fiercely independent, overly opinionated and stubborn in protecting her personal space. However, she also seemed averse to spending any length of time on her own. Sophia's father never stood a chance, really.

Not that he had fought to stay with Sophia or to get in touch since.

Given the first opportunity, he had left and didn't look

back. Still, sometimes it crossed her mind that perhaps Christina had orchestrated it that way.

Sophia had watched the other boyfriends come and go, had learned not to get too attached. Thankfully, they had all treated her with kindness, but she kept a distance between them so that she couldn't get hurt when they inevitably walked away without a backwards glance.

Colin's days were numbered. Sophia had noticed how Christina was looking at him with a tell-tale mix of mild revulsion and tight-lipped impatience.

There was a knock on her bedroom door and Christina walked in, a red, satin robe now knotted over the garish bikini.

'Baby? You ok?'

'Aren't you too busy to talk to me? Don't want to intrude on your me time,' she said petulantly, hating the way she sounded like a toddler. She clutched the teddy tighter.

Christina shrugged. She pulled the bottle of prosecco and two glasses from behind her back. 'That wasn't me time. It was Colin time – and I think I'd rather share this with you than him.'

Sophia sighed. 'Mum, I have revision to do later. I can't drink now.'

'Oh, shush. Have a drink with your mother and talk to me. No sulking. And put that stupid teddy down. How old are you?'

'What about Colin? Left him in the hot tub in his budgie smugglers all on his own? He'll get all wrinkly.'

Christina laughed. 'No, I told him to get dressed and go home. He was getting on my nerves anyway.'

'If he's been drinking, he can't drive home.'

'Oh, you are so responsible sometimes. He can catch the bus or get an Uber. He'll figure it out.' She flopped down on the bed, the gown temporarily flapping open, and lay back against the pillows, her head next to Sophia's and her dark, curly hair fanning out around her head. 'It must be bad if you're cuddling that disgusting thing. Is it boy trouble?'

'No.'

She sat up and poured two glasses to the brim, then handed one to Sophia.

Sophia paused, looked at her with as much annoyance as she could muster, then sat up and accepted the glass. She held onto the teddy stubbornly, though.

They readjusted themselves so that they were sitting shoulder to shoulder. Christina put her arm around her daughter. Sophia used to love moments like this. There had been many nights in between boyfriends when the two of them would sit just like this in Christina's bed and watch a film together, laughing at a comedy or crying into each other's shoulder at a rom com. It had been a while since they had done it though and Sophia felt all traces of annoyance dissolve away as she sipped on the prosecco and felt herself relax a little for the first time since she had bought the pregnancy tests. Next year when she was away at university, it would be these moments she would miss.

'If I tell you this, you have to promise not to freak out or anything, ok?' she said.

'Ok, I promise.'

'Just hear me out and don't say anything until I'm done.'

'Oh God, you're not pregnant, are you?'

'Not me, no.'

Christina looked at her closely then. 'Ok. So who then? Daisy? Electra?'

'Emma.'

'Emma who?'

'Emma Marco.'

Christina said nothing. The silence stretched out between them. Then Christina laughed. 'You are joking, right?'

Sophia shook her head. 'She found out a few days ago and I've helped her to get an appointment for the medical abortion pills. It's what she wants. She's properly freaked out and hasn't told Lisa or Ben, so you can't say anything to them. It was a huge shock, as you can imagine, and, well… let's just say she doesn't even remember the *deed*.'

Christina remained silent.

'Say something,' Sophia said.

Christina took a deep breath. 'Oh my God, so many questions! Who? When? How did you know how to book an appointment? How are you able to it without an adult?' The words rushed out of her on the exhale, like the bubbles in the prosecco that Sophia really didn't want any longer.

She set the glass aside. 'Well, I won't tell you who the father is because that is her copyright. She is only a few weeks gone and Electra kept me completely up to date when she had a medical abortion earlier in the year, so I already knew where to go to arrange it. There's this place in Twickenham and it's really easy – a video consultation, then they send you the pills by post. No adult necessary if you're over 16, as long as you can pay.'

'Right.' Christina looked almost impressed as she processed all of this new information. 'Ok, so let me get this straight. Emma has a boyfriend, got herself pregnant, but doesn't know how, and asked you to help her.'

'She doesn't have a boyfriend. She got a bit drunk when she was here the other week – you know, the night of the quiz?'

'She was here? I swear Lisa said she was at home.'

'They didn't know she was here. There's a lot they don't know about Emma.'

'Oh God, it happened here? If Lisa ever finds that out... Hmmm, ok. Wait, back up. Are you saying that she can't remember sleeping with him?'

'Yes.'

'That means it wasn't consensual.'

'Well, I... I don't know. She's not really saying anything about it, so I haven't pushed her on it.'

'Do you know who it was?'

'Yes.'

They sat in silence. Sophia reached for her glass and drank, then felt grotesque at discussing something as serious as this while drinking fizz. She put it down again. 'Mum, you can't say anything. She is really freaking out and wants it done and dusted before we do our exams.'

'Ok, but I really think there should be an adult involved here. I mean, what if something goes wrong? That is a lot for you to have to deal with, baby girl.'

'It'll be fine. It was dead straightforward for Electra. She took one pill, took another a day later, there was some cramping like she had a heavy period and it was done.'

'Wow, as simple as that, huh?' Christina chewed on her lip. 'I think you'll find that emotionally, there is a lot more to deal with than simply swallowing a pill like you have a headache. She will need a lot of support to get over this – and to make sure it is what she wants in the first place, despite what she's saying.'

'She has me.'

Christina looked at her carefully. 'Why you?'

Sophia's face tightened. 'What do you mean? Do you not think I am capable or something?'

'Oh, I know you are capable, but it's not like you two are good friends. Not anymore. So why you? Why has she come to you?'

Sophia paused, thought about it for a second and then said, almost ashamedly, 'Because she has no other friends.' Sophia picked up the glass and gulped at it, then carried on. 'She's been getting a lot of abuse at school – there's been rumours, people picking on her, sending her rude messages on Snapchat, photos, that kind of thing. It's been going on for quite a while, started before that night, but then it kind of got pretty dark pretty quickly afterwards. Someone filmed her drunk, going upstairs with him, and they started calling her names and stuff. She doesn't make it easy for herself, but it went too far. I guess I'm the only one that has the time of day for her.'

She felt ashamed that she couldn't quite bring herself to admit to her mother that she had started it, that she was helping because it was her problem to fix.

Eventually, Sophia said, 'What are you thinking?'

'I'm thinking about the little girl that used to play in the garden with you, how she had a very serious side and rarely laughed, but when she did, it sounded as though it came right from the pit of her belly and it would make her ponytail bounce.' Christina smiled at the memory. 'It was usually you who made her laugh like that. And then there was that whole thing with Lisa. Maybe if I hadn't kept you two apart, if I'd found a way to move past it, then you would still be close now and she may well have been a different kid.'

'I guess, but she doesn't do herself any favours, Mum. She can be really mean to people too. She sometimes gives as good as she gets. She is so patronising sometimes, you know?'

'Just like her mother. Well, I'm proud of you for helping her, but... Lisa does need to know.'

'Are you saying that just because you want to have something over her? Rub it in?'

'Wow, Soph, no.' Her mother looked hurt. 'If it was my daughter, I would want to know so that I could help and look after her. I assume, much as I hate the woman, that she would want to do the same – and would do the same for me if the tables were turned.'

'Ok, sorry,' Sophia mumbled. 'It doesn't matter, though. You can't tell her. I promised.'

'Ok, but if you won't let me tell Lisa, at least let me talk to Emma, let her know she is not alone. And I can be here for the assessment, just in case it is too much for you to handle. Would that be ok?'

Sophia thought deeply, absently chewing on her fingernail, a habit that had persisted since she was little. Eventually, she said, 'Ok, I'll ask her to come over tomorrow after school and you can talk to her. But no pressure – it has to be her decision.'

'Her body, her choice.'

34

Lisa

Now

Lisa felt like she was going insane. In the time that they had been sitting in this room waiting for news, she had lurched from shock, despair and anger, all the way through the spectrum to joy at seeing Ben shove Owen up against a wall in a jealous rage.

He did care after all. Who knew? Certainly not her, anyway. She figured his general disinterest was a sign of an affair or having fallen out of love with her, but his reaction had been anything but that. Or was she mistaking jealousy for male pride?

Owen's head had rocketed back and his nose splattered. It was one punch, but it was timed to perfection. Owen hit the floor and cupped his bleeding nose in his hand while Ben loomed over him, telling him to get up if he wanted another one.

A nurse had rushed in with a security guard and Owen was shuffled away to be attended to while Ben made good with the security guard. She could hear him saying he was under a lot of pressure and Owen had been goading him.

Lisa watched it all with a weird sense of pride that Ben had shown such passion. She walked over to where he was still talking to the security guard and said, 'Excuse me, but my husband is under a lot of strain. We both are as we wait for details about our daughter, who has just been in an awful accident. Tempers are frayed and I will keep the two men apart from now on. You have my word.' She gave him her best, most innocently pitiful smile.

The guard looked unconvinced until she heard a voice behind her. 'I can confirm that the other man was goading him, if that helps.' It was Christina. Lisa felt cold.

She didn't need or want her help.

The guard looked from one to the other, decided he didn't want the aggro today and said that he would talk to the victim. If he wasn't pressing charges, then it would all be forgotten. He walked away in the shoes of a tired man who didn't want to be working the night shift, who wanted to go home and put his slippers on instead.

Ben looked at Christina. 'Thank you, Chris.'

She shrugged. 'We've all wanted to punch him at some point. You ok? I can talk to Owen, make sure he doesn't take it further.'

'Thank you, Christina, but I can take it from here,' Lisa said coldly.

'Well, I suppose he would listen to you more than me, wouldn't he?' Christina retorted. She turned to Ben then and said, 'Have you heard anything more about Emma? Sophia asked me to come and find out.'

'No, nothing. She was having some sort of scans done. She… er… hasn't woken up yet.'

'Ok, well, Soph wants to stay for a bit, so we'll be round the corner in the waiting area if you need anything.'

'Thanks Chris, I appreciate it.'

She reached out and put her hand on his arm for a second, then walked away. Lisa watched her, feeling much the same anger that Ben had just demonstrated.

'What was that about?' Lisa hissed at him.

'He pisses me off. And I should be asking you that anyway. You two looked very friendly,' he sneered.

'Says you! What about you and her? And for your information, he's actually been paying attention to me in the last few weeks, unlike you.'

'I've had a lot on my mind, Lisa.'

'Oh really? Like what? Or should I say who?' She was aware her voice was rising, the frustration and anger that had built up over the last few weeks now bubbling over and turning her into a hideous, spitting snake.

When had they turned into the kind of couple that argued and threw punches in public?

'What are you on about, Lisa?' He looked weary suddenly.

'You! With your healthy eating and going to the gym, working late all the time and rubbing up to Christina.'

'Now is not the time for this.'

'You know she's the one that gave them the drugs, don't you?'

'Oh, come on! She wouldn't do that.'

'Really? You know how relaxed she can be, the cool mum, the one who gives them free rein in her house to do God knows what. I saw her! I saw her give something to Emma the other day and from where I was standing, it looked suspicious.' Lisa was spitting the words. 'You know Sophia was pregnant, right? Had to have an abortion recently. Now, are you really telling me that you don't think she could be responsible for all of this? How naïve are you, Ben?'

35

Emma

Two Weeks Ago

Emma watched as the yolk of the poached egg ran, glutinous and thick, onto the plate. She gagged and lurched from her seat into the downstairs toilet, where she vomited up nothing but milky tea that hadn't been sitting right in her stomach anyway.

She rinsed her mouth with water straight from the tap and returned to the table, just as her mother came back into the kitchen after shouting at Lucy to come down and eat her breakfast.

Lisa stopped in the doorway, looked from Emma's plate to her face, and said, 'You need to eat.'

Emma snapped, 'I'm not hungry.'

'If that's because you are worrying about Sophia or she kept you up all night talking, then I will be annoyed. This pregnancy is her problem, not yours. She got herself into trouble and it is not your job to get her out of it, no matter how admirable your intentions.'

Her mother's lack of sympathy was startling, but Emma

bit back what she really wanted to say. About how you couldn't trust anyone these days, even your own mother.

'No, it's nothing like that. Spent too long revising last night, that's all,' she said instead. She obediently cut off a corner of toast that wasn't touching the egg yolk and chewed mechanically.

Her mother looked relieved. 'Good. The hard work will pay off,' she said and turned to unload the dishwasher.

Emma took deep breaths and tried to eat around the egg, but the smell was hard to ignore.

Lucy came up behind her with a face like thunder. She plopped down heavily in her chair and scowled at the plate in front of her. Emma tried to catch her eye, but Lucy merely stared at the eggs like they were deadly poison.

'Oh stop scowling, Lucy. If you had prepared better for today's test, then you wouldn't be having apparent tummy aches and wanting to bunk out of school. You're going and that's final. Maybe you can learn to prepare properly for a test one of these days. Take a leaf out of your sister's book. Fail to prepare and you prepare to fail,' Lisa said over her shoulder without turning around.

Lucy flipped her middle finger at her back.

Emma smiled despite her nausea. She played with the toast some more, got another strong whiff of egg and pushed her plate away before she began to retch again. 'Oh no! Is that the time? I have to go. I said I would meet Sophia before school and go over some revision notes with her – since she hasn't had much time to revise lately,' Emma said loudly.

Lisa turned, about to say something, but Emma subtly shook her head and nodded at Lucy, hoping Lisa would realise what she was hinting at. Lisa flicked her eyes at Lucy and closed her mouth again.

Emma grabbed her bag. 'Bye, Luce. Have a good day, yeah? Good luck for your test.' She turned to go, then on a whim turned back to her sister and gave her a hug. Lucy looked momentarily stunned. It had been ages since there had been any affectionate physical contact between the two of them. Lucy hugged her back stiffly, picked up her knife and fork, and started to eat.

As soon as she was outside the front door, Emma felt lighter. She couldn't even look at her mother at the moment, but also didn't have the energy to waste on even trying to comprehend what was going on between her and Owen. She had a packet of ginger nut biscuits tucked into her backpack and she grabbed one to nibble on as she made her way to school. It was still early, so there were very few people she had to avoid. She moved quickly as she entered the school grounds and made her way up onto the roof where she was meeting Sophia.

She sat on the edge and dangled her white Nikes over the side. Resting her hands on the roof, she leaned over a little and looked down at the ground below, at the weeds growing between the paving slabs and the litter blowing in the wind. The sky was grey above her, the cement was grey below her and her mood was grey in between. A crisp packet had caught on a tree branch, and it writhed and twisted to try and get free. She could sympathise.

Her mother's reaction to all of this had actually surprised Emma. She had hoped for some signs of understanding or empathy, concern maybe, but there had been merely smug satisfaction. Lisa had been their babysitter for about six months during their first year at school when Christina was working full time. From what she had been told, instead of sending them both to an after-school club, Lisa had offered to look after them since she wasn't working anyway. It was a win-win for everyone. Christina got cheaper childcare and could keep doing her job, Lisa earned extra money and could be there for her daughter, and the girls were able to hang out as best friends.

Emma remembered those days in patches, like Polaroid photographs. The little plays that Lisa had directed them in after rummaging in the fancy dress box; making Mother's Day cards and Christmas advent calendars covered in glitter and glue; healthy fruit and vegetable platters for snack time as they giggled on a blanket in the garden. It had all been so simple then and she remembered it through a haze of innocence. And then something happened one afternoon and Lisa and Christina hardly spoke again. Emma couldn't remember what exactly, but it was bad enough that Christina had made sure Lisa was nowhere near Sophia after that.

Emma had never asked Lisa about what happened as it hadn't seemed important, but now that Sophia and her were finding their way back to each other, it suddenly bothered Emma why Lisa was being so unkind about the idea of the pregnancy. What had happened that had been so awful that it had torn two friends apart?

Would Lisa act the same way if she knew it was Emma who was pregnant? Would she be so judgemental? Emma didn't want to think about that because deep down, she didn't want to know the answer. Lisa had always pushed her hard, particularly academically. Nothing short of 100 per cent was ever good enough. If she lost marks in a test, Lisa wanted to know why, what could she have done better, how could she improve. She couldn't remember a time when Lisa had just said *well done*.

And this? This would kill her. The ultimate disappointment.

She felt more than heard Sophia behind her, but kept staring at the ground, her weight forward, her fingers clutching the edge, as Sophia sat down beside her.

'Can we move back a bit? I don't like being this close to the edge,' Sophia said.

Emma looked at her. 'God, you are such a baby.' She paled, then said, 'Excuse the pun – ha!' The laugh was brittle. She shuffled her bum back from the edge and crossed her ankles over each other.

'How are you feeling?' Sophia asked.

'I nearly threw up on my poached eggs this morning.'

'I don't blame you – I can't eat eggs first thing either.'

'Did you do it? Did you start telling people – about Kai, I mean?'

Sophia looked out over the school below her, spread out like a playroom map. It looked so unremarkable and yet could be the most toxic place on earth.

'Not yet. I've been trying to sort out the... you know.'

'Abortion. You can say the word, you know.' Emma paused. 'I'm sorry, by the way.'

'For what?'

'Telling my mother that it's you. I'm all over the place and I should've thrown the test away in the bin outside.'

'Hey, it's fine. I don't care what your mother thinks of me, actually. And that's what friends are for.'

Emma smiled. 'She says she won't tell anyone.'

'Do you believe her?'

'Yes. I think if I've asked her to keep it to herself, she will.'

Sophia picked at a weed growing through the roof felt. 'So, on that note...'

The panic swept over Emma as quickly as the nausea had earlier. 'Who have you told?'

'No one! Well, except my mother.'

Emma jumped onto her knees, felt tiny pricks of pain as gravel stabbed at her skin through her jeans. 'Fuck.'

'No, listen to me, please—'

'I thought I could trust you. You said you wanted to help.' She could feel tears building, the flood she had worked so hard to hold back threatening to burst through.

'Ems, listen. I was worried about the... you know... next week. What if something goes wrong? What if you're in pain or something? She won't tell anyone, ok? She's promised.'

'Are you sure about that? What if she wants to get back at my mother?'

'What?'

'They hate each other, Soph! I don't even know what happened, but your mother hates mine for whatever she did. What's to say she won't tell her just to get back at her?'

'If you knew my mother, you would know she is not like that. And the same could be said for your mother too.'

They glared at each other, Emma still perched on her knees, Sophia with indignant warmth in her cheeks.

'I just need to know I'm helping you in the right way, that's all. You kind of dumped a hand grenade in my lap the other day and walked away. I'm just making sure it doesn't go off. You know what I mean?'

Emma sunk back onto her bum and brushed the stones

from her knees. 'I guess,' she said in a tiny voice. 'So what did she say?'

'My mum? She's worried about you. She wants you to come to the house and talk to her.'

'I'm not changing my mind.'

'Not for that. She says it's your body, your choice. She's worried about *you* – you know, your head, how you're coping, how you'll cope afterwards.'

'Oh.'

'She wants to be there next week for the assessment and stuff. Just in case something goes wrong or… I don't know, you have a mental breakdown or something.'

'You'll still be there, though?' Emma said quickly and grabbed Sophia's hand.

'Yes, I'll still be there, but it makes sense. You can do it on our laptop – no chance of your mother overhearing anything – and then she will get us to school in time for the afternoon exam. Just talk to her. Please. Come over during lunch today and hear her out. She won't try to change your mind, I promise.'

Emma chewed on her lip, thought about it, thought about Christina and how larger than life she always seemed, so in control and sure of herself. 'Ok, I'll come.'

Sophia leaned over and pulled her into a hug. Emma resisted initially, still unnerved by such strong physical contact, then melted into it. The sob that had been choking her as they talked now escaped into Sophia's shoulder. They sat that way until they heard the first bell below and saw the frantic scurrying of legs, heard the crescendo of voices and knew they had to go.

'Meet me at the gate at lunch,' Sophia said as they parted. 'It will all be ok.'

Emma shuffled from foot to foot, feeling like she was presenting herself in front of the headmaster. Sophia used her key and called out a greeting when they stepped into the house.

Christina emerged from the kitchen, wiping her hands on a tea towel. Emma was suddenly embarrassed to see her. How could she have let this happen? Christina must think she was such a loser.

But Christina said nothing, just walked straight up to her and folded her into a huge embrace. They stood like that for a moment, then Christina released her and said, 'Come through to the kitchen. I've made you both lunch.'

'You have?' Sophia said, surprised.

'Yes, toasted sandwiches – with added tortilla chips for crunch.'

'Thanks, Ms Valdecchi, but I haven't really had much of an appetite. I've been feeling quite sick.'

'Ah, yes, I was awful with Sophia, but these toasted sandwiches were the only things I could keep down. You'll see. And since when have I been Ms Valdecchi to you?' She put her arm around Emma's shoulder and led her through to the table in the kitchen. A plate of sandwiches sat next to a big bowl of tortilla chips and glasses of orange juice. It smelled amazing. For the first time in ages, Emma's mouth began to water.

'Chicken, spinach, mozzarella and mayo tortilla crunch sandwiches,' Christina said proudly.

'You've never made these for me before,' Sophia said.

'You've never needed them. They're my rescue food and they make me smile.'

They sat around the table and the girls grabbed for the sandwiches. Christina sat back and watched eagerly.

'So?' she said eventually. 'What do you think?'

'They're delicious,' Emma said, reaching for another one.

'Thanks, Mum, perfect,' Sophia added.

'Excellent. Right, talk to me, Emma. Soph has told me some of it, but I want to hear it from you.'

'There's nothing to tell. I'm pregnant. I'm getting rid of it. End of,' Emma said briskly, setting down the rest of her sandwich and wiping her mouth.

'There's more to it than that, though. Soph says you were drunk.'

'I don't want to talk about that.'

'Ok. But know that what happened wasn't ok.'

'He was drunk too.'

'That's no defence.'

'And he's not on trial.'

'Should he be?'

Emma went to stand up, but Christina reached out and put her hand on Emma's. 'Ok. Ok. One thing at a time. We can tackle that another day. You aren't going to like this either, but are you sure you don't want to tell your mother? She would want to know. She would want to help.'

'No, definitely not. She's got all this stuff going on and it would just freak her out. She must never find out. You should've heard her when she thought it was Soph who was pregnant. It would be even worse if she knew it was me.'

'Wait, what?'

'Oh, yeah, I didn't tell you that bit,' Sophia said. 'Lisa found one of the tests and Ems panicked, said it was mine. So Lisa actually thinks I'm pregnant.'

Christina's lips tightened so much that they disappeared into a thin line. 'So you're telling me that she thinks *my daughter* is pregnant, and yet she hasn't come to tell me herself?'

'Yeah, but Mum, that's because Emma made her promise, just like I made you. So I don't think you can read anything into it.'

'Trust me, with our history, she will be loving this.'

Sophia could see the shutters starting to come down on Emma's eyes.

'Mum, please. This isn't about you and Lisa. It's about Emma,' she pleaded.

Christina looked down at her bare feet, the toenails painted a bright turquoise. When she had inhaled and exhaled again, she said, 'Ok, so perhaps she may surprise all of us and keep it to herself. Now for this appointment of yours, I think I should be there in case there's a problem or there's something you need, support afterwards or more toasted sandwiches. I respect your decision – it is your body after all – but you are young and may need more emotional support than you think.'

Emma sighed. She had thought a lot about it. She hadn't heard a word the teachers were saying, had spent the morning watching the grey sky through the window and thinking. Kai had tried to talk to her. She could hear him saying he had been texting her. She knew he had, but she wasn't reading any of it. She couldn't wait for Sophia to start spreading the word that she was the victim after all. They would all change their tune then. Things would get easier.

All of it would be easier once this was done.

But maybe Christina was right. Maybe this might be harder than she thought. She thought she would be relieved, but there was a voice in her head that recognised this was a *baby*. That she was a mother already. She felt her eyes filling up with the emotion she had been stubbornly holding at bay. 'Ok, you can be there. Thank you. But if you tell my mother, I'm gone. I have some money, I will disappear for good, sort it on my own.'

'You'd do that?' Sophia said, looking visibly upset at the idea.

'Yeah, I was thinking of doing that when I first found out, before I told you. Maybe just getting on a train and going somewhere, anywhere. Fuck exams, university, all of it. But now... I don't know. But if I'm pushed, then I'll leave. I don't think anyone would miss me anyway. My mother would be relieved to not have the stress anymore.'

'You know that's not true,' Christina said. 'She loves you so much.'

'She loves the idea of me going to Oxford more than me the person. She only wants me to go there because she didn't. Nothing I do is good enough. There's always room for improvement in her eyes.'

'Look, we mothers get it wrong sometimes, a lot of the time, actually. She loves you, I don't doubt that, and she wants the best for you. But if Oxford isn't what you want, you have to tell her. University isn't everything.'

'We have to go. Lunch is nearly over,' Sophia interrupted as she stood up with a loud scrape of the chair.

'Ok, so that's decided then. I'll see you next week, yes?'

'Yes – and thank you. For listening.'

'You know where I am if you need to talk.'

They walked to the front door. 'Ugh, I have such a headache,' Emma said.

'Wait, I'll get you some ibuprofen,' Christina said and returned to the kitchen.

Sophia opened the front door and walked out, her face pinched.

'You ok?' Emma said.

'Yes, it's just... just like your mum doesn't hear you about university, same with mine. She doesn't understand why I actually want to go.' Sophia sighed. 'I haven't even told her I'm applying.' She walked away then, back towards school. Emma watched her go to the end of the street and turn the corner, torn between running after her and not wanting to be rude to Christina.

Christina returned then with a little plastic zip-lock packet of pills and gave them to Emma. 'There's some extras in there in case you need more.'

'Thanks – for everything. I've got to catch Sophia up.' She paused and spontaneously reached up to give Christina a tight hug.

36

Christina

Now

'What the hell are you on about?'
Christina could hear the raised voices from along the corridor.

She was torn between going to see what was going on between Ben and Lisa, and staying well out of it. She knew her presence would not be appreciated, by Lisa at least.

She looked over at Sophia, who sat, motionless, in the hard chair, her free hand clutching onto her elbow through the sling, her face ghostly white.

She hadn't really said anything yet about what had happened and Christina didn't want to push her. She would have to tell the police sooner or later anyway. They couldn't leave the hospital until she had.

'Mum, is that Ben and Lisa arguing?' she said.

'Yes, I think so.' Christina shrugged, trying to sound nonchalant. 'They're under a lot of pressure.'

'I hear my name. They can't think this is my fault, can

they? Of course, they do. It was always going to be my fault,' she said, answering her own question.

'No, baby girl, I'm sure that's not it. They're under a lot of pressure and they're scared, ok?'

'Has she not woken up yet?'

'Not yet.' Christina reached out and stroked her daughter's beautiful mane of hair.

'What if she doesn't?' Sophia asked in a tiny voice.

'She will, baby girl. She will.'

Christina folded Sophia into her arms, like she would when she was a tiny girl, and hugged her close, feeling her own heart break for her.

'I saw you,' a voice spat at them over their heads.

Lisa appeared from around the corner, her face twisted in fury. She was pointing a trembling finger at Christina. 'Two weeks ago – *I saw you.*'

'You saw what, Lisa? I think you should take a breath and calm down.'

People were staring. Christina felt like a moth trapped in the glare of a lamp. Sophia had pulled away and shrunk into the corner.

'I was on my way to your house and I saw Emma on your front step. You gave her a bag of pills. You gave her the drugs! And now she's dying!'

'You have no idea what you are talking about.'

'Lisa? What's going on?' Ben came up behind her, looking from one to the other. 'What are you talking about?'

She turned to him, her eyes wide and manic, that one pointing finger still shaking. 'I saw her. She gave Emma a bag of pills two weeks ago. She's been waiting all this time to get back at me, to get revenge, and now this! This is what she's done!' She turned back to Christina. 'You wanted this to happen. I swear if Emma doesn't make it through this, I will come for you.'

Her voice dripped acid. Sprays of saliva hit Christina in the face and she swiped at her cheek with distaste. 'Oh, go and sit down, you stupid cow. You have no idea what you are saying.' She turned away, but Lisa grabbed her shoulder roughly.

'You're loving this, aren't you? Something went wrong, though, didn't it? What was it? Sophia wasn't supposed to be there? She wasn't supposed to get caught up in it? Or do you hate me that much that you would put your own daughter in danger too?'

Christina rose up out of her chair to her full height. 'Ben,' she said, her voice ice cold. 'I suggest you tell your wife to shut up and walk away before she says something she regrets.' Christina's fists clenched at her sides.

'Lisa, you're not making sense. Come on, you've had a shock and you need to just breathe.' Ben reached out for Lisa's shoulders, tried to turn her away from Christina, but Lisa pushed him off.

'You've waited years for this moment. They say revenge is a dish best served cold, but you are the expert.'

'And you are delusional if you think I care that much about a nobody like you.' Christina squared her shoulders, which gave her another inch in height so that she was well and truly looking down on Lisa. 'You act like you're all high and mighty, the best mother in the world, but let's be honest, you didn't know what you were doing when they were little and you don't know what you're doing now. You don't know your daughter at all.'

'Don't you dare! I have always done what I thought was best for all of the kids, including yours. Sophia was doing so much better when I was looking after her. She had structure and routine. Now she's drinking, getting herself pregnant, making a tart of herself. Like mother, like daughter.'

Christina laughed. 'Oh, you really don't get it, do you? It wasn't—' She stopped herself then, refusing to stoop to Lisa's level and betray Emma or Sophia, despite every fibre in her body wanting to shut this troll of a woman up.

Lisa wasn't hearing her anyway. 'I told you then that you were too relaxed with Sophia, too interested in being her friend rather than her mother. Now we are all in a hospital and there are drugs involved and my Emma's life is in danger – all because you would rather be a friend than a mother.'

'And you're the best example of a mother, are you? You hit Sophia! You hit my daughter! That is not doing what's best for her!' Christina spat back.

The silence that followed was broken by a subtle cough. A doctor stood behind Lisa. They all swung to face him.

'Mr and Mrs Marco. Would you come with me, please?'

37

Lisa

Two Weeks Ago

Lisa stood across the street and watched coldly as her daughter hugged her former friend with more emotion than she herself had felt from Emma in quite some time. The anger she felt was surprising in its ferocity. When last had Emma ever hugged Lisa with that much affection? It was like she was gripping onto her, drawing energy from her.

But that was Lisa's job as her mother. Not Christina, a woman who seemed to be the polar opposite of Lisa on every level.

Lisa had been thinking about Christina all morning. Should she confront her about Sophia? Worrying about her motivation for doing so. The thoughts swirled through her brain, to the point where the yoga session she was teaching at the community hall had descended into shambles as she forgot to complete the poses on the left side, then forgot to turn off the lights and play calming music when in savasana. One of the older ladies had complained at the end and she had to lie and say her phone had been acting up.

She had then received a text from Owen as she walked home, saying he couldn't see her today. She had been pushing for another 'coffee and chat', but he had been blowing hot and cold – all very interested in their late-night online chat sessions, going beyond flirtation to outright suggestion, but then running lukewarm on the idea of meeting up in person again. She was in knots about him, at once feeling ghastly for the incident in the alley, but also feeling the flip in her gut when she remembered what it had felt like.

It was made all the more confusing by Ben, who had been oblivious to her when he arrived home from work yesterday. He'd said he wasn't feeling well and had gone straight to bed at 7 p.m. without any dinner, where he had stayed until he got up for work that morning. The television had been playing to itself when she had gone up at 11 p.m., the curtains were still open and he hadn't stirred when she climbed into bed next to him. He had been snoring very quietly, curled into a foetal ball, and he had looked like the young student she had fallen in love with, the one who had his whole life planned out, who had love-bombed her in the early days of knowing her. He had once had dozens of red roses delivered to her tiny flat to disguise the awful smell when a mouse had fallen into the wall cavity and died. She had been his entire focus then, apart from his fledgling career.

Where had he gone? What had changed? Was it her?

It was probably her.

How had she turned into such a bitter person who didn't even like herself? It was no wonder she had no friends. Her tunnel vision with her children and the desperate need for them to succeed and to be protected at all costs had pushed everything and everyone else away.

Even Ben.

But Owen seemed to understand. They had a shared vision of who their children could be and what their role in getting them there entailed. He had given his career up to be a parent, which Lena didn't seem to be able to understand or forgive, but Lisa understood. Someone had to take the lead in parenting; someone had to make a sacrifice. They had to be single-minded. It was a scary world out there.

Ben's phone had been sitting on his bedside table and she was tempted to reach over and steal it to check his messages, but then she had reminded herself about some of the incriminating messages she had on her own phone right now and realised that she was no better than him when it came down to it.

She was a hypocrite.

When she woke up this morning, Ben had already left without a sound or a word. There was a cup of cold tea on her bedside table, the only sign he had been in the room at all, apart from his crumpled pillow. She had thrown the tea down the sink, watched it swirl its way down the drain like her marriage.

And that's when she decided that she would tell Christina about Sophia. Maybe it was the realisation that she was losing control of her own family or a weak attempt to give herself something else to think about, but she had an urge to do something, right a wrong perhaps, or throw a grenade into someone else's house.

Someone had to be the parent, right?

She would tell her without judgement, just one mother to another.

When her yoga class was over, she walked briskly over to Christina's house, not even bothering to change out of her billowing yoga pants and sports bra. She just threw on a sweatshirt and shoved her feet into her Birkenstocks. The street was quiet, leaves blowing around her feet as she mulled over what to say, how to begin, how to arrange her face so that she didn't look smug. However, as she rounded the corner and looked up before crossing the road, she stopped in her tracks.

Four houses down from where she was ready to step into the road, she saw Emma standing on Christina's front step. They were talking, smiling. Christina handed what looked like a little bag to Sophia. They had both then looked up the street in Lisa's direction, like they were checking for witnesses. Lisa had stepped back into the shadows.

Then Emma had pulled Christina into that hug.

That was what burned inside her gut the most. Emma had instigated it.

Lisa stepped further behind the tree providing her camouflage and watched as Emma ran down the opposite side of the street, right in front of her without seeing her, shoving the packet into her jacket pocket.

Lisa felt like the ground opening up beneath her.

Why was Emma here? And what had Christina given her? Had Emma told Christina herself, therefore beating Lisa to it? An unfathomable annoyance latched onto the thought and twisted it. Now she had nothing to dangle in Christina's face if Emma had pulled the pin on the grenade herself.

Yet Christina hadn't seemed upset or angry. She had looked calm, in control, which just proved how different their mindsets were when it came to their children. Christina had been smiling, like she was proud; perhaps the thought of being a grandmother in her late forties was not at all upsetting to her.

How could she be ok with it?

Lisa would be climbing the walls with fury, disappointment and fear if she was in a similar position.

The anger was now metastasizing with the realisation that Christina was handling it all too well and Lisa knew that if she crossed the street to confront Christina, it wouldn't end well. Her earlier veneer of decency had been stripped away to leave only outrage leaking out of her, raw and unfiltered.

She turned around and headed back home.

38

Ben

Now

'What the hell are you on about?' Ben said.

He had no clue what his wife was talking about anymore. She was spitting and snarling accusations at Christina, something about being a drug dealer, which anyone could see was preposterous.

He could understand her need to blame someone, to try and make sense of all of this. She had always been so black and white about everything. There was always someone at fault, no shades of ambiguity, no shared blame or responsibility.

She had wanted children so much when they got married and was determined to be the best mother she could be. When they were babies, he had tried to get involved, but everything had to be done her way because she knew best. So he had stopped trying and sat back instead. She liked to be in control, so he let her, but being in control of her children meant she had stepped out of every other aspect of her life, from friendships to a career to her marriage.

He had been thrilled when she made friends with Christina because for a while the old Lisa was back, full of laughter, letting her hair down, having a few drinks, letting the girls stay up late watching Disney films while she drank margueritas in the kitchen with Christina. He would come home from work, loosen his tie and crack open a beer, feeling the weight of the week falling away as he joined them.

But that day when he came home, Lisa had been quiet, saying that Christina had accused her of the unthinkable. He had tried to persuade her to talk to Christina when the dust had settled and the anger had cooled, but she had refused, said that Christina owed *her* an apology for overreacting.

Then the rumours had started. Lisa was the talk of the playground and Ben watched her fade into herself, not wanting to go out or socialise, the stigma of what she had done following her like a stench that couldn't be washed away.

Christina had taken it too far, but Lisa hadn't fought back and, although she had explained to him what had happened that day, he had often wondered if she had been completely honest with him. Surely someone with nothing to hide would have more outrage and fight in them?

Only Lisa and Christina knew what had really happened that day.

The whole incident had simmered down eventually and they slowly integrated themselves back into their social circle, but the damage had been done by then, friendships and reputations forever tarnished.

But as he looked at Lisa now, almost like he didn't recognise her, he realised that none of it had ever really gone away. It has been lurking beneath the surface all this time, just waiting for one fissure to appear before it erupted once more.

39

Emma

One Week Ago

The brown box sat on her desk, nondescript, inoffensive and yet so powerful. Emma picked up the box and sat on her bed with it in front of her on the duvet, the pink flowers obscene against the plain, brown cardboard.

Her breath was coming in fits and starts, gulping, then shallow, heart racing, hands shaking. For a second, just a second, she asked herself if this was really what she wanted to do. She opened the lid and looked at the packets of pills and medical leaflets packed neatly inside. After a moment, she closed the lid and shoved it to the bottom of her backpack.

She thought the hardest part would've been the assessment with the questions and probing to make sure she was doing the right thing and was in the right frame of mind to be making this decision. Every time she had faltered in her answers, had felt emotion trying to engulf her, she had looked over at Christina and Sophia, sitting just out of camera, and they had smiled at her with encouragement and support. They had scooped her up and looked after her, given her the strength to face it, and then followed it all with a cup of sweet tea and a chocolate digestive.

She exhaled, grabbed her backpack and headed downstairs.

Her mother sat in the kitchen, a mug of coffee untouched in front of her, her head in her hands. She jumped when Emma came into the room, her mind clearly elsewhere, and plastered a fake smile on her face.

'Hey, you ready for your exam? You feeling good?' she said.

Emma mirrored her with the same fake smile, but it came out like a sneer. 'Yes, all fine.'

'Good, good.' Her mother looked strained, the lines around her eyes deeper, her lips pulled tighter.

'Has Dad gone already?'

'Er, yes, he had an early meeting.'

'I didn't even see him last night.'

'He wasn't feeling well, so went to bed really early.'

Emma hadn't had a proper conversation with her father in weeks. He walked around the house like he didn't really belong. The truth was Emma and her dad hadn't been close for some time, not in the easy, fun, playful way that young children had with their fathers. She got the impression that teenage girls baffled him somehow, that he couldn't understand the emotion and drama that walked hand in hand with everything they did, that he had no time for it.

Yet one more reason why he couldn't ever find out about this. His disappointment would be worse than anything else. A large part of why she was going along with their plan for her future was to see them both heavy with pride rather than disappointment when she finally made it to Oxford. That might help to fix them. She felt her hand stray to her non-existent belly, something she had found herself doing lately, and shoved it into her jeans pocket instead.

'I better go. Don't want to be late,' she said.

'Do you want something to eat? Or a cup of tea before you go? And have you double-checked to make sure you have everything you need?' Lisa said, getting to her feet.

'I'll grab a banana, but I don't want to drink tea in case I need to pee in the exam or something. And yes, I've got everything.'

Lisa stood up and pulled her into a tight hug. Emma stiffened, wondered for a second if she knew something, if she suspected what Emma was about to do. The hug felt tight, loaded, almost desperate.

No, she couldn't know, not unless Christina or Sophia had told her and they wouldn't. It was these damn exams. It was her dream of Oxford and she couldn't seem to see anything past that.

'I'm so proud of you for doing this, working so hard at school. You know that if you are worried, you can talk to me. You know that, right?'

Emma pulled out of the embrace impatiently and said, 'Sure, Mum. I'll see you later.'

Lisa stepped back. 'Good luck, you'll be amazing. You always are.'

Emma rushed out of the room, a swell of unwelcome emotion creeping up on her. She couldn't cry. Not now. Because if she started, she didn't think she would stop. And then she'd end up telling her mother everything, which wouldn't do.

That wouldn't do at all.

*

She immediately felt more in control as soon as she closed the front door behind her. It was a lovely day. Warm spring sunshine, no hint of a breeze, the kind of morning that would make you smile if you took a moment to appreciate it. But Emma had a plan to execute. No time to smell the roses.

She secured both straps of her backpack over her shoulders, straightened her back and walked briskly, keeping her mind empty. Once at the corner of the street on which Sophia lived, she paused, looked around, took a deep breath and crossed the road, heading towards the door that was painted in a bright fuchsia pink.

You could tell Christina had lived alone for many years. Her house was an eclectic photograph of her own individual taste. There were no white walls, beige carpets or masculine accents here. It was all bright colours, interesting artwork and books on subjects that Christina found fascinating. Even the colour of the front door was vibrant.

In Emma's house, everything was beige, like her mother was afraid to stand out in case someone didn't like it. And her father hated colour, wanted everything neutral with no clutter or fuss.

Emma knocked and the door opened instantly. Sophia leaned out, grabbed her by the arm and pulled her inside.

'Did you bring it?' Sophia looked more nervous than Emma.

Christina emerged from the kitchen, carrying a tiny, doll-like cup of espresso. 'You're here.'

Emma smiled, but it felt insubstantial. She followed Christina into the kitchen and they all took a seat.

'Where's Colin?' Emma asked, expecting to hear his deep voice and not relishing having to explain why she was here.

'We're... on a break,' Christina said.

'Does he know that?' Emma felt a bubble of a giggle float into her mouth.

Christina frowned.

'Sorry, it's a *Friends* reference,' Emma mumbled. She reached into her backpack and placed the box on the table in the middle of them. They all stared at it.

'So...' Christina said. She looked at Emma intently. 'I'm going to ask you once more. Are you sure? If there is even a flicker of doubt in your mind, then let's talk some more.'

'I'm sure.' Emma sounded firm, decisive, in control – everything she was not feeling on the inside.

'Ok then.' Christina opened the lid, and took out the leaflets and the packets of pills. 'We know how this works – we heard the nurse, we watched the videos.' She took a moment to read the leaflet, then inspected the pill packets. Emma and Sophia watched her silently. Christina set the smaller packet to one side and put the larger one back in the box with the leaflet, closed the lid and passed it back to Emma. Emma reached out with a trembling claw of a hand and hid it away securely in her backpack once more.

'Soph, get her some water please.' Christina had the voice of a headmaster – calm, collected, in control. At least someone was in charge of what was going on.

Sophia got up at once, poured some water from the tap into a glass that was cloudy from the dishwasher and put it down in front of Emma. Some of the water slopped over the rim of the glass.

Emma gazed at the packet in her hand.

'You know how this works – we've gone through it a few times – but do you have any questions?' Christina said.

'No, I just want to get this over with and get on with my life.'

Emma took hold of the glass of water, tipped a pill into her other hand and swallowed it quickly.

They looked from one to the other, none of them sure what they were waiting for or expecting.

'Shall we go and revise at school maybe?' Sophia said eventually. 'Or do you want to stay here until the exam?'

'Can I stay here, please?' Emma looked from Sophia to Christina and back again. 'Just in case something happens.'

'Of course you can. I'm going into my studio to work, so you guys spread yourself out – or watch TV, anything. Come and knock when you're going, though – so I can say goodbye.'

The chair scraped loudly, jarring in the heavy atmosphere of the room.

'Thanks Christina – I couldn't have... well, just thanks,' Emma said with wide eyes.

'No problem, kiddo, no problem,' she replied with a supportive smile.

When they were alone, Sophia was unsure what to say. She broke the silence with, 'How are you feeling?'

'Fine. There won't be any real effects until I take the pills tomorrow anyway.'

'Yes, but... are you ok?'

'I'm relieved, I guess. Not looking forward to tomorrow. Didn't sleep at all last night, so tired.' Emma picked at the skin around her fingernail, pulled at it until it tore. A bead of blood formed. She picked some more, ignoring the sharp sting.

'Have you thought about… telling him?'

'Have you thought about doing what I asked you to do?' she snapped back.

'I've been kind of focused on this.'

They sat awkwardly, then Sophia said, 'I need to get some more revision done before this afternoon. We can go upstairs or we can work here at the table?'

'Can I just watch TV or something?'

'Sure, yeah. Can I get you anything? Cup of tea or something?'

'Nah, I'm good.'

Emma wandered into the lounge on heavy legs. She lay down on the slouchy couch, feeling herself sink into the cushions, as Sophia turned on the TV for her and then handed her the remote control.

'I'll just be in there if you need anything. We'll leave at about quarter to one, yeah?'

Emma didn't respond. Her mind was numb, her skin was cold to the touch, and she wanted to close her eyes and sleep for a thousand years. Then, at least when she woke up, it would all be over.

The desks were lined up in neat rows, one behind the other all the way across the hall. There was something so institutional about it, but Emma felt no real nerves as she filed in with everyone else. The others around her were chewing on their lips or staring wide-eyed and panicked, but Emma felt numb. She had almost forgotten to check her seat number on the board outside, but Sophia had come up behind her and said in a stage whisper, 'You're in row M, seat five. Good luck,' then had disappeared to the back of the hall where her seat was.

Emma sat down and placed her clear plastic pencil case on the desk in front of her, then tied her hair back in a loose ponytail. She suddenly couldn't remember what exam she was writing, but there was no sense of panic at this. More a sense of resignation. She looked at her fingers where they were stained with ink from drawing late into the night last night. She had fallen asleep eventually, bent over sideways with the pen still in her hand. There had been a blob of ink on the duvet cover this morning that her mother would go mad about when she saw it.

The adjudicator was talking, running through the do's and don'ts, and Emma suddenly had an overwhelming urge to get up and walk out, then just keep walking until she was as far away as possible. Her feet itched to move, but she crossed them under the hard, wooden chair and dropped her chin onto her chest.

She looked up again when a test paper arrived on the desk in front of her. She looked over at the teacher, who gave her an encouraging smile. Emma scowled back.

The timer began and there was the rustle of paper, the scratch of a pen, an occasional cough or sigh, some kid behind her groaned loudly as he read the first question, but otherwise blissful silence. Emma turned her paper over, but the words blurred. She could hear her pulse in her ears. She clicked and unclicked her pen repeatedly, causing the girl in the desk next to her to glare at her. Emma ignored her, but stopped clicking and started chewing on the end of the pen instead.

Her stomach grumbled and rolled over. She froze. Was this it? Was something happening?

Her stomach groaned again, the hollow sound of hunger, and settled. Emma attempted to answer the multiple choice questions fading in and out of focus in front of her, but her mind was blank, all facts and figures falling into a bottomless chasm, so she made a random pattern from the letters instead.

Her stomach rolled over again, this time more forcefully, and she stopped breathing, convinced this time something would happen. Again, it settled and she exhaled.

And this was how it went on for one hundred and twenty minutes – every twinge, every gurgle, every grumble of her stomach – until the adjudicator told them to put down their pens and started gathering the papers into a pile. Chairs scraped across the worn floor; a low-level chatter began almost immediately. Someone to her left was crying. Emma stayed in her seat, letting them all file past her, ignoring the curious glances thrown her way. She felt the pointed gaze of someone across the hall and turned to see Kai watching her, frowning. He smiled at her, gave her a thumbs up, but she looked away and got to her feet slowly.

Sophia trotted up to Emma when she finally made her way out of the hall and into corridor. 'How did that go for you?' Sophia looked elated, almost giddy.

'Not great.' Emma saw Sophia's face drop immediately.

'Oh, sorry.'

'Hey, not your fault. How was it for you? You look happy with how it went?'

'Yeah, it was the past paper I went over this morning as luck would have it, so I'm well chuffed. Might have done alright in the end.'

'That's great – and I'm sorry I've heaped all of this on you now. I know it's not fair, but I really am grateful.'

Sophia put a hand on Emma's arm. 'Hey, it's fine. Really. But call me if anything happens or you're struggling and you want me to come over.'

'Can you maybe come over tomorrow when I take the next one?' she said in little above a whisper.

Sophia faltered. 'I've got a morning exam tomorrow – but I can come afterwards?'

Kai sauntered up to them then. 'Hey, how was it for you guys?'

Emma turned and walked away without a word. She felt them watching her the whole way and thought she heard Sophia call after her, but she kept putting one foot in front of the other until she was at home.

40

Lisa

Now

The doctor was waiting for her to respond, to follow him. He was going to take her to see Emma, but she couldn't hear anything past the fury pulsing in her ears, all-consuming in its intensity. Ben was staring at her, frowning, like he didn't even recognise her.

But all she could see was Christina in front of her, standing there innocently. Why was no one taking her seriously? Why was no one listening to her when she was saying that Christina did this? Where were the police now?

And now Christina was turning the tables and trying to blame all of this on her when all Lisa had ever done was put her family first. She was a good mother, had always prided herself on that. She set boundaries, expected discipline, made sure they strived to be the best. The complete opposite to what Christina thought was important.

Lisa remembered that day all those years ago when her friendship with Christina came to a sudden and juddering stop. It was still so clear in her memory, like a photograph she could pull from an album.

It was a Friday close to the end of the summer term. That day had been sticky warm. The girls were niggling at each other unusually, a mix of being overtired and hot making them snippy and whiny as they walked home from school. Sophia in particular had been in a sulk when Lisa collected them because she hadn't had a turn watering the vegetables in the nursery garden.

They had come in from school and Lisa had handed out their swimming costumes so that they could sit in the paddling pool with ice lollies after they had had lunch. She remembered the effort she used to put into just serving up a lunch. Sandwiches cut into shapes – crowns, unicorns, butterflies – and carrot sticks and cucumber with homemade houmous to dip them into. None of that shop-bought stuff. Grapes were cut into manageable sizes after she'd read all those stories about choking and the flapjacks were freshly baked. That day, Sophia had eaten very little, saying she suddenly didn't like cheese sandwiches and asking for crisps instead.

Eventually, Lisa had compromised and provided a packet of Pom Bears for them to share, but Sophia's stubbornness had irked her. Sophia liked to be contrary when it came to food.

Emma and Sophia had sat in the garden at the little plastic kids' table, chatting like old women about everything and nothing, while Lisa had pottered about, filling the paddling pool, finding some plastic bowls, watering cans and cups for them to play with in the water.

When they had finished their food, they'd hopped in the paddling pool and Lisa had cleared away the plates, one eye on the pool to make sure everything was fine.

And they had been happy, splashing each other, making pretend drinks for their toys, eating ice lollies that dripped into the water. Even Sophia had lifted out of her earlier mood. Lisa had left them to it and sat in her garden chair to read a magazine in the warm sun.

It was a blissful afternoon – until it wasn't.

After an hour or so, Lisa told them she needed to put the paddling pool away. Christina would be over soon to collect Sophia and she needed to dry off and get back into her clothes. But the girls were having fun and didn't want to come out of the pool. Emma had argued with Lisa and threw a tantrum, forcing herself to cry in protestation, while Sophia sat quietly and watched.

Lisa could hear the telephone ringing in the house. She made one more attempt to reason with Emma, who was having none of it, so she agreed that they could stay in the pool until Lisa had finished with her phone call.

Then she went into the house.

It had been her mother on the phone, complaining about something or other – Lisa couldn't remember what now and it hadn't been important – but the call had gone on longer than expected.

When she finally managed to hang up fifteen minutes later, she came outside to see Sophia standing over Emma, who was face down in the paddling pool.

Sophia was laughing.

Cold washed over Lisa's body. She shrieked, ran to the pool and scooped Emma out of the water. Emma's eyes were closed initially, but as soon as Lisa lifted her up, she opened her eyes in fright as Lisa clutched at her and shook her hard, screaming her name in her face.

Emma started to sob. Lisa put her down, her heart still racing, then saw Sophia standing and watching them. Anger bubbled through Lisa, mixed with panic and fear, and she screamed at Sophia, 'What did you do? What did you do?'

Sophia stepped away from her and started to cry too.

'No, you don't get to cry. You nearly killed her!' Lisa screamed. Her hand shot out and slapped Sophia hard across the back of her bare legs, just as Christina let herself into the back gate.

Lisa remembered so clearly the panic and fear that had ripped through her, the pure and transparent relief when Emma opened her eyes, and the rigid fury upon seeing the shadow of a smile still on Sophia's face. To this day, Lisa was still convinced that in that moment it had looked like Sophia had been standing over Emma as though she had pushed her into the water on purpose.

She couldn't go so far as to say Sophia had wanted to hurt Emma, but it had niggled in the back of her head, churned up into a bigger notion by the guilt of knowing that she had been on the phone instead of watching them.

Lisa also remembered the look on Christina's face as she walked into the garden to see her friend hitting her daughter and her daughter crumbling in fear. Sophia had run to Christina and fixed herself to her leg, had refused to let go, while Christina has screamed at Lisa, demanding an explanation as to why Lisa had needed to resort to violence.

It was only later that night when Lisa was watching Emma play in the bath that Emma had leaned forward and dropped her face into the frothy water, then came back up seconds later, her face covered in bubbles, saying, 'Look, Mummy, I'm blowing bubbles. Like I showed Sophia today.'

That's when Lisa realised that perhaps she had made a mistake. Perhaps she had jumped to conclusions in her panic.

But by then, Christina had set off a rumour flare at the school that Lisa had hit Sophia for no reason, that she had lost her temper and lashed out at an innocent child. Women she had previously met up with for coffee no longer answered her calls. Her yoga classes started to thin out until she found herself sitting in an empty community hall with only seventy-six-year-old Brenda for company. Mums even stopped inviting Emma to their children's birthday parties. She became something of a pariah overnight and it was years before the collective memory faded and the invitations started up again.

But by then, Emma was used to being a loner, used to being left out and marginalised.

Lisa knew there were more important things to think about right now, but she found herself fixated, needing to hear Christina say this was her fault. She needed someone to blame – anyone – so that this was a little bit more bearable. She wasn't going to listen to that doctor until she knew where she could direct all of her outrage and fear and panic.

The doctor was still speaking. He was asking them to follow him, telling them they could see Emma now.

Ben was pulling on her arm. 'Lisa, we need to see Emma.'

His voice broke through and she stepped away from Christina, followed like a sheep, her feet moving on autopilot, but her brain still screaming, terror and fury rippling through her like cramps, sharp and brutal and debilitating.

You did this, Christina.

You wanted revenge and you got it.

I will kill you for this.

41

Christina

One Week Ago

Christina watched as Sophia shuffled around the kitchen, humming under her breath, her AirPods in her ears. She looked so at ease with herself. She was wearing an oversized sweatshirt that was far too thick and heavy for the welcome sunshine outside and a pair of loose-fitting jeans that were torn at the knee so that her pale skin showed through.

Christina was about to ask her how her exam had gone that morning when Sophia stopped abruptly, holding the jug of milk in her hand, and grabbed her phone from her back pocket. She looked at the screen, then put the milk down and answered the call.

'Ems, are you ok? Ok, slow down, it's to be expected. Yes... yes, that's what they said. Do you have any ibuprofen you can take?... Do you want me to come over? Please don't cry. I can come over – or I can ask my mum to come?... Ok, call me later. Ok. Bye.'

She hung up the call, pulled out her AirPods and tossed

everything onto the countertop with a clatter. She looked at Christina, her skin ashen.

'It's started. She says she's cramping really badly. She's taken some ibuprofen and told Lisa she thinks she ate something bad at school.'

Sophia started to cry. Christina pushed away from where she had been leaning against the counter and pulled her into a tight hug. 'Oh baby girl, it's ok. She'll be ok.'

When her crying had abated, Christina released her and said, 'You ok now?'

'Yes, it's just been a lot to deal with, you know? I want to be there for her, but it's hard when I'm the only one who knows anything – and I can't say anything to *him* either. And he's a friend too, says he doesn't know why she won't speak to him. I feel like I'm being pulled in two.'

'You can talk to me, let me know what actually happened that night – I won't say anything.' There was a burning curiosity in Christina, like a physical need, but she wasn't going to force Sophia into telling her anything she didn't want to. She would give her time and space, and she would tell her eventually. She usually did her tell her most things, although all of this with Emma had illustrated to Christina just how little teenagers chose to share with their parents as they got older.

She found herself wondering more about Sophia and what she was getting up to with the boys she dated, what she was doing at the parties she went to, what example Christina had set over the years with her boyfriends coming and going, her drinking and glamorising alcohol. Christina had always wanted to be a cool mum, someone her daughter wanted to spend time with, but what if that was wrong?

What if she should've been more like Lisa: strict, controlling, pushing her rather than letting her take the lead?

Christina trusted Sophia implicitly and was a firm believer in letting the kids make mistakes as the best way to learn and grow, but it was also hard to sit back now and watch without commenting, silently hoping Sophia had learnt the right lessons from her and not the wrong ones. There were so many layers to what had happened to Emma, so many mistakes that had been made, and Christina could see how keeping it all inside was affecting Sophia.

Sophia opened her mouth to speak, then shut it abruptly as Christina's phone began to ring. Christina glanced at the screen – Colin again. He had been phoning constantly since Christina had told him that she needed space. Apparently, space to Colin meant not physically being with her, but still pestering her constantly with calls, texts and memes that he thought she would find cute or funny. They weren't cute or funny – and neither was he.

'Sorry, it's Colin,' she said as she aired the call.

'Is it over for you two then?'

'I guess – he was a bit much, wasn't he?'

'Well, I wasn't going to say anything, but I'm pleased I don't have to see his budgie smugglers in the hot tub anymore,' Sophia said with a small laugh.

'You ok?'

'I'm fine – I made a promise to Emma and I'm not going to break it. In a week's time when all of this and the exams are over, we can get back to the way things were.' Sophia smiled weakly and grabbed her books from the kitchen table. 'I'm going upstairs to revise.'

Christina didn't want to say that it may take Emma more

than a week to get over this, because she knew Sophia didn't want to hear that right now. She needed to think that she could go back to her regular teenage life and not have to think about it again.

Christina went to make herself a coffee, suddenly needing a hit of strong caffeine, but her attention was diverted by a buzzing sound coming from somewhere. She followed the noise and noticed that Sophia's mobile phone was pushed behind the cushion on the chair. It must've fallen when she tossed it aside. Christina picked it up, saw a missed call from Emma and was about to call up to Sophia to tell her when she also noticed the number of social media notifications on the home screen that had come in while Sophia was listening to music.

She paused, not wanting to betray Sophia's trust, but still feeling that desperate curiosity creeping its fingers up the back of her neck. Her phone and Sophia's looked almost identical except for a different photo on the home screen, so she put her own phone face down on the table for when Sophia inevitably realised she was naked without it and came looking. Christina then pocketed Sophia's phone and called up to Sophia to tell her she was going out to her studio.

As soon as she was safe behind the closed door of her studio, she began the process of trying to guess her daughter's passcode. She was no James Bond and the usual birthday guesses were immediately wrong. She then tried all zeros, thinking that teenagers weren't that imaginative sometimes, and when that didn't work and with one attempt left, she tried the date of her anniversary to Sophia's father on a whim.

The phone unlocked. Curious.

She opened Snapchat and saw the number of messages stacking up one on top of the other. It looked like Sophia was airing quite a few of her friends. Christina pulled some of the message alerts to the side without fully opening them so that they wouldn't show as read, a trick Sophia had taught her when she was airing Colin recently.

There were plenty of messages from boys, many of which had been opened, read and in some cases saved, so she could open these fully. Christina was shocked at the number of unsolicited photos that seemed to have been shared with Sophia in just one day, but was proud to see the responses she sent back – laughing emojis and verbal put-downs that left the sender under no illusion what she thought of them.

But the messages that burned into her eyes were those from so-called friends, girls talking about girls, spreading vitriol and nastiness as they discussed Emma and the party – and Kai.

Then she found a video that Sophia had saved in her camera roll. Posted yesterday, it showed Emma talking directly into the camera, her hair pulled back in a tight ponytail, her eyes rimmed with red, her skin sallow. She talked about the party, how she knew what they all thought of her. Then she told them she had not consented to it, that she had been taken advantage of when she was drunk, that she was incapacitated by alcohol. She called on the girls that were listening to stand up to boys like that and she asked for the boys to call out their friends who were doing the same thing to girls. It was a call to arms for girls to support girls, not to tear them down, and for boys to have the balls to do the right thing.

It was strong and powerful, delivered in a voice that barely shook.

And through it all, one name was mentioned over and over again.

Kai.

Christina flicked through some of the comments under the video. There seemed to be a split between those supporting her in solidarity and those blaming her for being drunk and leading him on as her reputation persisted in colouring their opinion of her. Some comments were just mean: name-calling, exaggerated rumours, comments about Emma's looks and her body, praising him for doing her a favour, and generally laughing at her expense. But as the comments stacked up, the tide began to turn. Girls started labelling her a victim and discussing how they were always allowed to say no and that boys had to honour it. Anything else was not ok.

This was the judge and jury right here, in the palm of her hand.

There were also a number of messages to Sophia from Kai himself since the video had been posted. He seemed to be asking a lot of questions about Emma and now Christina was under no illusion that it was Kai that Emma had been with that night.

He was the father of her baby.

He was the one who Emma claimed had raped her.

From the messages, it was clear he didn't know Emma was pregnant, but he was concerned about her and about what she had told Sophia. A guilty conscience, perhaps?

Christina was shocked to her core. She had always liked Kai. He was quiet, came across as polite and respectful when he was at their house, greeting her warmly and spending time clearing up afterwards. Before this, she would've liked something to have happened between Sophia and him, but certainly not now.

Social media was a blessing and a curse for the younger generation. Thank God it wasn't around when she was younger. They had all debated the facts and convicted both Emma and Kai of various crimes – and they'd done it with spite and viciousness. If Christina knew those kind of things were being said about Sophia, she would step in, talk to the school, something.

The words were meant to wound.

Tramp.

Whore.

Paedo.

Ugly bitch.

Pervert.

She deserves everything she gets.

He deserves to have his dick cut off.

Someone should push her under a bus and put her out of her misery.

Someone stab him and save us all from this happening
to another girl.

I hope she dies.

He deserves to die.

The more she scrolled, the crueller and more shocking
it became, the words burning into Christina's eyes. Then
she realised that some had come from Sophia herself.
As she scrolled backwards and forwards, she started to
build a picture of the role Sophia had played, from initially
being firmly in the camp that were trolling Emma to shifting
towards urging people to stop listening to rumours and to
build their own opinions of people.

Christina was confused. That couldn't be right. Surely
Sophia had been on Emma's side all along? She had seen
how Sophia had been with Emma in the last few days.
Caring and considerate and kind. She wasn't malicious or
hateful. That was a side of her Christina had never seen
before. So where had her initial nastiness come from?

But the evidence was clear on the screen in front of her.
Nowhere near as bitter and acidic as some of the abuse, but
engaging in the conversation all the same, all from before
Emma publicly accused Kai.

There was nothing from Sophia after the video was
released, though. No support of Emma and calling out Kai.
Why was that?

Christina put the phone down, deep in thought, shock
leaving her with goosebumps on her arms and an emptiness
in her chest. Perhaps she didn't know Sophia at all.

And then there was Lisa. Christina couldn't help but think she would want to know that her daughter was being bullied at school, that her daughter may have been assaulted – and that it was Kai. But of course, she didn't even know her daughter was pregnant.

Christina caught sight of movement through the frosted glass door of the studio and quickly locked Sophia's phone and slid it into her back pocket, then grabbed a paint brush from the worktable.

The door opened. 'Mum, I think you picked up my phone by mistake,' Sophia said, holding out Christina's phone.

'Did I?' She feigned innocence as she pulled the phone from her pocket. 'Oh, sorry, you're right. We must get different cases or something. Here you go.'

She handed the phone to Sophia.

'What's for dinner tonight?'

'Ugh, I don't know. Shall we order in pizza?'

'Sure, why not.'

Sophia left, closing the door behind her, and Christina slumped into her work chair. She couldn't shake the feeling that she should be doing more to help Emma by speaking to Lisa, especially if what they were saying about Kai was true, but how would she explain it to Sophia when it came out that Christina knew about the online abuse? She would have to admit that she had snooped on her phone. And what if Sophia was involved? These days, you had to go along with a lot of stuff or you could be frozen out too, ghosted by your friends or – worse – become the subject of their taunts and abuse. Sophia had always enjoyed being popular, so would she quietly go along with all of it if it meant protecting herself? Although Emma and Sophia had known each other for years, they were certainly not close until recently. There had been no loyalty there until after this had all happened.

So, if she spoke to Lisa, she opened up the possibility of Sophia getting into trouble if Lisa complained to the school and there was an investigation – and she would betray Sophia's trust.

No, her daughter was all she had. She wasn't about to jeopardise her incredibly close relationship with her for someone like Lisa. Not after what Lisa did to Sophia all those years ago. And besides, didn't Christina do something similar when she spread the rumour through the schoolyard that Lisa was dangerous and prone to lashing out? That she couldn't be trusted? If social media had been as dominant then, she would've done the same and used it to spread the word as far as it would go. She was just as bad as all the other bullies in the school playground when it came down to it, even if she had been wronged. Christina had never felt a flicker of shame about it until now. It was like Sophia was holding up a mirror to her and showing her the example she had set.

And Emma was the victim at the centre of all of it.

Above all else, there was also the question of consent and what had actually happened that night. That was a much more emotive problem and one that shouldn't be ignored.

It was something that Owen and Lena should know. But was that her responsibility too?

She needed to talk to someone, to use a friend as a sounding board.

Because if it was true, then she couldn't sit back and do nothing. She couldn't let Kai get away with it.

He deserved to be punished for it.

It was becoming harder to keep her promise to Sophia and stay quiet. The time had come when she had to decide.

Was she a mother or a friend?

42

Christina

Now

She watched Ben and Lisa follow the doctor up the corridor like they were being led to the gallows. She was still shaking from Lisa's verbal attack, but despite what she thought of Lisa and the things she had said, no parent deserved to hear the news that their daughter was in a coma. The doctor had mentioned a tainted batch of drugs, that they had finally received the toxicology results and knew what they were dealing with. The more they heard, the worse it sounded.

She slumped back into the chair, the seat still warm.

'You ok, Mum?' Sophia said.

Christina nodded, not trusting herself to speak just yet.

'She shouldn't have said what she did. That wasn't fair of her.'

'She's just scared and looking for someone to blame.' She sat forward and dropped her hands between her legs, letting them hang heavily.

'Yes, but you weren't even there!'

Christina sat up again. 'Soph, what did happen? I think it's time you told me, don't you? And I know. I know about Kai.'

As she was about to speak, a voice called behind her. 'Soph.'

They both turned to see Kai and Owen heading towards them.

'Soph, are you ok? Have you seen her yet?' Kai said.

'No, they won't let me. Are you ok?'

'They've just let me go – the police, I mean.'

'What did you tell them?' Sophia said, her eyes wide.

Christina was confused. If Sophia knew what Kai had done to Emma, why was she being so calm and friendly to him? Why had he been with them last night?

Owen came to stand next to Kai and said, 'Sophia, pleased to see you are ok. How's your arm? Not too painful, I hope?'

She shrugged. 'It's ok, it's nothing compared to what Emma is going through.'

Christina turned on Kai. 'Haven't you done enough? Why are you even here? Can you not leave that poor girl alone?'

'Christina!' Owen said.

'You have no idea what he's done, have you? What he is capable of. I don't want him anywhere near my daughter.'

'Mum, what are you on about?'

Christina turned to Sophia. 'I know, ok? I found out last week about what happened, what he did, and I've been trying to figure out what to do about it ever since.'

'How?'

'I saw some of the messages on your phone.'

Sophia was indignant. 'You snooped on my phone?'

'It wasn't snooping. It was safeguarding. And I'm pleased I know now because he deserves to be in jail for what he did. He raped her – and it wouldn't surprise me if he gave her the drugs. He did, didn't he?' she said, only then noticing the police officers standing at the nurses' desk behind Owen.

43

Lisa

One Week Ago

She heard the key in the front door and checked her watch. It was gone eight o'clock. His dinner would be cold, sweated out under clingfilm on the kitchen counter. She had eaten with the girls already, their conversation stilted, before they disappeared to their bedrooms. The dishwasher was loaded, everything neat and tidy again. Everything in its place.

Lisa quickly replied to Owen's messages, telling him that Ben was home, that she had to go, and then she locked her phone. She drank some more rosé wine, feeling the ice cubes clatter against her teeth, then set down the glass and waited, her feet curled up under her where she had folded herself into the corner of the couch, her arms hugged in tight.

He seemed to take a while to take off his suit jacket, kick off his shoes, and clatter his keys, wallet and spare change into the bowl in the front hallway. He went straight into the kitchen and she heard him turn on the microwave. Only then did he come to find her. The television was on,

EastEnders shouting in the background on catch-up. She turned the volume down a little and tried to arrange her face into something that might resemble a smile, but already knew he would look through her like a pane of glass.

He came over, pecked her on the cheek and said, 'Hi.'

'Hi, how was your day?'

'Long.'

'Your dinner is in the kitchen.'

'Yeah, thanks.' He hovered for a moment, his eyes on the television. He hated *EastEnders*, but he watched for a few minutes anyway, making her feel uncomfortable as he hovered, his arms crossed, his face betraying how pointless he found the programme. She wondered if he was going to say something else, then when he didn't, she wondered if she should say something, but couldn't think of anything.

The beeping of the microwave called him back to the kitchen.

She sighed as he left, recalling what her sister had said to her in their phone call earlier. She wished her sister lived closer to her, but the occasional snatches of conversations they managed in between her sister having to parent an autistic son and work full-time as a lawyer were still small blessings. Her little sister Carla had a way of seeing things from a different angle to Lisa. She'd always been empathetic, sometimes to a flaw, but she pointed out to Lisa this morning that perhaps Ben was struggling to relate to her as much as she was struggling to break through to him, neither of them knowing what the right words were and both instead saying nothing for fear of making things worse. But one of them had to stick their necks out and try if they still thought it was worth saving. Carla reminded

Lisa that she had found no evidence that Ben was having an affair, so she owed him the benefit of the doubt at least.

Carla was the success of the family, the child that had gone on to a respectable legal career and could still parent a child with special needs. Her mother had often used Carla as an example when they were younger, reminding Lisa that she wasn't as smart, didn't work as hard, would always be in Carla's shadow despite being the older sibling. It was this that had shaped Lisa's need to push her own children so that they would never feel so inadequate and lacking.

She never wanted her children to feel like she had.

And yet some days she could hear herself making the same mistakes, comparing Lucy to Emma, telling her to be more like her sister.

Lisa drank greedily from the wine glass and slid her feet into her slippers. She found Ben sitting in the kitchen with one elbow on the table, shovelling chicken curry into his mouth while his eyes stared at his plate. He had the look of a man who was eating on autopilot, not tasting, just refuelling.

She sat opposite him. He looked up briefly, then back at his plate.

'So how's things?' she asked.

He shrugged. 'This is nice, by the way.'

She nodded in recognition of the offhand compliment.

His fork paused in mid-air and he looked up, then repeated, 'I said, this is nice,' with a glare.

She recoiled a little. 'Sorry, I… er, thanks.'

He looked down again.

She tried again. 'So not a good day then? Do you want to talk about it? Perhaps I can help.'

'No, thanks.'

She sat with a moment of panic then. What else should she say? Was that it? How could she find so much to talk about with Owen, someone she had only really known a short amount of time compared to Ben, and yet she could find nothing to talk to Ben about that wouldn't escalate into some sort of argument?

'I think Emma's exams are going well.'

'Good.'

'I think she's doing enough revision. She's gone back to revising in her room and I'm leaving her to it so that I don't put too much pressure on her.'

'You should trust her more.'

She could feel the annoyance starting to bubble beneath the surface. She wanted to tell him that it was easy for him to say that when he wasn't here every day worrying about whether she was doing enough, lying awake at night agonising about what her future held.

Silence.

'She has another two exams over the next few days, then she's done. She wasn't feeling well today, though – luckily, she didn't have an exam, but she said she had stomach cramps and felt sick. I hope it's not stress.'

'Could be. But she needs to learn to handle stress. It will always be a part of her life.'

'Well, I'm doing my best to monitor it.'

'What about Lucy?' He put his fork down and pushed the plate away from him. Half of the food was left. He mustn't have liked it after all.

'She's fine. Is there something wrong with the dinner?' she snapped, her well-intentioned patience starting to wear thin.

'No, I told you it was nice. I've just had enough.'

'I'm sorry, the chicken was a bit dry and it is bland, but I made it bland so that it would suit Lucy. I know you like your curry hotter than that.'

'I said it's fine.'

He picked up his phone and started scrolling through Instagram.

'Right, well, good talking as always,' she said.

She left the room, curled back into her spot in the corner of the couch, her feet pulled up, her arms crossed, the glass of wine within easy reach. She berated herself for not grabbing the rest of the bottle from the fridge as she passed so that she wouldn't have to go back into the kitchen – and there would be another glass for her tonight because every fibre in her body was now strumming with annoyance. He hadn't asked about her day, hadn't shown any interest in talking about the girls or given her any insight into why his day had been so difficult. Instead, he had managed to make her feel invisible by saying very little and merely rearranging his face into its usual expression of disinterest at best and disdain at worst.

Had he used up all his words on someone else? Was that it?

She looked around the room, all neat and tidy and beige. She could see an edge of the stain on the rug in the far corner, peeking out from under the couch, where Lucy had spilled juice one day when she got too excited while watching *Strictly Come Dancing*. At the time, Lisa had been annoyed as she knew the blackcurrant wouldn't come out of the beige rug, but now she thought about how much Lucy had loved to dance along with the celebrities, and how she and Ben would laugh and encourage her. There had been noise and laughter and silliness then.

He would never watch *Strictly Come Dancing* with them now.

She thought about the number of dirty fingerprints she had cleaned from walls and windows and furniture, the grass stains she had washed out of clothes, the broken bits and pieces she had thrown away, all with a certain degree of annoyance then but now she realised they were all snapshots of a once happy home, with carefree children and memories being made before the stress of school and achievements and accolades had set in. She had a fleeting moment of nostalgia, carrying with it a tinge of sadness that those signs of happiness had been cleaned and tidied away so quickly. She inexplicably thought of Christina then, with the chalk marks on the wall measuring how much Sophia had grown, Sophia's artwork still stuck to her fridge, the corners curling with age, the dent in the wall in the hallway where Sophia had crashed her bike while practising up and down the corridor. Those memories still lived and breathed in her house. They hadn't been washed away and sterilised.

Lisa was annoyed that she had let the need for order erase what was left of the spontaneity in the house.

She grabbed her phone from where it had slipped down the side of the couch cushions and opened the conversation she had been having with Owen. She read back over his comments, smiling at the loaded compliments and veiled flirtation, needing to read the comments again to get her out of her own head. She still didn't know where she stood with Owen or where he expected this to go. She had suggested meeting again, but he had swerved the idea. After their initial encounter in the alleyway, it had all played out on text or in hushed phone conversations, like a dirty little secret.

She wondered if he found her too needy. She did initiate a lot of the text conversations. Looking at the messages now, they sounded whiny and pathetic, full of grumbling and creating an image of a woman dissatisfied with her perfect life. Was that how he saw her too? Did he now wish he hadn't initiated that kiss? Her head swirled with paranoia, what if's and questions, driving her crazy with self-doubt. In the gaps of time between messages, she wasn't sure if any of this was worth it – and then he'd send an incredibly sweet message of support or he would be openly suggestive in his choice of words and she would be left confused all over again.

She fired off a message now, telling him about her conversation with Ben, then immediately regretted sending it. He didn't want to hear about her marital frustrations and petty domestic disputes. No wonder he was cooling off. She went to delete the message before he saw it, but he was already typing. She waited, annoyed at herself but still feeling a buzz of pleasure that he was answering so quickly.

The little dots continued, then he stopped typing and no message appeared. What did that mean?

The dots reappeared as he began typing again, but Ben then walked into the lounge, his face strangely dejected, his shoulders slumped.

'I'm sorry, I'm not being fair,' he said. 'We need to talk.'

She tucked her phone under her leg.

'I know it's a very stressful time for you with Emma writing exams. I should be more supportive. I'm not trying to tell you how to do things or criticising you for what you are doing. I think you are doing a great job. It's just… you can be so hard on her sometimes. I'm tired and… never mind.' He looked like there was a lot more he wanted to say, but the words were stuck in his throat.

She sat forward.

'Ben…'

The sound of a loud claxon filled the air, a notification that he had received a text message. The noise cut through the moment.

He glanced at his phone, then looked at it more carefully.

'Who is it?' she asked.

'It's no one.'

She narrowed her eyes. He looked shifty suddenly. He moved to leave the room.

She launched out of her seat and grabbed the phone from his hand.

'Lisa!'

'I want to know who it is.'

She looked at the screen, then said, 'Why is Christina texting you?'

'I don't know. I haven't read it.'

Then her own phone chimed. She was still holding his phone in her hand. It felt weighty and hot in her palm.

But she also knew who was texting her. She was no better, was she?

'Really, Ben? Christina? How unoriginal.' She thrust the phone back at him and returned to her corner of the couch. She glanced down at her phone, then placed it screen down on her knee.

'Look, Lisa, I don't know what you think is going on, but I can guarantee you are wrong. But there is something we need to talk about.' He took a deep breath. 'A few weeks ago, I—'

Her phone chimed again. This time, she jumped and the phone fell from the couch where it landed face-up on the floor. She looked at it as though it was now the loaded gun. Owen had sent another message and from this distance, she couldn't read what it said. Before she composed herself enough to bend over and pick it up, Ben said, 'You're popular tonight,' and stepped forward to pick it up himself. He glanced down at the screen. Lisa's breath caught in her throat.

He handed the phone to her and said, 'Owen sent you a message,' and left the room.

She sat with her hand outstretched, the phone in her fingers, her mouth open, scared to look at what Owen had sent. She heard Ben stomp upstairs, the moment when he was about to open up to her now long gone.

She closed her eyes, as though that would blot it all out, then opened them and looked at the screen.

You're too good for him. You deserve better.

Ok, not great, but it could be easily explained if she told him that her and Owen had struck up a close friendship and that she was struggling to talk to Ben. He would surely understand.

Would she understand if she thought Ben was sharing advice and texts with another woman? No, probably not. As it was, he was doing just that with Christina of all people. And she didn't understand.

She needed an explanation.

She got to her feet, already formulating in her head the questions she needed to ask.

She stepped into the hallway to find Lucy standing at the foot of the stairs in her pyjamas, her hair in a messy ponytail.

'Mum, something's wrong with Emma. She's being sick in the bathroom.'

44

Lisa

Now

She looked so tiny and frail. There were tubes and wires, beeping machines, nurses checking this and that. Lisa wanted to scream at all of them to get out, that she was sleeping and they would wake her. Then she realised she wanted her to wake up, that this wasn't the peaceful sleep of a stroppy teenager, but the medicated sleep of the broken.

She looked across the hospital bed to where Ben was sitting on the other side, mirroring her, each holding one of her hands, each of them staring at her, willing her to move, open her eyes, twitch, anything.

It was late, well after midnight now, and although they had only been at the hospital a few hours, it felt like a lifetime had passed.

She sat up straighter with a jolt. 'Ben, we need to tell Lucy. She doesn't know about any of this.'

Ben looked at her with vacant, haunted eyes. 'What?'

'Lucy! She's at home alone. We need to tell her. What if something…'

'No, that isn't going to happen.' He shut her down straight away. 'I will go and get her in a minute. I just… I just want to sit here a little longer.'

'I don't understand how this could've happened. She doesn't drink. She doesn't go out.' Lisa's mind was flipping over itself trying to understand why it was Emma in this bed and not Sophia. She hadn't heard how they had got here as yet, but she did now know that only Emma had been admitted. Kai and Sophia were fine, able to go home. No one was talking about how Emma got the drugs and why she had taken them.

'Well, maybe we don't know her as well as we think we do,' Ben said. 'I should've asked more questions… The other night, we had hot chocolate and she seemed… well, she wasn't herself. I should've thought to ask more questions.'

'Maybe we never really know anyone. People lie,' Lisa said with bitterness.

He looked at her again. 'What does that mean?'

She sighed, let her finger stroke the top of Emma's warm hand.

'Where have you been these last few weeks, Ben? You've pulled away from us. I feel like I'm parenting on my own and living with a stranger.'

'Are you saying this is my fault?' His anger was quick to bubble over.

'No, I'm just… I've been distracted, worried about you, suspicious, making up the worst scenarios in my head when I should've been focusing on Emma.'

'So you are blaming me.' He sighed again and dropped his head.

'No, I'm trying to understand.'

'Well, why don't you ask Owen? I'm sure he has some theories – and a shoulder for you to cry on.'

'I only started talking to Owen when I couldn't talk to you, Ben.'

A nurse came in, checked the monitor, checked the IV, smiled at them both in sympathy and left again.

Silence fell, the only sounds coming from the machines that were helping their daughter to breathe.

'I had a health scare,' he said eventually.

'Pardon?'

'The reason I've been… distant. I had a health scare.'

This was not what she had expected. 'So you aren't having an affair?'

He laughed at that. 'My God, Lisa, I could think of nothing worse! No, I was feeling really tired, run down, thirsty all the time, so I had some blood tests done. Turns out I'm pre-diabetic – and I struggled with it. I didn't know how to tell you because it felt like I had failed, like I'd let you down somehow. And it's my fault – it's a lifestyle disease, so it's my own fault for drinking too much, eating too much junk when I'm at work, the tubs of ice cream and all those energy drinks to keep me awake at my desk.'

Lisa saw the regret in his face. 'You should've told me. I could've helped.'

Was she that hard to talk to that he couldn't tell her he might be ill, that he was worried? She felt wretched.

He carried on. 'I thought that if I made some changes myself, started getting more exercise, looking after myself, I could reverse it and you would never know. But then, they wanted more blood tests and the worry, the guilt… it's been hard.'

'I thought you were having an affair.'

'And is the truth better or worse?'

She didn't answer that. 'At least I can help you, support you, work through it with you now.' She paused. 'Does Christina know?'

'Christina? No, why would she?'

'The texts from her, the whispered conversations.'

'No, Lisa, I never even got in touch with her to see what it was she wanted to talk about. She had said she wanted to run something by me, get my advice, but I didn't reply. I had other things to worry about.' He sat for a moment, then said, 'And what about you and Owen? Are you sleeping with him?'

'No, I'm not,' she said, looking him straight in the eye.

'Ok then.'

'Ok,' she repeated.

They turned their attention back to Emma, watched her chest rise and fall, kept their eyes on the heart monitor, willed her to wake up.

45

Emma

One Week Ago

Emma felt like her insides were going to drop out. In fact, it looked like they had already. She changed the sanitary pad yet again, her hands shaking, a cold sweat beading her forehead. They had said to expect some period cramping and blood, but this was on another level. They had also said to expect some nausea, but so far it was beyond nausea. It was what she imagined the worst case of food poisoning mixed with a tequila hangover would feel like.

She was floundering in hell.

She splashed water on her face and rinsed out her mouth, then crawled, doubled over, back to her bed. She curled up under the covers, at once cold and shivery while also feverishly hot and sweaty.

She closed her eyes, but they sprung back open when she heard a light tap on her bedroom door.

Her mother walked in, carrying a mug.

'Lucy says you're not feeling well? She says you've just been sick?' She sat on the end of Emma's bed. 'Here's some camomile tea to settle your stomach. Do you think it's something you've eaten, maybe?'

'Could be – I had a chicken sandwich at school yesterday, could've been that.'

'But that would have hit you last night, not today.'

Emma kept quiet. She had hoped Lisa would just accept that it was a bug and leave it at that. But her mother had to be right. Emma used to think like that too. She knew the kids at school used to roll their eyes when her hand was always up in class, when she would cut people down, tell them they were wrong, dismiss them for being ignorant. Once she had thought being right was the most important thing. Now she knew being liked was a bigger deal.

'Is it stress? Are you worried about your exams? You dad thinks it might be that, but please don't let stress make you ill. As long as you've put in the work, these exams should be a mere formality. And you always work hard.' She reached out and stroked Emma's damp hair away from her forehead. 'Maybe I should call you in sick tomorrow. You do feel clammy.'

'No, I need to do the exam in the afternoon. It's probably a twenty-four-hour bug and I'm sure I'll be miles better tomorrow.'

'I blame Sophia for putting extra pressure on you. She has plenty of other people she could ask for help with her *little problem*. I've a good mind to call Christina about it.'

'It's not that, Mum. I think it is a bug or something. And you promised you wouldn't say anything. Thanks for the tea, but I'm tired. I'm going to go to sleep.' She rolled over onto her other side, hoping her mother would take the hint.

She kept her eyes closed, but her mother remained where

she was for a moment. Emma was about to ask her to leave when she felt the weight lift from beside her and heard her leave the room, softly closing the door behind her.

She gave it a few seconds longer, then propped herself up on her pillows and sipped at the tea. Her phone was on silent, but it kept vibrating and lighting up on the bedside table. She had been feeling too weak mentally and physically to look at it, but it was incessant, so she grabbed it with the intention of turning it off altogether.

Her eyes fell on a Snapchat from Sophia, asking how she was doing. She opened it and replied that she felt awful and thanking her for checking in. Out of all of this, she was grateful that her and Sophia were friends again. At least, she hoped they were. Sometimes, she wondered whether she could completely trust Sophia yet, but she seemed to have her back now and that was all that mattered at the moment.

Then she saw the list of unopened Snapchats below Sophia's message. Her fingers hovered over the messages, her brain telling her to look away, turn off the phone, don't read them, but her fingers took over and she opened the top message. It burned into her eyes, leaving a searing scar.

Wouldn't it be hilarious if the stupid bitch was pregnant? That would teach Miss Smarty-pants! If we're lucky, she'll die in childbirth.

Emma felt the panic take over from the nausea. Did they know? How could they know? Had Sophia told everyone? Such an idiot for trusting her.

Then she read it again. No, they were speculating, that

was all. She didn't even register the death threat. She was almost immune to such things now. She flicked through some of the other messages, the bitterness and abuse no longer cutting through her defences.

Then she saw the other messages about Kai. The video had been seen and shared, and while it had taken a little while for anyone to change their opinion of her, the seed had been planted and was growing fast. She had paused for only a slight moment to consider if she should post the video, but only for a second. If Sophia didn't have the balls to say anything, then she had to do it herself. She had nothing left to lose.

She read some of the messages of support and solidarity that were pinging through, soaking them up like a sponge.

Then she turned her phone off and rolled over to face the wall, feeling marginally better.

Emma woke up some hours later, surprised that she had actually slept at all. The house was quiet. She sat up, feeling groggy, like she had had the deepest sleep of her life. Half the cup of camomile tea still sat where she had left it, cold, staining the cup with a greenish ring. She checked her phone; it was past midnight. She took a moment to check in with herself, take stock of how she was feeling. Better, perhaps – certainly not so nauseous and feverish. Her stomach felt distended and uncomfortable, but more like mild period pains now than the agonising cramping of earlier.

She felt weak, though. She threw on a dressing gown and crept out of her room. The lights were all out upstairs, so she made her way carefully along the corridor and down the stairs, avoiding the noisy fifth stair from the top.

She held her breath at the bottom when she saw light flickering in the lounge. She peered around the door and saw her dad fast asleep on the couch, a blanket tossed over him, the television volume turned down very low but playing away to itself. He spent most nights sleeping there these days. He claimed it was because he was tired and often fell asleep in front of the television, but she wondered if there was more of an element of choice involved. She knew her parents hardly spoke.

She went into the kitchen, closed the door behind her and turned on the light. She blinked rapidly as the light burned into her night vision before settling. Everything was spotless, tidy, organised. She thought back to Christina's kitchen the other day with the crumbs on the counter, dirty cups in the sink and an unidentifiable herb plant that had long since died still sitting on the windowsill. The difference was not cleanliness but how at home she had felt – and she didn't feel at home here now. She felt like she was the mess her mother was trying to clear up. She suspected that was how Lucy felt too. She would love to see Lisa just leave a dish out one day, maybe forget to load the dishwasher or keep a teaspoon on the counter pooling tea. But that wasn't how she rolled. She turned off the light again.

She found some bread and made some toast, slathering it thickly with butter. Eating it quietly at the table in the moonlit near-dark, she steered herself away from any sort of analysis of how she might be feeling mentally. The physical torture was helping to distract her from any deeper thoughts and feelings, but tomorrow might be different. She could feel the thoughts tapping her on the shoulder, wanting to be acknowledged, but she shooed them away.

Instead, she thought about those messages from people who had barely tolerated her before, showing support and encouragement, praising her for being brave. She started composing a message of gratitude in her head, something that she could post tomorrow maybe.

Feeling more human after finishing the toast, she sent Sophia a message saying that she was feeling better, only expecting her to answer tomorrow, but was surprised when Sophia replied straight away. Rather than use what little strength she had on typing, she decided to call Sophia.

'Hey, you're not asleep then?' she said.

Sophia sounded wide awake, wired. 'No, getting some last-minute revision in for my exam tomorrow.'

'I should probably think about doing something too,' Emma said with a humourless chuckle.

'I think you've had other things on your mind.'

'Yeah.'

'So you're feeling ok?'

'Yeah, but it was rough there for a while. But I guess ending a life shouldn't be easy, should it?'

'Don't say it like that.'

'That's what I did, though. Did you see my video?'

Sophia didn't reply, but Emma could hear her breathing. Eventually, Sophia said, 'Yeah, I saw it. Maybe you should have told him first?'

'Who? Kai? No way.' Emma realised her voice had risen an octave and, conscious of her dad in the other room, she took a breath and lowered her voice again. 'I don't need anything from him.'

'He's been worried about you.'

'That's guilt, not worry. You haven't told him about the baby, have you?'

'No! It's just... all the messages and stuff. There's been a lot and it can't be easy to read them.'

'Am I supposed to feel sorry for him? He deserves it.'

'No, just... he feels really bad about what happened.'

'Again, not my problem.'

'Maybe you and him should talk. He says he was drunk too.'

'He was drunk too? That's his defence?'

'He doesn't need a defence, does he? Or are you thinking of taking this further?'

'What do you mean by taking it further?'

'You know, not just talk at school, but actually calling him out for what he did, what you both did. If you're thinking of telling anyone... It could ruin his life, you know.'

'You mean like it ruined mine?' Emma could feel tears coming thick and fast. 'You know what, if you're so much on his side, then stay out of my life.'

'No, Ems, wait, I'm sorry. I'm just... caught in the middle a bit and I don't know what to say to him. Fuck, this is such a mess.'

Silence fell.

'I'm sorry,' Sophia repeated eventually. 'I'm tired, too much caffeine, and I'm not saying the right things, I guess.'

Emma chewed on her fingernail, didn't reply but also didn't hang up.

'Listen, I've got some tickets to a gig on Friday night when the exams are over. There's a couple of us going. Do you fancy it? A change of scenery, a chance to have some fun, put the last few weeks behind us? It's in town, so it should be good fun. Please come.'

'I don't know.'

'Think about it.'

The door to the kitchen swung open and Emma's dad stood there, his hair on end, his eyes blinking away sleep.

'I've got to go,' Emma said and hung up.

'What are you doing up?' Ben said, sitting down opposite her. He rubbed his eyes and yawned.

'I was hungry.' Emma indicated the plate with the toast crumbs on it.

He nodded. 'Fair enough. Not a bad idea, actually. I might have some myself.' He got up and started making himself some toast. 'I think toast needs hot chocolate too though, don't you?'

Suddenly, all she wanted was to sit with her dad, drinking hot chocolate in the moonlit kitchen, the sky twinkling darkly outside, the house silent. 'I think you're right.'

She watched as he warmed milk in a pan, buttered his toast and cut it into triangles, then stirred chocolate powder into the steaming milk before setting the mugs down in front of them.

'Who were you talking to so late?'

'Sophia. She's still revising.'

'You two friends again then?'

'Yeah, I guess. We've grown quite close lately.'

'That's good. I always thought she was a good kid.' He chewed thoughtfully. His eyes were puffy with sleep and his skin was pale.

'You ok, Dad?' Emma said.

He paused in his chewing, looked at her, then smiled. 'Hey, I'm the parent. I'm supposed to ask you that.'

'Sometimes we all need to be asked.'

He reached out and stroked her hair, like he used to when she was little. 'When did you get so grown-up and wise?'

Emma suddenly felt like crying. She swallowed it down.

'So are you?' Did he know about her mum and Owen? Should she say something to him?

'Yes, I'm ok. Tired, stressed at work, feeling a bit run down, I guess. Sometimes, it hard being an adult. What about you, kiddo? How are the exams going?'

She didn't say anything for a moment, the cracked dam wall threatening to burst. She sipped at the hot chocolate and shrugged, which seemed the safest response. What good would come from honesty right now?

'You'll do great, kiddo, you always do.'

She stared into her mug. 'Dad, would you be really disappointed if I didn't get into Oxford?'

He sat back, ran his fingers through his already upright hair and wiped the crumbs from his T-shirt. 'Why do you ask that? I have no doubt you'll get in.'

'Yeah, but it's not guaranteed though, is it? Anything could happen. I could completely mess up my exams or the interview or anything.'

'That's just panic talking. But what I really want is for you to find your place, wherever it is. If it's Oxford, then great. If it's another university, so what?'

'And what if it's not university at all?'

He frowned at her then. 'Why wouldn't it be? I thought

you wanted to go to university? A degree is important if you want to be successful in life.'

She nodded, cradled her drink between her hands.

He watched her closely, then continued, 'I am slowly coming to realise that life is too short to do something just to please someone else. You don't know how long you have, so you should fill it with things you enjoy, people you enjoy being around, so that when it comes down to it, you have no regrets.'

'Way to get morbid, Dad,' Emma said.

He smiled. 'Maybe I'm feeling old.' He shrugged. 'I guess it's a balance of finding your happy place and paying the bills, but the choices you make now and the work you put in now will mean you can have options later. And that's important. So yes, I think university is important, only in that it will open doors to enable you to be financially secure enough in the future to do the fun stuff you really want to do.'

'You're not old. But I do wonder what fun stuff you do. All you do is work.'

He didn't reply to that and they sat in silence for a moment, sipping and swallowing.

'Do you think Mum would think the same, though? About university?' Emma asked then.

'The one thing about your mother is that she wants the best for you. She wants you to succeed. Everything she does for you and Lucy is to make sure you are given the best opportunities to excel.' He drained his mug. 'Now, I don't know about you, but I could do with going back to sleep. And you've got an exam tomorrow, haven't you? You better get some sleep too.'

He stood up and she followed his lead. Then he stopped and turned to her. 'They don't give you a manual for being a parent, you know. We are all just figuring it out as we go along – and that means we make mistakes, have regrets, don't always say the right thing. I'm sure one day you'll understand when you have your own children. Cut her some slack.'

He kissed her on the cheek and walked slowly up the stairs.

She watched him go, heard the creak of the fifth stair from the top, and only then let the tears she had been holding in leak down her cheeks silently.

46

Ben

Now

He sat in the driver's seat, hands gripping the steering wheel like a life preserver. He hadn't even started the engine yet. He just needed to sit.

The moon was dull, clouded over. It wasn't silent – a car horn sounded, a siren squealed somewhere, the traffic lights at the pedestrian crossing beeped as a couple of teenagers messed about on the street – but in the car, the dark muffled all of it so that he felt like he was in a padded cell.

He looked down at his hands as they wrung the life out of the steering wheel. He watched them, disembodied, then forced himself to loosen his grip, to let go altogether. They landed heavily on his legs, palms up.

Instead of relief at having finally told Lisa what had been going on, he felt weighed down with guilt. The look of disappointment as he told her about his diagnosis had cut straight through his middle. He had mistakenly thought that keeping it from her was better than having her worry about his health. Now he knew that was wrong. That one look from her had made that clear. It wasn't the condition itself that fazed her; it was the idea that he had kept it from her.

Pride had got in the way.

Yet none of it mattered now. His daughter was lying unresponsive in a hospital bed, having taken goodness knows what, and he was sitting in his car again in the dark, paralysed by fear and shock.

Right now, he didn't care about his own health. All he wanted was for Emma to wake up. He couldn't even begin to fathom how he would cope if she didn't. How any of them would cope.

He thought of Lucy then. That was why he was hiding in his car. As soon as Lisa had mentioned Lucy, he had felt the unavoidable urge to get out of there, away from the sterile hospital with its muted hallways and pistachio-colour palette, but then panic at what he would say to Lucy, how he would explain it had rooted him to the chair. Eventually she had said, 'So are you going to get her or not?' in her typical impatient manner and he had left.

He rubbed the palms of his hands on the legs of his jeans, over and over, as though trying to get some feeling back into them, to fire up the nerves and push back against the numbness that had settled over him.

A horrible thought intruded into that numbness. What if something happened while he was hiding in the car? He would never forgive himself if he wasn't there when she woke up – or worse, didn't wake up. He needed her to remain in limbo for the next hour while he drove home and broke the news to Lucy. He willed her to stay as she was, frozen in time and space.

He felt traitorous and repugnant at thinking it, at even contemplating that no change would be preferable, but that was the reality of it. He was a selfish coward and the longer he sat in the dark, the more he hated himself.

He reached down and turned the key, heard the engine purr into life. His hands gripped the wheel again, the knuckles still white.

47

Christina

Yesterday

Christina was pleased the whole sorry episode was over. Sophia could get back to normality. None of this being locked in her room or poring over books. No dark circles under the eyes and constant grazing on ultra-processed carbs and sugar. She could go back to being a regular teenager who liked parties, boys and underage drinking. Christina had hardly recognised her in the last few weeks.

Ben had never returned Christina's message asking if she could talk to him, so there was still the issue of what to do about what she knew.

That was a conversation she still needed to have with Sophia too.

She'd turned into such a studious kid. Not that Christina wasn't proud of her because she was, but people like Christina and Sophia didn't go to university. They were creative souls, liberated, free spirits. She wanted Sophia to feel alive every day, not chained to a desk or driving herself to boredom in an office somewhere, not gadding about with posh folk at some institution where they were out of touch with reality and the lives of the regular people in the street. She had watched Sophia lock herself away, become a shadow of herself, focused only on books and facts over the last little while, and she missed the funny, lively, energetic girl that had been there before.

However, she had to give kudos to her for being so dedicated, especially with everything they had dealt with, what with Emma and the abortion, the constant, frantic phone calls. The walls in their house were thin and Christina had heard the mumbles of late-night conversations, the gentle support Sophia had offered.

Those calls seemed to have stopped now though and the exams were over as of today. She sat in the kitchen, waiting for Sophia to come home from her last exam with a shop-bought Victoria sponge on the table. She had no idea how Sophia would do in these exams, but she would be fine either way. They would be fine. She liked the idea of the two of them packing up and travelling to exotic places, finding bar work and living their best lives together.

Last night Sophia had mentioned her university application and how she would like to look at some universities over the next few weekends. Christina had been surprised and a little taken aback because it had hit her all at once that their time together was coming to an end.

And if she was really being honest with herself, she would recognise that she just didn't want Sophia to leave home, to leave her here on her own.

It had been the two of them for so long that she was terrified of who she would become if Sophia went to university, who she was if she wasn't Sophia's mum. She also had no idea where she would find the money for university fees. So she could secretly hope that Sophia had messed up the exams, that Emma's drama had pushed her off-track – and she would keep her delight private when the exam results came back and Sophia's aspirations were deflated.

Did that make her an awful person? Probably.

There was a little voice in her head that told Christina she was horrid for ever wishing that her daughter would fail. What kind of mother did that?

Selfish, she knew that, but she couldn't stop the thoughts swirling around her head like whispers and she knew that she was letting those inner whispers influence what she said to Sophia. Christina had fought hard to create a home environment that was a creative space of self-expression and non-conformity, and yet her daughter was wanting to conform to a life less lived in Christina's opinion.

She heard the key in the front door and acknowledged the delight she still got at seeing her daughter every day. There hadn't been a day go by when she hadn't seen Sophia since she was born. No wonder Christina felt an uncomfortable tug in her stomach when she thought about her leaving.

'Hi,' Christina called out.

Sophia stuck her head around the door. 'Hey Mum.' She looked bone weary.

'How was it?'

'Ok, I think, but who knows, right? It could go either way, I guess.' Sophia threw down her bag and fell into the chair.

'Baby girl, you look tired. But all done now and you can

put it out of your head for a bit. Have some cake – it will perk you up. It's a Victoria sponge. Your favourite.'

Sophia smiled despite her exhaustion. 'Thanks Mum.' She helped herself to a moderate slice.

Christina was mildly annoyed that she didn't eat more. She pushed the annoyance aside and cut herself a much larger slice in silent protestation. 'So, got any plans to celebrate?'

'Not tonight,' Sophia said as she played with the cake. 'I just want to sleep. But tomorrow, I've got that gig I told you about? With the twins and a couple of others? And I think I might have persuaded Emma to come too.'

'To a gig? In London?'

'I know. I don't think she's ever been to one, but she didn't say no when I mentioned it and I have a spare ticket now that Daisy can't come, so yeah.'

'I used to love a gig in town – drinking beer on the Tube, and then the bustle and stress of trying to catch the last train home. Ending up on the night bus with everyone else instead. I can get you some of them pre-mixed cocktails in the cans if you want? For the journey? Preloading in case it's expensive at the gig. It usually is expensive.'

'Sure, thanks Mum.'

Sophia stared at the rest of the cake on her plate, poked at it with the fork, tearing the cake into crumbs.

'So what's up then? I thought you'd be happy exams are over.'

'I am. I just… I know you don't think it's a big deal and you maybe don't want me to go, but I really want to have done well in the exams. I'm worried I've not done enough though, what with everything with Emma. I know you don't want me to go to university, but I really do want to go. So much.'

'It's not that I don't want you to go. It's that I don't want you to be disappointed if it doesn't happen.'

'So you don't think I'm smart enough. I've set my sights too high, is that it? I get it. That's what everyone thinks.'

'No, that's not what I said. The truth is, I think university can be a waste of time. It doesn't teach you life lessons. It delays you getting onto the career ladder and earning money, and you will leave there after three years with little experience and the extra burden of debt to pay back. I just think there are better ways of starting out in life. But if you are so keen on the idea, I would suggest maybe taking a gap year first. We could travel a bit, you and me, see some of the world out there and you could take your time deciding what you want to do.'

'And how would we pay for this travel?'

'That's my problem, not yours. And we can always work while we travel – you and me working behind the bar on an island somewhere? What do you think?'

'Mum, this is my time now. It's up to me how I spend it and what I do with my future. You've had your time.'

Christina felt the sting of that.

'You know, Emma doesn't even want to go to uni anymore. She's basically been forced into applying and she'll be lucky to get a pass in these exams – I don't think she revised for any of them. Of course, you probably think she's smart enough to pass without even trying. Maybe you can go travelling and clubbing with her instead of me if I'm so disappointing.'

'Hey, that's not fair. That's not what I'm saying at all.'

'Be honest, Mum. If you don't think I'm smart enough, just tell me.'

'Honey bee, you are smarter than most kids your age – look at how amazing you have been with Emma. I have no doubt you are smart enough. Any university would be proud to have you.' She sighed. 'I'm a selfish cow, aren't I? I'm sorry.'

Sophia shrugged, ate a bit more cake. 'I'm a little worried about tomorrow night if Emma does come.'

'Why?'

Sophia picked at the crumbs, squishing them together between her fingertips. 'There's been a lot of stuff going around about her at school, horrible stuff on social media and Snapchat and stuff. Some of the people there tomorrow sent some of it and I'm not sure how they'll all get on.'

Christina looked at her closely. 'Did you send anything?'

Sophia didn't reply, which spoke volumes.

Christina asked the same question in a different way. 'How much did you send and does Emma know you may have contributed?'

'At the beginning, it was because I was angry and annoyed that she slept with Kai because she knew I liked him.'

'You like Kai? Since when?' Christina ignored the admission that Emma had slept with him.

'For a while now. But he doesn't see me as anything other than a friend, never has. I only sent the initial stuff because I was jealous, but then we got talking and I could see the effect it was all having. Then she told me that she couldn't remember what had happened that night and I felt terrible for her. Because, well, that's a consent issue, isn't it? But Kai says he was drunk too, so they were both as bad as each other – and he swears he did nothing wrong. He swears she was up for it, even initiated it. So I don't know what to think. He's coming tomorrow night and she doesn't know he'll be there.'

Christina sighed. There was so much to unpack here. 'Ok, first of all, you have to tell her he's coming, but I also think this is between them. Being drunk and getting into such a situation is dangerous for everyone involved – and I'm not dismissing what she says when I say that. I'm not saying she brought it on herself. But getting in the middle of them will only end with you getting yourself into trouble with one or both of them. She has to decide if she wants to take it further. Only the two of them know what really happened.'

Sophia looked so wretched, tiny, like the little girl she had left behind.

'Hey, don't worry,' Christina said as she grabbed onto her hand across the table. 'Forget about everything that's going on. Go out tomorrow night, have some fun and the rest will take care of itself.'

Sophia's phone buzzed then. She read the message, then looked up at Christina. 'It's from Emma. She's going to come tomorrow night after all.'

48

Lisa

Now

Now that she was on her own, she was surprised to find she felt calmer. The fury that had blistered through her when she had confronted Christina has been visceral. It hadn't dissipated when she'd walked into the room and saw Emma, so small and helpless, but she had pushed it down, let it simmer while she focused on the doctor and what he was saying, concentrated on holding Emma's hand and letting her know she was there.

As soon as Ben had started telling her about his health scare and how he had kept it from her, she had felt the anger bubble, again reminding her it was there. It had taken all of her strength not to walk around the bed and hit him as hard as she could – for being selfish, for underestimating her, for invalidating her.

She'd encouraged him to go and get Lucy because she didn't want him around more than anything else. She needed space from him. She almost wished it had been an affair. Then she wouldn't feel like this was all some sort of judgement on her, that no one believed she was strong enough to take on any sort of trauma or difficulty. Did he really think she was that incapable? That he had to protect her by lying through omission?

She sat holding Emma's hand, her forehead clenched as tightly as her jaw. Her chest was tight, her breathing shallow, like she was holding in every breath instead of letting it out. She dropped her forehead onto her arms and sat hunched over, her back screaming at the angle it was being forced into, but her head accepting the discomfort with relish. At least with pain, you knew where you were. She sat that way for some time, trying to squash the fight out of her chest.

She heard a gentle knock behind her and sat up quickly. Sophia stared through the glass panel in the door, her face ashen.

Lisa hesitated, but nodded for her to come in.

Sophia looked afraid. She flicked her eyes at the bed, then away again. 'How is she?' she said in a tiny voice.

Lisa shrugged. 'You can see for yourself, can't you?'

'I'm sorry. For all of it.' She hovered at the end of the hospital bed, her arms crossed tightly over her chest.

'What happened, Sophia? What happened to my little girl?'

'It was... it was an accident. I don't know, really.'

'What do you mean, you don't know? You were there!'

Lisa didn't realise she was shouting until Sophia took two steps backwards towards the door. Lisa shot out of the chair and closed the gap between them.

'You did this. She's a good girl, but you? You're a mess, just like your mother. You did this to her, didn't you? Was it a sick joke? Let's see if we can get the conscientious

student high? See if we can mess with her a bit? Is that
what happened? I bet you took photos, spread it across
your socials. I bet you laughed and laughed. Am I right?
You make me sick. How can you get away with a broken
bone and she is left like...' Her voice crumbled. She had
pushed Sophia right up against the wall. Sophia had tears
running down her cheeks, but Lisa couldn't see any of it
through the red veil over her eyes. 'You tell me right now
what happened or so help me God—'

'Get the hell away from my daughter, Lisa.'

49

Lisa

Earlier

Another day, the same routine. Lisa was bored of all of it. Getting up after her husband had already left for work. Her morning ritual of trying to turn back time with a pot of expensive moisturiser. Watching her teenagers chew on sugary cereal that was undoubtedly bad for them, but was the only thing she could get them to eat before school. Waiting patiently for them to get off to school, arms folded, until she could focus on her clients, then waiting patiently to get through her sessions with her shallow clients and their endlessly petty, skin-deep anxieties. The monotony of deciding what to make for dinner, grocery shopping, laundry.

It was tiresome and mundane and she craved some excitement. Something out of the ordinary that would get her heart pumping and her pulse racing.

Some days, it felt like if she sat still for long enough, she would actually die from boredom – and she wasn't convinced anyone would notice for quite some time. They'd find her, still in the chair, Jester chewing on her long-dead foot, and wonder how long she had been there without them missing her.

She watched Emma play with the milk in her cereal bowl, remained tight-lipped as Lucy smeared way too much chocolate spread on her toast. She felt irritation nipping at her heels.

Emma pushed her bowl away. She looked exhausted, her skin a pale grey that her foundation wasn't masking very well. She caught her mother watching her over the rim of her mug.

'Oh, Mum, I've been invited to a gig tonight. Can I go?'

Lisa frowned. 'A gig? Where?'

'It's in central. Some people from school are going to celebrate finishing exams. There'll be a few of us, so it'll be safe. I won't be on my own.'

Lisa put the mug down on the counter. 'I don't like the idea of you going into town on a Friday night.'

'We'll be travelling there and back together. It's a straight train, then Tube journey and we'll be in a group.'

'Who are you going to see?' Lucy asked.

'None of your business,' Emma snapped.

Lucy raised her eyebrows.

'Please, Mum, I don't normally get invited to these things and I just want to have some fun with my friends. You won't know the bands anyway.'

'Loser,' Lucy muttered under her breath.

Lisa chewed on her lip, her mind already creating disaster scenarios in her head of what might happen – train crashes, muggings, kidnap, spiked drinks. The list was endless. Of course, if Ben was here, he'd say *let her go, let her have some fun for a change.* That was enough to make her mind up.

'No, I don't think so, Emma. You look exhausted – I think it's best if you have an early night, catch up on some sleep. Self-care is important when you are revising.'

'But the exams are over now. After this morning, anyway. And I really like these people.'

'Who are these friends? Do I know their parents?'

Emma paused, found her fingernails very interesting, mumbled, 'No, you don't know them.'

'Well, even more reason not to let you go. I'm sorry, Emma, but I don't think it's safe.'

Emma scowled, her cheeks now enflamed. She shoved her chair back and swiped at her backpack.

Lisa felt awful. She didn't want to be picking a fight with her just before she left for an exam. 'Ems, darling, maybe we could all go out for pizza or something instead?'

Emma left in silence. Lisa managed to shout, 'Good luck!' before the front door slammed.

Lucy was still at the table, staring at her phone intently, barely touching her breakfast.

Anger bubbled through her. 'Lucy, put that damn phone down at the table or I will take it away!'

'But Mum, there's something about Em—' Lucy was pale, her eyes wide.

'I said put it down.'

Lucy did what she was told reluctantly, then left in much the same mood as Emma had.

Ten minutes later, Lisa's phone buzzed with a text from Emma asking if she could stay at Sophia's house instead of going to the gig. Sophia wanted to thank her for helping her revise apparently, so had suggested chilling with pizza and watching Netflix.

Lisa was relieved. She had been feeling guilty about how she had handled the conversation with Emma and even worse about snapping at Lucy afterwards. At least if Emma was texting her, it meant she had forgiven her.

A sleepover was by far a safer option than a gig in London, but it meant that Em would be spending the night at Christina's house, which did not thrill Lisa at all. God knows what she would be exposed to. She picked up the phone and rang Ben. He was dismissive to say the least. It sounded like he was walking somewhere in the street from the amount of background noise, but he should've been at the office for a while by then, considering what time he had left that morning. When she quizzed him on where he was, he said he had a meeting to get to, but was very short with her, as though she was accusing him of something, which she was.

She told him briefly about the argument with Emma and mentioned that she wanted to stay at Sophia's.

'So what's the problem?' he said as what sounded like a truck rumbled past him.

'Because it's Christina's house.'

'If I know Christina, she won't be home tonight. And it would be good for Emma to get out and have some fun. Let her go – stop micromanaging her so much. She'll be living on her own soon enough and then you will have no control over what she does. Look, I have to go.' He hung up.

How did he know Christina was going to be out? He had sounded so sure. Was he still talking to her, messaging her? It couldn't really be her, could it? He surely wouldn't be so cruel as to have an affair with Christina of all people?

He was right about one thing though, which annoyed her even more. She knew the time was coming when Emma would be living independently. She had never been the kind to get into trouble, so letting her have a night to hang out with a friend she had been helping wasn't the worst idea in the world, despite what Lisa thought of that friend and her family.

She texted Emma back, saying that she could go to Sophia's, then put her phone down and breathed deeply, trying to dislodge the awful feeling of dread that had settled upon her.

Emma checked over her answers half-heartedly. She glanced to her right and saw Kai chewing on the lid of his pen, stress creasing his forehead. Over her left shoulder, she could just glimpse Sophia, still scribbling away. There was still ten minutes left of the exam, but she wanted to stand up, flip over her desk and run screaming from the hall. Instead, she began to doodle in the corners of her answer paper, drawing caricatures of her biology teacher as he sat in the front of the hall, reading a book and occasionally looking up to make sure no one was openly cheating.

A bit of light illustration for them when they had to mark her paper.

When the time was up, she was one of the first to stand

and leave. On the way out, she wormed past Sophia, who was still sitting down.

'Hey.'

'Hey,' Sophia said. 'What did you think?'

Emma shrugged.

'I think I did ok in the sixteen marker, but I don't know about the first section,' Sophia said.

'My mum says I can come tonight,' Emma blurted.

'Really?'

'Yeah, but she said we have to go together, so can I travel with you?'

'Ok, that's fine. Come over to mine for about five then and we can get on the train by six. I think it will be fun.'

Emma was only making a point of going because her mother had said she couldn't. It was as complicated and as simple as that. She had this burning bile in her stomach that made her want to rebel, lash out, do something crazy – and her mother trying to control her just made the bile rise even further. She walked away from Sophia, already thinking about what she was going to wear.

50

Christina

Now

'I said get away from her!' Christina reached out and grabbed Lisa's upper arm.

Lisa spun at her. 'Get your hands off me!'

'What are you going to do? Hit her again? I swear if you lay a finger on her, I will have you this time.'

'Mum! Enough! She's been through enough,' Sophia said with a sob.

They both turned to look at Sophia. After a second, Christina released Lisa's arm and held her hands up in surrender. Lisa stepped back and put some space between her and Sophia.

'Sophia, I just need to know what happened.'

'She has told the police she doesn't know anything.'

Lisa glared at Christina, then swivelled her glare on Sophia again. 'Who are you protecting? Because that's what you're doing, isn't it? Is it because your mother *did* get you the drugs? And how did you break your wrist?'

'Lisa, you are so far off the truth, you look foolish right

now,' Christina said and walked towards the bed. She gazed down on Emma, leaned over and gently pushed a lock of hair from her forehead.

'Get away from her,' Lisa growled.

'The problem here, Lisa, is you. You have no idea who your daughter actually is, who she wants to be. You have to take control of everything and that has pushed you away from her. Did you know about her art? Her comic books?'

Lisa looked confused. 'What comic books?'

'Your daughter is an incredibly talented artist who wants to create comic books for a living. If you took any real notice of her or even asked her what she actually wanted to do, she would tell you that.'

'You know nothing, Christina.'

'Is that right?' She turned to Sophia. 'Tell her, Sophia.'

'Mum, please.'

'No, go on, tell her.'

'Yes, tell me, Sophia,' Lisa sneered.

Sophia squared her shoulders. 'Mum is right. She has loads of notebooks of comics that she has drawn and they're brilliant. She is talented and that is what she wants to do. She doesn't want to go to university.'

'You're taking rubbish. I know my daughter.' She stepped towards Sophia again.

'And did you know about—'

'Mum! No. You promised.'

Lisa rounded on Christina. 'Promised what?'

Christina looked at Sophia, then backed away. 'Nothing.'

'Tell me, Christina! What else don't I know?'

'It's not my place and I promised my daughter. I won't break that trust. Come on, Soph.' Christina grabbed hold of

Sophia's hand and pulled her towards the door. She shuffled her into the corridor.

'Wait! Don't you walk away from me!' Lisa shouted after them.

'Come on, let's go home,' Christina said quietly to Sophia.

'Fine! Then I'll just have to find Kai and ask him. Owen will know what's going on,' Lisa shouted through the open door. 'Look, there he is now!'

51

Sophia

Earlier

Sophia threw her phone down on the bed. Emma's video had caught fire and she was well and truly cast as the victim now. It was Kai who was the demon and Sophia knew his life would be unbearable over the next short while.

She still had a niggle at the base of her throat that something wasn't quite right and she couldn't decide if it was that she really hoped it wasn't true about Kai or that she didn't believe Emma. Sophia had seen how drunk Emma had been that night, but she had also seen her flirting with Kai, so it wasn't like she was blameless, surely? She knew what they'd been told at school about consent, but who was to say what had actually happened behind closed doors? Kai was also her friend and she couldn't not believe him just because he was a boy. That wasn't fair. But then, she couldn't not believe Emma either because what if she was telling the truth? She felt like she was being torn in two and so she couldn't bring herself to respond to the posts. She couldn't bring herself to side with either of them.

She did find it ironic how these same girls were now Emma's biggest cheerleaders when just a few weeks ago, they had hated her because she was doing better than them, could outsmart them all in a test and clearly didn't care what any of them thought.

And she had been one of them. She had let her mother's opinions colour her own and when Kai had shown an interest in Emma, Sophia had wanted to see her fall.

Tonight was going to be interesting. She was worried – and a little curious – about what Emma would say when she found out Kai was coming with them. She knew she should've told her and she wasn't entirely sure why she hadn't. Perhaps she was hoping that seeing them together in the same space might help her to pick a side.

She sighed and bent down to lace up her Converses just as she heard the doorbell ring downstairs. It was a few minutes before Emma appeared in her bedroom doorway, no doubt because Christina has chewed her ear off, quizzing her about how she was feeling, whether her mental health was currently a nine or a four, was she eating, was she sleeping.

'Hey,' Sophia said. Emma looked pale – not deliberately made-up pale, but stress pale. Regardless of how she had gotten into the situation, she had had a hell of a week. Sophia walked over to her and gave her a hug. 'How are you doing?'

Emma pushed Sophia away and rolled her eyes. 'Can everyone stop asking me that please? I just want to have some fun and forget about all of it.'

Sophia stepped back. She recognised the same attitude in

Emma that she had shown that night when all of this began. 'Um, about that. Kai is coming with us.'

'What?'

'I'm sorry, I should've said – but he was the one to get the tickets and he was fine with me asking you to come along.'

Emma was backing away. 'I bet he was.'

'Emma, please – just come. It's a gig, it'll be loud and noisy, and there is a group of eight of us, so you don't have to speak to him if you don't want to. Besides, what else are you going to do? Go home?' Then she added lamely, 'And he is really sorry for what happened, if that helps?'

'Sorry? Sorry? It's ruined my life!'

'But… you must've known what would happen if you were flirting with him all night, then went into a bedroom with him?' Sophia knew as soon as she said it that it was the wrong thing to say.

Emma glared at Sophia, but her voice was ice calm. 'You think it's my fault.'

Sophia took a step towards Emma. 'No, I think there was a miscommunication maybe? He says he asked if it was ok with you – he's beside himself that you think he… raped you, because that is what you are saying. That's what everyone is saying he did. And it's only a matter of time before the school finds out, his parents, even the police.'

'I can't believe you.'

'This is serious, Em, like life and death serious, because it could ruin his life, so you need to be sure. If what you say is true, then his life is over. He could go to prison, he'll be on the sex offenders register, no chance of university or a job or even a girlfriend any time soon. That's it for him – so you need to be really clear about what happened because just a sniff of a rumour like this could ruin his life.' She paused, thinking she had gone too far, but needing to say it anyway. 'You've known him a long time. We all grew up together. Tell me what happened and I'll believe you, no matter what, no judgement. And if he did rape you, then he deserves what he gets and I will go with you to report him. I will support you all the way.'

Sophia held her breath.

Emma continued to glare at her. Time ticked over. Sophia could feel every second in the pulse of her wrist. Then Emma's face scrunched up and she sat heavily on the bed.

'You're right. I can't do that to him.'

Sophia frowned. 'What are you saying?'

It was Emma's time to sigh, a long, lion's breath of an exhale that seemed to dispel a multitude of guilt particles into the tense atmosphere.

'He didn't rape me.'

Everything stood still.

And then in one second, the weight of all that responsibility she had been carrying lifted from her shoulders, leaving behind space for anger to settle in. Words leapt into her mouth, ready to be shouted, but Emma was crying, looked so tiny and diminished.

Instead, Sophia sat next to her and kept quiet, waited for Emma to say what needed to be said.

Emma stared at the carpet, couldn't look Sophia in the eye. 'I lied about not remembering. I was drunk, yes, but not as much as I made out.' The tears fell slow and steady, but silent. 'He was kind. He did ask and I said it was ok. Then afterwards, I panicked. When I came out of the room, everyone was sniggering, judging, laughing. I mean, they hated me before, but this was something else. This was cruel and I really did come close to wondering if any of this was worth it, if anyone would miss me. Then there was my mum. She would be so disappointed in me if she knew. And I was in a weird place after it happened. Then I saw my mum and Owen... I don't know, I think they're having an affair or something.'

'Her and Owen?'

Emma glanced over at her, then back at the carpet. 'I saw them once a few weeks ago – in the alleyway alongside the house, kissing.'

Sophia's eyes widened. 'Whoa.'

'That's nothing to do with why I said what I said initially, but it was part of why I made the video, I think. At first, I panicked, told you that I didn't remember. Then I think part of me thought that if I blamed Kai publicly, then it would be enough to break them up, my mum and Owen I mean. I guess I figured there'd just be a lecture on consent at school and that would be it, you know? And then everyone was suddenly so kind and supportive. Suddenly, I hadn't brought it on myself and I wasn't as awful as they always thought I was. I sat back and watched it all burn around me, saw the likes rack up on the post. But then it was like this freight train that had lost control, rushing down the hill and everything started getting too big too quickly and I just – I couldn't take it back even if I wanted to.' She sobbed then. Big and loud and gut-wrenching. Just one, but that sob said everything. 'She's going to think I'm a slut, like everyone else does.'

Sophia pulled her into a tight hug. 'Hey, she has no room

to talk! We will fix this. We will fix all of it, ok?' She felt Emma nod into her shoulder. 'First things first, you need to apologise to Kai.'

'He'll hate me.'

'Maybe, but I think initially he will be relieved. And it hasn't got so far that the police or school are involved yet. The rumours can be squashed. I can redirect things. I'm good at that. But if you leave it much longer, it will be too late.' They sat in silence for a moment, then Sophia pulled back and said, 'I'm going to ask one more time though, just to make sure, because I don't want you to just be saying it because you feel guilty or whatever. Did he rape you?'

Emma looked her in the eye, direct and steady. The trickle of time slowed in the hourglass, the grains more like heavy boulders.

'No, he didn't.'

Sophia exhaled long and slow, tried to keep her face impartial but inside, she was raging. How could she lie about something like that? There were girls out there where this kind of thing had happened, painfully, wrecking them from the inside out, who couldn't bring themselves to say anything because they were convinced they wouldn't be believed.

And then there were the girls who lied, who made themselves into victims as a distraction, who played social media for their own gains, who ruined boys' lives like they were dispensable in all of this. Sophia had to remind herself that she was guilty of weaponizing social media herself. What crime had Emma actually committed originally other than liking a boy that Sophia liked? And she had been crucified for it by the social police, to the point where she was a quivering wreck standing on the edge of a roof. Sophia had manipulated the narrative to make her into a villain, so Emma had manipulated it some more to make herself into the victim.

And none of it was real.

But Sophia verbalised none of this. She clenched her fists at her sides and felt her fingernails dig into her hands like tiny, sharpened claws.

Her voice remained calm but cold as she said, 'You need to make this right with him. And your mother need never find out. My mum won't say anything, I promise you.'

'Please don't hate me.'

Sophia looked at her, with her big eyes and perfect hair, but imperfect in many other ways. What would Sophia have done in the same situation? Would she have come clean straight away? It's easy to judge when you aren't the one in the eye of the storm.

Sophia had been a part of this all along. She carried some of the blame for the mess they were all in and she needed to step up now too.

'I don't hate you. It's done now. It's all over. The worst has happened. Now we fix it.'

52

Lisa

Now

L isa flung open the door and was relieved to see Owen and Kai standing in the corridor. Owen was talking to Kai in a low voice. Kai looked like he had been crying.

'Owen!' she called, ignoring the annoyed glare of the nurse.

He looked up, said something else to Kai, then they both approached Lisa.

Lisa stepped out of the doorway and let the door to Emma's room swing shut with a swish in Christina's face.

'Lisa, is everything ok? How's Emma?'

She ignored Owen and turned to Kai. 'You were there, Kai. Tell me what happened.'

The door opened behind her and she sensed Sophia and Christina standing there. Kai looked from Lisa to over her shoulder.

'Don't look at her! Look at me.' Lisa stepped closer to him and grabbed his upper arms, despite him towering over her. 'What happened?'

'Lisa, I know you've had a shock, but now is not the time. He has also had a shock and I think it's best if I take him home. We can talk another time.' Owen said.

'No! You all need to tell me now!'

Kai had started to cry again. 'It wasn't my fault, I swear! I didn't rape her, whatever she is saying. She said yes.'

The air stilled. They stood, open-mouthed, looking at him like he had appeared from nowhere to take them all by surprise.

Owen coughed. 'Kai, don't say another word.' He grabbed hold of Lisa's hands. 'Let him go, Lisa.'

'How about you let my wife go instead?' a voice growled. Ben marched over and shoved Owen away.

'Mum?' Lucy stood behind Ben, her eyes glassy with sleep.

'Lucy.' Lisa released her grip on Kai's arms and moved towards Lucy.

'Can I see her? Can I see Ems, please?' She looked tiny and frightened.

'Yes, yes, of course.' She turned to Ben. 'Ben, please take her in – I will deal with this.'

Ben didn't look convinced. 'Are you sure?'

'Yes, Ben, I am. Someone needs to be in there with Emma and Lucy. Please. I just want to talk to Kai and Sophia a bit more and then I will come in, I promise.'

Ben looked sceptical, but eventually took Lucy by the hand and led her into Sophia's room.

'How is she?' Owen asked quietly.

'She still hasn't woken up. We won't know more until she does – if she does.' Her voice cracked on those last words.

'Oh, Lisa, I am so sorry. You must be so worried,' Owen said.

'Which is why I need to know what happened.' She turned back to Kai. 'Who are you talking about, Kai?'

Kai sunk into a squat, his legs giving way, and put his head in his hands.

Sophia crouched down next to him and put her arm around his shoulders. 'Just tell them, Kai. There have been enough lies lately.'

He looked at her and nodded, took a deep, juddering breath. 'There was this whole thing that happened the night you were at the school quiz. We were all at Soph's house. Emma ended up coming too. She was drunk when she arrived, but she was still fine, you know? We were chatting like we haven't in ages, laughing, getting along so well.' He looked up at Owen. 'And I like her, Dad. I always have.'

'But Emma was at home that night – at least when we got home, she was,' Lisa said, confused.

'She wasn't. She sneaked out, turned up on my doorstep and I said she could join in,' Sophia explained.

'Ok, so what has that got to do with tonight?'

Kai took a shuddering breath and kept his eyes on his filthy trainers. 'We were getting along really well. I thought she liked me. She suggested we go upstairs—'

'Wait, you can't be talking about Emma. My Emma.' Lisa looked stricken.

'Lisa, hear him out,' Owen said. 'Go on, Kai.'

His voice was tiny when he did. 'We ended up sleeping together.'

Lisa tried not to gasp audibly. None of this sounded like her daughter.

'Anyway, these rumours started up afterwards – horrible stuff about her, saying she was sleeping around and stuff. I tried to talk to her about it, but she ghosted me, ghosted everyone – well, except Sophia.'

'That was my fault – I started the rumours, the bullying, because I was jealous of Kai and Emma,' Sophia admitted. 'But it got out of hand. They were doing some pretty mean shit – spraying her with cat pee when she walked past, putting condoms in her bag, stuff like that. I guess everyone wanted to poke the bear.'

'But that was weeks ago and she never said anything to me. Why wouldn't she say anything? I don't understand. If anything, she should've been staying away from both of you.' Lisa's voice was rising in frustration.

'Lisa, you should be waiting to talk to Emma about this,' Christina said.

'Well, that's great advice, Christina, but I can't, can I? How are you involved, anyway? Why was she at your house?'

'I think you should sit down. None of this is going to be easy to hear.' Christina tried to steer her to a chair, but she resisted, pushed her away.

'Just fucking tell me!'

'She asked Sophia for help in getting an abortion.' Christina rushed on before Lisa could react. 'I found out because Sophia was worried and I promised to be there for Emma if she needed support. I knew it wasn't something I wanted them to do on their own, but she was adamant she couldn't tell you or Ben.'

Kai was pale. 'I didn't know she had been through that. When she put up that video saying I had... that she hadn't consented, I was so angry and hurt, but I also knew no one would believe me, 'cos the guy is always guilty, isn't he? If she had spoken to me, told me what was going on... She must've been so frightened.'

'She didn't want you to know either,' Christina added. 'If we hadn't have gone along with her wishes, then she wouldn't have let us help her.'

Lisa put a hand out to steady herself against the wall. How could this have happened? How could she have been so out of touch with her own daughter? How could she have not noticed what was going on?

'And who's to say you aren't guilty? It's your word against hers.' Lisa's voice was made of pure ice and fire.

'Lisa, take a breath and listen to what he's saying.'

'What I can hear is that my daughter accused that boy of rape, then had to have an abortion, on top of being cruelly bullied, and I think I should be talking to the police.'

'Lisa, he didn't do it. Emma has admitted to Sophia that he didn't rape her. He has also been through enough.'

'Been through enough? My daughter has been through an abortion and now she is in a coma! How do I know that he didn't do this to her just to shut her up, to stop her from going to the police?' She towered over Kai. 'That's it, isn't it? That's what happened. You were trying to silence her.'

53

Emma

Earlier

The way Sophia was looking at Emma now burned into her, shame and self-disgust eating away at her like acid. She knew she had acted like a coward by trying to shift the blame onto Kai. But it had felt good after the cold reality of walking back down those stairs at Sophia's house and seeing the looks and hearing the sniggers, knowing that they all knew because nothing was private with their generation. Everything had to be documented, commented on, posted, liked, judged in black or white.

Even then it would've been fine – she figured she could handle the trolls and abuse. But it hadn't made sense how all the abuse was in her direction. Not at Kai. No, he came out of it almost like a hero, the kind-hearted, sweet boy who did her a favour, who was getting high fives for adding one to his list. Good on him taking one for the team.

The sad truth was that boys and girls were still treated differently, even now when outwardly, everyone made it sound like there was a semblance of equality. There wasn't. The scales still tipped in favour of those with the penis.

For the first few days, she ignored Kai because she was mad that he was coming out of it so well. She knew deep down that he had as little control over what they were saying as she did, but still she had felt angry at him and had ignored his many messages asking to see her, ghosted him at school when he tried to talk to her in between classes, refused to acknowledge him when he was defending her.

She didn't need him. She could fight her own battles.

Then the abuse picked up a notch. Someone even went to the trouble of leaving what looked like a used condom tied to her locker; someone else sprayed her school bag with cat piss. It was astonishing the lengths and trouble they could go to just to be horrible to someone, just to let her know they were better than her.

But even that would've passed eventually. Then her period was late – and that was when she realised that she had gambled with her entire future. The idea of her parents finding out was too much to bear. She knew they weren't on good terms, knew also that the idea of her going to Oxford was almost the only thing keeping them together.

And she was still furious at Kai. He wasn't being spritzed with eau de cat piss as he walked into school. She didn't even remember thinking about it before she asked Sophia to spread the word – and when that didn't happen, she realised that perhaps Sophia didn't believe her. The final straw was seeing her own mother actually acting like what Emma was accused of being, of seeing her with Owen, even when her dad was in the house. That had burned deep and she had wanted to act out, to do something that would affect not just Kai but Owen and Lisa too. Something so big that they wouldn't want to even look at each other again. So she took matters into her own hands.

She had desperately wanted Sophia to hate Kai too, to get angry with him and be on Emma's side. Sophia was her only friend and yet there was still this distance between them. Emma wanted someone to be wholly on her side, to have that one friend that they have in those television shows where they fight for you, defend you so fiercely that they would bury a body for you – that's the kind of friendship she craved. If it hadn't been for her mother, Emma and Sophia would've been those kind of best friends now anyway. She had hoped that Sophia would be outraged in a *you and me against the world* kind of way. However, what she hadn't realised was that Sophia was in love with Kai. She could see it now in the way her face betrayed her when she spoke about him. It complicated Sophia's allegiances and Emma knew that if it came down to it, she would lose and Kai would win. Because he was nice and kind and genuine.

And Emma was just Emma.

Unliked. Unnoticed. Unimportant.

The support she'd received after posting the video was unexpected, a nice bonus. Suddenly, she knew what it felt like to have people in her corner, asking if she was ok, wanting to support her, checking in on her instead of trying to push her over the edge and watch her fall.

But sitting here in front of Sophia now, shame was crawling over her skin like a million tiny spider feet. She scratched at her arms, her nails scraping at the surface, leaving red marks.

'Ok, now we fix it,' Sophia repeated with a sigh. She

stood up, tugged at her tiny dress where it sat centimetres below her crotch. Emma had never had the confidence to wear those tiny dresses. Sophia didn't wear it; she owned it.

Emma was wearing a baggy, oversized, black T-shirt over wide-leg jeans and filthy sneakers. Sophia looked at her and said, 'Is that really what you want to go to the gig in?'

'I don't really have anything else.'

'Ok, then. Let's get that sorted.' She turned towards her wardrobe, then paused and said over her shoulder, 'Can I ask you something?'

'Sure.'

'Did you do any of this to hurt Kai? Or was it more about saving your own skin and then about splitting up Owen and your mother?'

Emma hung her head. 'You really like him, don't you?'

Sophia didn't reply.

'I was angry – that I was being labelled and judged, but he wasn't. He was the lad, you know, getting away with it, like it's never a big deal for a guy, but the girl is a slut. Why is that fair? And then I found out I was pregnant... and I just wanted people to feel sorry for me, maybe? Be on my side for a change, I guess? I know – pathetic.'

Sophia nodded. 'I guess I get it.'

'So you and Kai?'

'He never sees me like that. I'm a mate to him, that's all.' She picked at a fingernail. 'Do you like him?'

Emma thought about it for a moment. 'Yes. Yes, I think I do, but I've ruined it for us. There's no chance now. So maybe now is your time. Tell him how you feel. But please don't tell him about the baby. No one needs to know about that – it's over with.'

Sophia sighed. 'Tonight is about sorting this shit out and then having fun. Ok? Now let's find you something to wear that doesn't make you look like you're hiding a sack of potatoes up your shirt.'

'Hey!' Emma said with a relieved laugh.

The doorbell sounded downstairs and Emma heard Christina shout up to them, 'Soph! Kai is here!'

Emma and Sophia looked at each other. 'Ok, ready?' Sophia said.

Emma swallowed, nodded her head.

'Then let's go.'

She walked down the stairs like she was being escorted to the gallows. Kai was in the kitchen chatting to Christina. She could hear them talking about the exams and what he wanted to do at university. Christina looked up as they walked in, her face giving nothing away about what she knew.

Sophia walked ahead of Emma into the kitchen. 'Hey Kai, listen, just so you know, Emma is here and coming with us.'

There was silence. Emma inhaled once more and stepped into the kitchen.

'Hi,' she said quietly.

His face was thunderous. 'Soph, you should've told me. I wouldn't have come. I can't be anywhere near her.'

'That's why I didn't tell you. I think we need to sort this out. You two do, anyway.'

Christina was watching from the other side of the room, her eyes curious.

'Soph, she's been telling everyone I'm a rapist! That video was all lies!'

Christina stood back against a kitchen cupboard, her arms folded. 'Maybe you both need to hear each other out.'

Sophia rounded on her mother. 'Mum, please?'

Christina shrugged, but kept quiet.

'I'm sorry, Kai. I panicked. I dunno – the trolling and everything, I guess I just wanted it to stop, and I thought if they saw me as a victim, I would be seen and supported. I didn't think about the repercussions for you and I'm sorry. I'll make it right. I promise.'

'And I'll spread the word too,' Sophia added. 'She really is sorry.'

'You need to make it right tomorrow – before school or before the teachers hear about this. If this gets out to the authorities, it would ruin my chances at uni and stuff.' He looked from one to the other. 'Please, tell me you'll fix it tomorrow.' He looked to be on the verge of crying.

'I will, I promise. I really am sorry. It was stupid and selfish and there is no excuse for it.'

His face was still tight and panicked.

'Are you ok with me coming tonight?'

His frown had softened enough for her to know he was thinking about it.

'Just keep her away from me for a bit, ok? I need to process it,' he said to Sophia. 'I'll wait for you outside.'

Sophia watched him leave, then said, 'Well, he could've gone home, but he didn't, so that's something, I guess.'

Christina pushed away from the cupboard and said, 'Emma, you have to make this right. That was dangerous what you did and wasn't fair on him if it wasn't true, not to mention what implications it could have for all those girls who really have been raped and want to report it, but aren't believed. You do know that, don't you?'

Emma looked stricken then, but Christina pulled her into a hug. 'Look, you've made a mistake – and a whopper at that – but you've paid your dues and what is important now is what you learn from it and how you fix the mess you've left behind, ok?'

Emma nodded into her shoulder.

'Now go and enjoy yourselves. You both be careful though, ok? And Emma, give him time – he'll come around.'

'Thanks,' Emma mumbled.

'Call me if there are any problems – any time, ok?'

'We will, Mum, thanks,' Sophia said. 'It's just a gig. What's the worst that can happen?'

54

Christina

Now

'Lisa, you need to be careful about what you're saying.' Owen's voice was a low growl and he looked thunderous, his perfect eyebrows knitted into one tight line.

'I will not until I know what happened tonight. You are so obnoxious sometimes about how amazing your son is, but look at him, look at what he's done.'

'And are you any better? For all we know, Emma is sleeping with everyone in a five-mile radius! You wouldn't know. She clearly tells you nothing,' Owen flung back.

'Oh, so it's all coming out now, what you really think of me. Were you just using me, telling me what you thought I wanted to hear?'

Christina interrupted then. 'Now, hang on a minute, Owen. I do know what's been going on and Emma did the right thing in the end. She was scared and came to me for help. She was responsible in her choices about the pregnancy and she made the choice that was right for her.' She turned to Lisa. 'You can be proud of her for that.'

Lisa was shaking and gulping at the air.

Christina carried on. 'And her and Kai discussed that she would make everything right tomorrow and they were going to draw a line under this whole sorry mess. I'm sure when she comes around, that is exactly what she will do.'

'If, Christina, if,' Lisa choked out.

'Pardon?'

'*If* she comes around. What if she doesn't?' Lisa repeated. The gulping was more audible and shallower.

'Lisa, you need to breathe. You're hyperventilating,' Christina said with concern. 'Sit down, come on.'

Lisa let Christina steer her into a chair. Christina crouched in front of her, her knees crackling as she squatted down. 'Take some slow and steady breaths, just like you teach in your yoga class. In and out, in and out.'

'Fuck, this is such a mess,' Owen growled.

Eventually, Lisa sat back upright. 'He's right. This is a mess – and I still don't know what happened tonight.' Her voice rose again as she said to Kai, 'And you! Has your useless father not taught you about birth control?'

'She said she was on something already,' he muttered.

'Oh, Kai,' Owen said. 'You know that shouldn't matter. You know you should be protecting yourself first and foremost. You don't know her history, who else she has slept with.'

'Excuse me?' Lisa shot to her feet.

'Well, he doesn't. This isn't over. She could've ruined his life with her false accusations. Who does that? You women are all the same, creating drama to cover your own arses when you need a bit of attention.'

Both Christina and Lisa gaped at Owen.

'Like mother, like daughter I think,' he continued.

'You what?' Lisa said.

'You were just as bad – as soon as things were rocky with you and Ben, you came sniffing around my door.' He put on a false soprano. 'Oh, Ben doesn't understand me. Please can I play around with you and maybe he'll get jealous.'

'That was not it. I thought you were my friend!'

Christina put herself between them. 'Owen, I think you should go, don't you? And stay away from my friend.'

They glared at each other, nose to nose. 'Gladly. Come on, Kai.'

'No,' he said.

'What?'

'No, I need to tell the truth. No more. I can't with any more of it. I need to take responsibility for what I did tonight and Lisa deserves to hear the truth. I don't want anyone else thinking I am something I am not. I made a mistake and I need to fix it, just like Ems will when she wakes up.'

55

Emma

Earlier

The train journey into town was tortuous. Emma sat between Kai and Sophia with neither really talking. They stared at their phones the whole way. The rest of the group were meeting them outside the venue and Emma was relieved to finally get there.

The air was heavy and unusually warm, the threat of rain hanging ominously over them. The gig was in a park in central London and she could smell cut grass, weed and alcohol getting headier as they walked towards the entrance. Kai trailed behind them, his hands shoved deep into his pockets. The twins stood to one side, chatting to a couple of girls and already swigging from cans of beer that Sally had given them to drink on the train. Kai went straight over to them and started handing out the tickets.

'He hasn't said two words to me yet,' Emma said.

'Ignore him. He's sulking. Come on, forget it and have some fun.'

She looked over to where Kai was now opening a beer. He scowled at Emma as he necked half of it in one go.

She also noticed Sophia's friend Liv, a tall, incredibly beautiful and rake-thin blonde who had squeezed herself into a bandeau top that was almost non-existent and skin-tight, high-waisted jeans. She was giving off huge Olivia Newton-John vibes. Emma had always felt uncomfortable around her and knew Liv hated her. She had seen some of Liv's responses to her video and her comments made it clear she was still siding with Kai. Soon everyone would be, so it didn't matter anyway. Liv was talking quietly to Kai. Emma saw her palm something small to him, which he shoved into his pocket.

Sophia saw her watching them and grabbed Emma's hand. 'Come on. Let's sort this.' She marched over to the rest of the group. 'Guys, Emma and Kai are both hanging out with us tonight, ok? Some shit has been said on both sides, all of it out of context, and they've agreed between them that it's all cool and done with. It was all consensual, no one to blame, yeah? So let's just be nice and have a good night.'

Liv frowned at Sophia. 'You've changed your tune.'

'Yeah, I have actually,' Sophia said.

'But weren't you the one who started it? Sending pics of her and telling everyone what a slapper she was not that long ago?'

'Yeah, so I got it wrong, ok? You're no saint, Liv. How many guys have you stolen just to get back at someone?'

Liv narrowed her eyes, but said nothing more.

'Yeah, that's what I thought. You've done things, I've done things. Who hasn't?'

'So you're saying she was lying about Kai?' Liv wasn't going to let it go.

Emma glared at her. 'What are you going to do, Liv? You've always been open about how much you hate me, so do your worst. I feel bad enough about it as it is, so no need to hold back on my account.'

Live took a step towards Emma.

'Liv, back off, yeah?' Sophia squared up to her – and there it was. The friendship Emma craved, the need for acceptance, to know someone was on her side. She finally saw it on Sophia's face.

'Yeah, Liv, back off,' Emma said, 'because there's some stuff I could probably tell everyone about you, stuff I've seen from a handy little viewpoint I've found at school. I'm going to keep it to myself in case I need it, but be under no illusion that I can drop that shit like a grenade if I need to.' Emma relished the doubt that rippled across Liv's perfect face.

She could hear the music starting up from the tents inside the park, could smell candyfloss and fried onions, saw people milling around and making their way inside, looking happy and relaxed. It was all so normal and they were caught out here, holding their breath and treading water.

'Carter, pass me a beer, would you?' Sophia said and pointed at the bag in his hand. 'Want one, Em?'

Emma was still glaring at Liv, but nodded. 'Definitely.'

Liv finally held her hands up and turned away.

'Kai, we good?' Sophia said.

He shrugged.

'Ok, then. Let's get in there. Kai, have you got our tickets?' Sophia asked.

He pulled some folded paper from his back pocket and a small packet fell out onto the dusty ground in front of them.

Emma bent down and picked it up. It was a bag of pills. 'What are these?'

'Nothing,' he mumbled and went to grab them.

Emma snatched them away. 'What are they?'

'They're just to take the edge off. It's been a shit time,' he said pointedly.

Emma looked at them curiously. 'Can I have one?'

'No, Em, you don't want to mess with that stuff. And neither do you, Kai,' Sophia said.

'You're so boring these days, Soph,' Liv said. 'If Emma wants one, let her. Besides, I think I might like "off her face" Emma.' Liv looked dangerously like all her Christmases had come at once.

'It's fine, Soph, just a bit of fun,' Kai said. 'Something to help us relax. I was saving them for later, but she can have one if she wants. We could all do with letting go a bit.'

Sophia looked from one to the other and shrugged. 'It's up to you, Em.'

Emma opened the bag and took one out. There were two left in the packet.

She opened the beer and swallowed the pill with a big gulp.

56

Christina

Now

'Kai, it wasn't your fault,' Sophia said. 'She was in a weird mood, the stress of everything, I think, as we all were. She was… edgy I guess, wanting to drink and stuff. Like she was wired anyway, although I don't think she had taken anything before we got there. I think it was all hitting her – she was convinced she was going to fail her exams and was looking to blow off steam after everything and I think she was looking to make it up to you by going along with what you were doing.'

'The stupid little bitch could've ruined your life, Kai,' Owen scowled.

'Owen, I swear to God, one more word from you—' Christina started to say, but Sophia interrupted her.

'Mum! Enough, please. That's part of the problem with all of you. Dictating, telling us what to do, who to see, where we're going wrong, but never actually listening to what we are telling you. And you're not listening now, any of you.' Sophia looked from Christina to Owen to Lisa in turn. 'Lisa, Emma really doesn't want to go to Oxford. She is terrified of telling you that, but she wants to be a comic book artist more than anything. And me?' She looked at Christina now. 'I really do want to go to university. I don't want to travel with you, working in dodgy bars for money. I want a degree, a good career, a family with a husband one day. I want to be boring! And I know it's not what you want for me and you don't want to see me go, but this is my time now. It's our time,' she said, gesturing at Kai. 'Let us be who we are. Let us make mistakes. We've heard you; now hear us.'

There was silence as the grown-ups digested what she was saying.

Then Lisa said, 'That's all fine, Sophia, but letting you live your lives in the hope you have listened to us has ended up with my daughter being bullied, having an abortion and lying in a hospital bed in a coma. I think maybe even you can see that we might know better than you sometimes.'

57

Sophia

Earlier

It wasn't Sophia's job to babysit Emma any longer. She'd done that so much lately, but watching her take that pill was one step too far. She made the choice to take it, just like she made the choice a few weeks ago to sleep with Kai without protection, and just like she made the choice to have an abortion. She was hitting the self-destruct button again and all Sophia could do was shrug and cross her fingers that it would be ok.

Kai was watching Emma too, but with a mix of disbelief and what could easily be construed as pride on his face.

'Let's go,' Emma said.

The bodies were packed in tight once they got through the turnstiles and closer into the mosh pit. They wriggled and squirmed to the side of the stage, feeling the music pulse and vibrate through their bodies. It was loud and aggressive; there was shoving and jumping and a mob-like energy to the crowd. The air smelled of smoke and sweat, with everyone moving to the music like a mass of writhing snakes in a pit. It was furnace hot too.

'Maybe we should head further back,' Sophia said, suddenly frightened that they might be crushed if they tried to move further in, the anxiety coming out of nowhere and taking her by surprise. She was starting to understand the need for the pills.

Emma was already swaying to the music, her face relaxed, her hands cutting the air like she was orchestrating a band.

'No, let's get closer,' Liv said.

Sophia looked around. All the beer stalls were around the edge of the arena. 'If we stay towards the edges, we are near to the beer stalls.'

Liv was adamant she wanted to be further inside. She got the huff and pushed through the crowd on her own, saying she would find her other group of mates instead, but the twins agreed with Sophia and headed to the side to set themselves up near a stall selling overpriced pale ale.

'What about you two?' Sophia said to Kai and Emma, hoping they would say they wanted to stay where they were. 'Going over there?'

Kai shrugged, said he wasn't bothered. Emma was exaggerating her dance moves now and not really listening. Sophia looked around again. There was a small space to her left that was closer to the crowds, between a group of boys who were all topless with their jeans hanging lower than their undershorts, and a foursome of girls all dressed identically in crop tops and tiny denim shorts. There was space for them to dance while still being close to the beer stalls.

'There – let's go there,' Sophia shouted just as a body

came crashing down over the top of her. She was shoved roughly to the ground and landed heavily on her arm, which twisted under her unnaturally. She cried out in pain and for a moment was convinced she would be crushed under the feet that were stomping and jumping and kicking near her head.

The boy who had been launched into the air by his mates in an ill-fated attempt at crowd surfing and had landed on her rolled off with a laugh and a whoop. Then he was up and dancing again. Sophia could taste dirt in her mouth and she thought her lip was bleeding. She tried to get her feet under her, but her arm screamed back in pain.

Then she felt herself being lifted and put back on her feet. Kai was looking down at her in concern. 'You ok?'

Lisa clutched onto her arm. 'I dunno.'

Emma was oblivious as she danced just in front of them. She turned around and said, 'I need water. I am so thirsty.'

'The pills will do that,' Sophia said. 'They can dehydrate you.' Sophia worried she would pass out with the pain that was rippling through her arm. 'Um, I'll go and see if I can buy some water, I think,' Sophia said to Kai. 'Don't move.' She just wanted to get out of the crowd, just for a moment. She walked away.

She was not having fun. She wanted to phone her mum, ask her to come and get her, but she didn't want to leave Emma here on her own.

She wandered aimlessly, looking for a stall that sold water and still holding her throbbing arm. Her wrist was turning purple already and looked to be swelling fast. There were people everywhere, dancing, smoking, drinking, having the time of their lives, and yet Sophia felt weirdly lonely.

She stopped at a stall selling candyfloss and bought two ridiculously expensive bottles of water, then headed back to where she had left Kai and Emma, resting one of the cold bottles on her wrist as she walked.

The bass was pulsing through her chest, making her insides feel hollow. As she approached Kai and Emma, she noticed a commotion to her right. A man dressed in baggy jeans and wearing a bucket hat decorated in a marijuana design was racing through the crowd towards her with a couple of policemen chasing him. As he rushed past Kai and Emma, he tossed something to the ground. It was a bag of what was clearly drugs, tightly wrapped in clingfilm. He then darted in and around the beer stalls and was gone.

The bag lay on the ground like an accusation. Kai and Emma turned to look at Sophia, then at the bag at their feet.

The police drew closer. 'Hey, you there,' one of them called to Kai. 'What have you got on you?'

Without thinking, Sophia kicked the packet into the heaving mass of people, but she knew Kai still had a bag of pills in his back pocket.

'They're going to search you for drugs,' she hissed to Kai. 'Get rid of the pills.'

Kai started tapping at his pockets in panic. He pulled out the bag. 'What do I do with them? I can't just throw them in the grass? I bought them off Liv – they cost me a fortune.'

'What's more important, Kai? The money you are losing or your future if you get arrested for possession?'

Emma looked from one to the other, then snatched them out of his hand.

The police were a few yards away now.

Emma opened the packet and spilled the two remaining

pills into the palm of her hand. She dropped the bag onto the ground and covered it with her foot.

'Look, I owe you, Kai, and I don't care about getting into university anyway,' Emma whispered, her back now to the policemen.

She grabbed the bottle of water from Emma's hand, unscrewed the cap and swallowed the last two pills in one go.

58

Lisa

Now

'It all happened so quickly after that,' Kai was saying. 'The police searched us and of course found nothing, but then Sophia started feeling faint. I didn't realise her arm was so bad. I told Emma we needed to find a first aid tent and I think that was a blessing in disguise because by the time we had fought through the crowd to the side, Ems... she collapsed and...' He broke down then, unable to finish his sentence.

'Jesus, Kai!' Owen said. 'What have we told you about that stuff?'

'I know! I just... what with everything going on, sometimes it helps to take the edge off, you know?'

'What was in the pills?' Lisa asked.

'I don't know. They were supposed to be weak Es or something. They looked normal. I just bought them from Liv. They must've been cut with something else.'

'Where did Liv get them from?'

Kai shrugged, looked down at his hands dangling between his knees.

It was like Lisa was watching a television programme of Emma's life, but with second-rate, stand-in actors that were doing a poor job. None of it made sense. They were talking about Emma, but this wasn't a version of her that Lisa recognised.

Kai was visibly shaking. Lisa looked down at him impassively.

Owen was pacing, his face like a mask. 'I can't believe how bloody stupid you are!' he ranted. 'Your mother will be furious when she hears all this.'

Kai rounded on him then. 'Oh yeah? And where is she, Dad? She's not on a business trip like you say, is she? You and her have split up, but you don't have the balls to tell me. I heard you arguing the other day. I heard her telling you she'd seen your messages to Lisa and the other women.' He looked at Lisa now and she shrivelled in shame at the look on his face.

'Emma knew too,' Sophia added. 'She saw you and Owen kissing outside your house.'

'But... but we didn't do anything,' Lisa said. 'I mean, there were messages and that one kiss, but otherwise nothing happened.'

'Yeah, but my dad has form,' Kai spat back. 'It seems he's quite good at collecting phone buddies, aren't you, Dad? And sometimes the conversations are not so innocent by the sounds of things. The walls are pretty thin in our house, Dad.'

Lisa was mortified. She looked at Owen, wanting to

see embarrassment or contrition, but his face was blank, unmoved. How could she have thought Owen had feelings for her? She was just one of many, someone to stroke his ego and to distract him from the monotony of his own life.

She was a fool. The realisation smothered her.

She stepped towards Kai and took his hands in hers.

'Kai, honey, I can only apologise. I am a fool. There is no excuse. Ben and I were in a bad place and, well, I was gullible, I guess. But thank you for being honest about what happened.'

He dropped his head. 'I'm going to go to prison, aren't I? I gave her the drugs, I've heard the stories.' He was just a kid in trouble and, despite his outburst and anger, he looked back at his dad and said, 'Dad, I can't go to prison.'

'Well, it would teach you a bloody good lesson,' was all Owen said.

Lisa shook her head at Owen, found herself wondering what she had seen in him. Such a small-minded man. How could she have been so blind? 'Kai, I promise nothing like that is going to happen. What have you told the police? Did you tell them where she got the pills from?'

'No, my dad told me to keep quiet about that, so I said I didn't know where she got them from.'

Lisa scowled at Owen. 'Lying is just second nature to you, isn't it?' She turned back to Kai. 'Ok, as far as we are concerned, you know what the pills looked like, but not where she got them from, what was in them or why she took them. You stick to that story. Enough people have been hurt tonight. The hospital has done a toxicology test, so they know what she has taken anyway. Is that understood?

Kai, listen to me! Is that understood?' She turned to Sophia. 'You understand too, right?'

'Yes,' they both mumbled.

'Owen, take him home,' Christina said.

Christina and Lisa watched Owen walk stiffly away with Kai.

'I'll get us some more coffee,' Christina said.

Lisa walked over to the window that looked into Sophia's room. Lucy sat in the chair, her phone balanced on her knee, but with her eyes only seeing her sister. Lisa couldn't see Ben, but she knew he was there in the corner, probably leaning against the wall, giving Lucy the space to be with Sophia, but also being there if she needed him to hold her up her if it got too much.

She felt Sophia come up behind her. 'Lisa, can I go in and see her?' Sophia asked.

Lisa looked at Sophia and said, 'Yes, of course you can.' As Sophia went to push open the door, Lisa said, 'Thank you, Sophia. For being there and helping her when I wasn't.'

Sophia paused with the palm of her hand on the door. 'She loves you and only wants to make you proud. And she's really talented.'

Lisa smiled weakly as Sophia disappeared through the door.

Lisa sat back down in the chair. It felt like the life had drained out of her legs. Her mouth was dry. Christina approached cautiously, holding two cardboard cups. She handed one to Lisa and sat down next to her.

'So it turns out you were right then,' Lisa said to her.

'About what?'

'That I'm a terrible mother.'

Christina shook her head. 'I was wrong to say that all those years ago. I was wrong to embellish what happened and make you out to be a villain. I was just as bad then as the teenagers are now. You're not a bad mother. Neither of us are. We might come at it from different sides, but we both want the same thing. We want them to do well, to be happy and healthy. And I think we've both been caught up in trying to get them to be who *we* wanted them to be rather than who *they* want to be.'

They sat for a moment in silence, just the sound of squeaking shoes and swishing doors.

'The one thing I can say from listening to them in the last little while is that they are good kids, all of them. They are strong and resilient and not afraid of making a mistake – or correcting one either.' Christina sighed, then continued, 'But it would be a lot easier if this parenting thing came with a user guide, don't you think?'

Lisa laughed. Then she started to cry again, despite not thinking she had any tears left in her. Her throat felt raw and her eyes were swollen to the point of almost shutting, and yet the tears still came – from somewhere deep down, somewhere visceral and raw. 'What if she doesn't wake up, Chris?'

'Hey, come on now. We don't talk like that.'

'I can see it in the doctors' eyes, the way they are talking to me. It's not good news.'

'But they haven't said that, have they?'

'They said that they don't know what she will be like if she wakes up, if there will be any long-term damage.' Her voice juddered and jumped. 'This is all my fault. I put too much pressure on her for Oxford. But how was I supposed

344

to know she didn't want to go? She never shared her art with me.'

'And that is not your fault. She should've had faith in you, in your love for her, that you would support her. I know because Sophia did the same to me. She didn't tell me how badly she wanted to go to university, but if she had, I would've supported her. I would've done everything to help get her there. I was too busy being selfish and worrying about myself, about whether I would be lonely without her.'

'I think I would've argued with Em, told her that the comics were a hobby, that she needed a degree. I think she knows me pretty well.'

Christina sighed. 'And maybe Sophia knows me too well too. She knows what I'm really worried about. I know she won't always be with me, but I can't stand the thought of not having her around, of not talking to her every day, of spending every day on my own. How selfish is that! I would prefer that my daughter gives up the opportunity to further her education than leave me on my own, all because I have managed to push away every man that ever loved me and I am now alone.'

'And I'm pushing my daughter to go to a university she doesn't want to attend because I am so scared she will make a mess of her life like I did, by not finding her place, ending up relying on a man and losing her independence until she is so reliant on him that she can't be alone, who would contemplate staying with him even if he had an affair because that is easier than being on my own. I don't know who is worse – me or you.'

Neither of them had noticed Sophia emerge from Emma's room. She stood with her back against the closed door, listening to the two of them as they sat, working it out between them, trying to figure out where things had gone wrong and where they went from there.

'I am sorry, Lisa. I was only trying to help Emma – I don't think she would've let me help her if she knew I was going to tell you about the abortion. But I made sure she was safe, I promise,' Christina said.

'Thank you, Chris. I really mean that. And I am so sorry for what I said about Sophia. I let my feelings towards you taint how I reacted to her. All those years ago, that day in the paddling pool, it was my fault. I left them unattended, and when I came out and saw Emma lying with her face in the pool, I panicked and lashed out at Sophia out of pure fear. What I never told you was that Emma showed me the game she had been playing later that night when she was in the bath. She had learned to put her face in the water and blow bubbles at her swimming lessons and that was what she had been showing Sophia. She wasn't in danger. Sophia hadn't pushed her like I thought.'

Lisa wasn't sure what to expect from Christina with this last revelation. Christina sat as still as a statue for a moment, then her arm shot out. Lisa flinched, preparing herself for the blow, but was pulled into a hug instead. 'Oh my God! How stupid are we!' Christina was actually laughing.

Christina released her and wiped at her eyes. Only then did she notice Sophia over Lisa's shoulder. 'Um, how much of that did you hear?'

'All of it,' Sophia said. 'Mum, I'm not going to leave you. It's just a temporary thing. I will always be here for you.'

Christina walked into Sophia's arms and Lisa wanted to weep at the raw emotion as she watched them.

But then, out of nowhere, there was a commotion behind them. Nurses charged into Emma's room, their faces tight. Sophia was shoved aside. Lisa could hear Ben talking loudly, calling Emma's name.

'Oh my God, what's happening?' Lisa shouted. 'Emma? Emma!'

Fear rooted her to the spot. She couldn't make her legs move at all.

She inhaled, then held the breath, afraid to exhale in case nothing would ever be the same again afterwards.

Then Ben opened the door and said, 'She's awake. Lisa, honey, she's awake.'

59

Emma

Later

Emma, Sophia and Kai sat with their feet dangling over the flat roof of the drama block, the envelopes containing their A Level results sitting unopened between them. They passed a bottle of cheap prosecco between them, taking sips as they looked out at the chaos unravelling below: the hugging, laughing, crying, relief palpable in the air.

Emma's phone began to ring. She glanced at the screen, then set it aside. Her mother was calling yet again.

'So are we going to open them or what?'

'All at once, yeah?' Kai said.

'All at once,' Sophia said.

They picked up their envelopes, tore them open in sync and pulled the letters out. Each one read them impassively, then they looked at each other.

'Looks like I'm going to Leeds to study concept art,' Emma said first, a wide grin on her face.

'Looks like I'm going to Nottingham to study law,' Kai said.

'Looks like I'm going to Birmingham to study English,' Sophia said.

'We did it. After all that, we did it,' Emma said. She felt like she was going to cry.

'Never a doubt, right?' Kai said and they all laughed.

Emma looked out across the school grounds and thought back over the last few months. By the time she was discharged from hospital, Sophia and Lucy had conducted a thorough social media campaign that had not only cleared Kai of any suspicion, but had also gone on to educate teenagers about the dangers of unprotected sex, the responsibility of consent and what that meant, and the dangers of drugs. It turned out that her baby sister was a bit of a whizz with video editing tools. She had worked with Sophia and Kai to produce a number of videos that had gone viral on TikTok. All Emma had had to do was repost and share, and concentrate on getting better.

And that wasn't the only thing that had changed. She watched now as Kai reached out and took Sophia's hand. 'Hey, Nottingham and Birmingham aren't that far away from each other. We'll be ok,' he said to her.

'You guys will be more than ok. Just don't forget about me,' Emma said.

Her heart ached to think that she had only just found the kind of friends in Sophia and Kai that she had craved for so long and now the band was splitting up and going their separate ways.

'No chance of that,' Sophia said and grabbed her hand too.

Emma's phone rang again.

'You have to put her out of her misery, you know,' Sophia

said. 'She'll be so proud of you for getting those results after everything. And you're pleasing her by going to uni while pleasing yourself by studying art. She'll be thrilled.'

'I know. It's just sad that this is it, all of this is over.' She indicated the school below them, the concrete and damp and ugliness that had dominated their lives for so long.

'You surely aren't going to miss this, are you?' Kai said.

'Not this, but you two, yes.'

Now it was Sophia's phone that rang. It was Christina.

Sophia answered the call. 'Hey Mum, yes, we are on our way... No, I'm not saying anything until we get there. Are Lisa and Ben with you? ... Good, ok. ... No, don't let Lisa drink all the champagne!' She laughed. 'You two are terrible when you get together. We'll see you in ten minutes.... No, I'm not saying anything until we get home! Ok, bye.' She hung up. 'They're already tucking into the champagne and all I can hear in the background is your dad telling them to slow down and leave some for the kids,' Sophia said to Emma.

Emma rolled her eyes and laughed. 'It's nice they are such good friends again, isn't it? They're going to need each other when we go.'

The three of them stood up, grabbed their results letters and made their way back down the fire escape.

'I'll see you two later at the party then,' Kai said. He leaned in to kiss Sophia and Emma watched them with a smile.

'You off to see your dad?' she asked him.

'Yeah, he's taking me for lunch. His new girlfriend seems nice, so that's good.'

'How's your mum?'

'She's good. The sale of her business is going through, so I guess that's the end of an era too. But she seems happy and she's moved on. We all have.'

They walked to the school gate and hovered for a moment.

'I'm proud of us, you know,' Emma said then, feeling tears prick at her eyes. 'We came through hell and made it out the other side, stronger than ever.'

'Oh no, she's getting emotional,' Sophia teased.

They all hugged once more, then Kai pulled away and said, 'See you at the party.'

Emma and Sophia watched him walk away.

'It's going to work out for you two, I can feel it,' Emma said.

Sophia hooked her arm through Emma's. 'It's going to work out for all of us,' she said.

Acknowledgements

Being a parent is hard and sometimes being someone's child is hard too. We all do our best, but sometimes it feels like it just isn't enough. But to all the parents out there, it is enough and you are doing fine.

I lost my dad very suddenly just after I started writing this book. He wasn't much of a reader, but he read every one of my books and I know he was proud of me. I miss him.

I am also a mum to two brilliant, smart, capable, strong-minded daughters, and I want to thank them and my husband for making me a better mother every day and for supporting me as much as I hope I support them.

As with every one of my books, there is a team behind me, to whom I am forever grateful: Jo Bell, my brilliant agent, who knows just the right things to say to keep me going; the editorial powerhouse that is Martina Arzu and the team at Head of Zeus; the wider writing community that is so supportive and generous; and my close friends who are always interested in what I am working on next. As always, any mistakes are mine and mine alone – chalk it up to creative licence if you will.

But the biggest thanks always go to you, Reader, because what is a story without an audience? Thank you, thank you, thank you – there's so much more to come, so bear with me...

About the Author

DAWN GOODWIN'S career has spanned PR, advertising, publishing and healthcare, both in London and Johannesburg. A graduate of the Curtis Brown creative writing school, she loves to write about the personalities hiding behind the masks we wear every day, whether beautiful or ugly. What spare time she has is spent chasing good intentions, contemplating how to get away with murder, and immersing herself in fictitious worlds. She lives in London with her husband, two daughters and her British bulldog Luna.